Apr 2015

THE SCAPEGOAT

THE
SCAPEGOAT

SOPHIA
NIKOLAIDOU

TRANSLATED FROM THE GREEK
BY KAREN EMMERICH

MELVILLE HOUSE
BROOKLYN · LONDON

THE SCAPEGOAT

Melville House Publishing   8 Blackstock Mews
     145 Plymouth Street   and   Islington
       Brooklyn, NY 11201   London N4 2BT

mhpbooks.com   facebook.com/mhpbooks   @melvillehouse

Library of Congress
Cataloging-in-Publication Data

Nikolaidou, Sophia, 1968–.
    [Choreuoun hoi elephantes. English]
    The scapegoat / Sophia Nikolaidou ; translated from Greek
by Karen Emmerich
        pages   cm
      ISBN 978-1-61219-384-7 (hardcover)
      ISBN 978-1-61219-385-4 (ebook)
      I. Emmerich, Karen.   II. Title

PA5638.24.I36C4613 2015
889.3'4—dc23

                                                    2014039611

Design by Christopher King

1 3 5 7 9 10 8 6 4 2

My center is giving way, my right is retreating, situation excellent, I attack.

—Ferdinand Foch, French field marshal

1948

"PEACEFUL, WITHOUT SHAME
AND SUFFERING"

"Every crook in Greece is in the government," the villager told the CBS correspondent.

At first this declaration sounded extreme, but the man spoke with no emotion at all, a fact that impressed the foreigner. Barefoot, filthy, dressed in rags. Scratches on his ankles, dried blood, bruises everywhere. A man who took life as it came and made the most of it—or so he seemed to the American, who'd been raised on eggs and bacon, had studied at expensive schools, had seen plenty of poor people in photographs. Now he wrote dispatches about them, and he did so with compassion.

He hadn't intended to interview the villager, he was on his way to meet someone else, a man of power and status, he'd been told; a man with political credentials and strict party discipline; a man of action. Something suddenly compelled him to have the driver stop the car. The villager was watching from across the way. There wasn't a green leaf in sight, though in the outside world spring was bursting into bloom. Here it smelled of ash and scorched earth; days later the odor still filled their nostrils.

The correspondent scanned the bare mountains. The interpreter feared a trap. Tricky times, an unsuspecting American who never thought of trouble, who trusted life to treat him well. That trust had become a torment to the interpreter. Now, for instance, the man had decided they should stop here, on the edge of nowhere. *My instincts are never wrong*, he said—sharply, yet with the courtesy of a man who knows he'll get his way.

Not long after, the correspondent's photograph was published in the newspaper. After days in the water, his corpse had turned white.

•

The local authorities knew right away what a mess they were in. An American—a CBS correspondent, no less—had been missing for ten days. A boatman found him in the waters of the Thermaic Gulf, fifty strokes from the White Tower. The boatman had seen dead men during the war, had buried bodies with his own hands, but he'd never seen a drowned man. The corpse floated serenely. The waves a caress, the clothes untouched, no trace of blood. A film of cuttlefish eggs over the dead man's eyes. *They eat the eyes first*, the boatman had heard older men say at the taverna, deep into drink.

Hands and feet loosely bound with marine rope, clothes that pegged the dead man as a foreigner. You'd never find a jacket like that in Salonica, sturdy fabric, cut and sewn with the attentiveness of a tailor who knew nothing of war, with lighthearted details, wasted fabric on the pockets. And the shirt open at the neck, *What a shame, such a strong young man*, the boatman thought, because the water had bleached the skin an arresting white. The sea had taken no pity. They call her mother but she's a mean-hearted bitch. Youth means nothing to her.

The boatman threw a rope and towed the corpse to the port police. It seemed wrong to touch the head, so he left it in the waves and dragged the body by its bound feet. Then he grabbed it by the elbows and lifted, a few boys helping from shore. The body was as heavy as a sack of stones.

The coroner carefully examined the wound, a bullet hole at the back of the head. The hair around it was scorched but he could find no exit wound. The bullet had, it appeared, exited directly through the victim's nose, *It can happen*, the coroner asserted with confidence, *of course it can*. The victim had dined on lobster and peas, he added once he had opened the body with a scalpel. Food unchewed, the man must have been in a hurry. En-glish food, hard to come by in this city, the authorities observed, jotting notes in their little books.

—An American, the Chief of Police muttered to himself. An American reporter. Just what we need.

He poured himself some ouzo. In a tin cup, no water, on a desk piled with papers.

—We're in it pretty deep, he said, setting the cup down on the coroner's report.

Around that time some gypsies had stolen laundry off the Gris family's line. Manolis Gris, eldest son and young head of the household, immediately reported the theft. He made a list of the stolen items, as his mother had advised: his white shirt, missing its third button, which his mother hadn't had a chance to sew back on; two double sheets of white poplin with tiny blue angels on the hem; another sheet, his favorite, cotton printed with orange flowers; three nightgowns; two slips; and six pairs of pan-ties, pardon the word.

On Saturday, August 14, 1948, the eve of the Assumption of the Virgin, Manolis Gris, thirty-eight years of age, reporter for the newspaper *The Balkans* and assistant correspondent at the news agency Abroad, was waiting for the bus to Kalamaria, heading home after work. He was standing on Tsimiski at the Agia Sophia stop. He'd lit a cigarette.

A plainclothes police officer came up to him and asked him to come down to the station. The officer spoke politely, looked Gris in the eye.

Manolis asked if they had news about the theft of his laundry. The officer nodded.

It was twelve years before Manolis Gris made it home. His eyes were still chestnut brown, but his hair had turned gray.

He was fifty years old.

SCHOOL YEAR 2010–2011

"SCHOOLS ENLIGHTEN ONLY
WHEN THEY BURN"

MINAS

My name is Minas and I don't want to go to university.
I DON'T WANT TO GO TO UNIVERSITY.
I stuck it on the door of my room. So they'd see it and finally stop asking.
I don't want a diploma in a frame.
I don't want memories from lecture halls.
I don't want former classmates.
And I don't have to prove anything to anyone.
All the kids at my school have lost it. They pretend not to care, but they've seriously lost it. Too much school rotted their brains. There's just no way you can memorize all the nationalist uprisings in southeastern Europe in chronological order and the casualty count for each one and still have the brain of a normal person, Jesus.
They stuff their heads with useless information. They memorize the kinds of phrases that impress exam graders: *in summation, moreover, nevertheless.* The handouts and photocopies from their cram school classes have sample essays that all end in exactly the same way: *in the critical era in which we live*—pure, unadulterated bullshit. They drive themselves crazy just to score a fraction of a point higher. In class the other day, Soukiouroglou, who teaches history and language arts, asked us what the phrase "they impaled Athanasios Diakos" from our textbook meant. Not one of them had anything to say. Of course not, details like that won't be on the exams. Soukiouroglou let a minute of total silence to go by. Then he told us about the practice of impalement. He used Dracula as an example, mentioned Bram Stoker, then played the opening scene from Coppola's movie on the projector. All the girls in the class thought it was gross. The only one who didn't close her eyes

9

was Evelina Dinopoulou, little miss perfect, who's in charge of the attendance book. Soukiouroglou lingered on some truly disgusting details. He's amazing when it comes to things like that. Useless knowledge, sure, but if you ask me when I'm eighty, I bet I'll still remember that class.

Soukiouroglou isn't like the rest. He's in a category all by himself. The first-years hear about him even before school officially starts, at the benediction ceremony. Until they take his class they're terrified of him. But once they've had him as a teacher they love him. At school Souk doesn't hang around with the other teachers. He never chaperones field trips, doesn't show up for graduation or Carnival parties. He's always free during break. He keeps a running tally of how many times he's caught each student unprepared. Scary, but it works. They say he was taught by the devil himself— and one thing he learned was how to petrify any parent, colleague, or student in seconds flat.

The devil has a name, Dad says, *and his name is Asteriou.* Dad knows everything that goes on in the city, it's his job. He's a career reporter. He's told me the story about Souk and his dissertation advisor, Asteriou, but of course I can't remember. Too many excruciating details, like notes from grammar class. An academic dispute, someone betrayed someone else, who took some kind of revenge, and soon enough it was one big mess. Pretty classic. The important thing is that Soukiouroglou blew his chance at a university career and ended up at the high school, teaching us.

A few days ago Mom came to school for a parent-teacher conference. Soukiouroglou met with her in the teachers' office. Our Latin teacher needed someone to make photocopies for our class during the break, so I volunteered. Evelina made some snarky comment about my finally doing something for the common good. *When it comes to the success and well-being of my beloved classmates*, I replied, *there's no sacrifice I'm unwilling to make.*

The copy machine is right outside the door to the teachers'

office, but I still couldn't hear what they were saying. Soukiouroglou asked me to come see him, though, during the next break. One thing I'll say about Souk, he's got style. He doesn't play good cop. He doesn't even pretend to like us kids. And he doesn't try to turn you into a replica of himself. Which is pretty rare for someone who spends his days at a high school.

—Your mom came to see me. I told her you don't study.

I fixed my eyes on the floor.

—I also told her your grade in my class is still fairly respectable, thanks to the outside reading you do, even if your knowledge is often chaotic and disordered. But I don't think you'd do well on the exams. She informed me of your decision not to take them.

Pause.

—Your mother objects, but right now that's not our concern. Can you tell me why you've given up on trying to get into university?

—I just don't want to go through all that, I answered with as much indifference as I could muster.

—You mean you can't handle it.

—I'd rather jump off a balcony.

—Fine, he said, and turned to leave.

Days passed. Then, on Thursday morning, Soukiouroglou asked to see me again during third break, the long one that lasts a whole fifteen minutes. I felt like I was standing in a circle of snakes. I found him in the schoolyard, by the basketball hoop. He was surveying the passes, the dribbling, the three-pointers. He was bored and it showed. He nodded me over to where the others wouldn't hear.

—Do you like our book? he asked.

I must have been staring at him like an idiot, because he did that thing he does with his eyes when he's trying to keep himself from crushing someone.

—The book for our history class, he clarified.

—Oh.

—Well? Do you like it? he repeated the question.

—Am I supposed to? I asked.

With Souk you never know what the right answer is. It works well for him when he's teaching, but outside of class it's too much.

—Do you understand it? he asked.

—I don't know, I usually can't follow the thread from one sentence to the next.

—It's not the most elegant text, Souk agreed, nodding.

I decided not to tell him about the hand. Every time I open the stupid book, a huge white hand appears and passes in front of my eyes. Within seconds it wipes away whatever I've just read.

—Listen, Georgiou, Souk went on. Since you're not really interested in taking your exams this year, I've got another suggestion. Forget the book. Would you like to do some actual historical research?

Only Souk could come out with the craziest idea as if it were perfectly normal.

—There's a case, well, there are lots of cases, but there's one I think might suit your temperament. I propose you research it. I'll give you whatever guidance you need in terms of bibliography. You'll work on it for the rest of the quarter, and then present your findings at the end of February in front of an audience of teachers and fellow students. Your grade in my class will depend entirely on this project. In other countries, students are introduced to basic research methodology during the last two years of high school. They go to libraries, look at primary sources, learn how to cite scholarly works. They cultivate their own views. If we lived in Australia, you wouldn't be staring at me right now as if I were an alien.

The bell rang. Souk told me to think it over. If I kept a diary, that day's entry would read: *Friday, November 5, 2010. There is a god. His name is Souk and he works at our school.*

·

I used to be an excellent student. Used to as in up until last year.
Mom was so proud. And even though Dad teased me about my
"sissy" grades, he still photocopied my report cards to show to his
colleagues at the newspaper. A row of perfect, sparkling twenties,
every time.

Their blood froze when I told them about cram school.

—You're wasting your money. You might as well hold on to it
and give it to me at the end of the year, when I'll really need it.

—What for? Mom asked, completely baffled.

—Mom, ever since I was born you've been saving up to send me
to university. Did it ever occur to you that I might not want to go?

From the look on her face, you'd think I'd just told her I only
had two days to live.

—And what are you going to be, Minas? A plumber?

I could see her counting the seconds in her head, the way her
shrink taught her to. Her face was bright red.

—You mean I'm only allowed to become a lawyer or a teacher?
Those are the only jobs that count?

I won't bore you with the whole conversation. In the end she
lost it and called Dad. She said she didn't want to do something
she might regret.

That night I heard her crying in the bedroom through the
closed door.

In our house education is everything. There are bookshelves in
every room with books lined up two rows deep. Both my parents
studied literature. They met at university. Dad became a reporter.
He's always complaining about the long hours and how his cell
phone never stops ringing. But when he's not at the newspaper,
he paces like a beast in a cage. His mind is moving twenty-four
seven, and always in the same direction. News is his sickness. For

13

him reporting is serious business. To be a reporter means to be out walking the beat all the time, eyes and ears peeled. You have to know who to talk to and what kind of information you're looking for. I mean, sure, he has a pretty high regard for journalists who write features and stuff, too. But for him, they're a different breed. They don't have to deal with the pressure of the quick turnaround, the day-to-day, they have more time to digest what they're writing. They're not out there in the trenches with the real reporters.

Mom comes from a long line of literature majors and teachers, and she's proud of it. Her uncles and cousins all studied literature, and most of them are teachers. It's in her genes, she says, since her mother studied literature, too.

Grandma Evthalia is a classical philologist of the old breed. In her day the Faculty of Philosophy accepted very few students, all of them top-notch. The girls who got in were the cream of the crop—rich or poor, they all knew their stuff. Grandma Evthalia speaks in proverbs, ancient Greek sayings and phrases from old schoolbooks. She reads Plato in the original, but she's crazy about John le Carré, too. She'll watch any thriller or police drama they're showing on TV. She loves beating the detective to the punch. She always calls out the murderer's name as soon as she figures it out, which Dad gets a kick out of, though it infuriates Mom.

Grandma Evthalia keeps close tabs on my education. When I was four, she taught me about ancient mythology. *I don't know any fairytales, child, someone else can tell you about Little Red Riding Hood, what you'll get from me is Poseidon*, she would say, raising her hand as if gripping a trident. She taught me syntax when I was eight, in the second grade, because she didn't approve of my teacher, or of the modern teaching methods the Ministry of Education decided to implement. Subject, verb, object: she made me mark them with a pencil. She left the butterflies, bugs, and *flighty structural approaches*, as she called them, nostrils flaring, for kids whose mothers and grandmothers didn't have literature degrees.

She was the one who bought me my first dictionary—and she didn't mess around, either, she went straight for Triandafyllidis. *We graduates of Aristotle University don't approve of the Babiniotis approach*, she told me, as if an elementary school kid would have any clue what she was talking about. She insisted on teaching me how to use it. She always took it down off the shelf carefully. But one afternoon it slipped from her hands and smashed my favorite toy car, a red one. She waited patiently for me to stop crying. Then she asked me to look up "assemble" in the dictionary and made me copy all the synonyms and antonyms into my notebook.

Mom found it amusing, but she also basically agreed with Grandma's approach. Grandma advised her to take charge of my education, and she did. What we learned in school wasn't enough. That was just the basics, *the absolute minimum*, as Grandma was always saying. I had to do my homework on my own. Mom, meanwhile, taught me the extra stuff, the above-and-beyond, the frosting on the cake that makes the difference between a diligent student and an exceptional one. We filled endless notebooks with language drills and math exercises, *the twin pillars of knowledge, the salt of all sciences.* Dad just looked on. He went along with my mother's decisions—after all, he didn't have time to waste on questioning her judgment.

I liked school. During summer vacation, when we'd go out to a place by the beach in Halkidiki, I was bored out of my mind. Sure, I chased frogs, collected ants, raced down the hill on my bike. I scraped my knees on brambles, did underwater flips in the sea, dug for worms in the dirt. I had to sit quietly in my room during siesta, even if I wasn't sleeping. Which meant hours of computer games and piles of comic books. Sounds great, right? Maybe, but who could possibly stand it for eighty-six days in a row? In the afternoons Mom would prepare me for the next year's schoolwork. Sure, I whined, but studying was what saved me.

I don't know when things took a wrong turn. Mom blames Kitsiou, the mule-faced history and language arts teacher we had last year. She filled my notebooks with red ink. *Is this really what you believe?* she would scrawl in the margin, enraged at my ideas. *He'll never get far if he keeps going down that path*, she once let slip when Mom went in for a conference. My essays suffered from *a lack of organization and an overly aggressive sense of irony*. Mom's angry comment to me when she got home was, *Her brains aren't worth a fig*. Usually Mom tries to maintain some kind of solidarity with the literature teachers, but with Kitsiou things got so bad she wrote a letter to the principal. The perfect twenty on my report cards of previous years had dropped to a seventeen, then a sixteen, and it looked like it might go even lower. *I know my child*, Mom insisted to the department head, *there's no way his performance has gotten so poor*. But no one could do anything about it. Inside her classroom, a teacher is queen of the realm, as Mom should have known.

I don't think it was Kitsiou's fault. At a certain point, school just became unbearable.

But I kept gritting my teeth and bearing it. If it were up to me, I would drop out before graduation. I started getting leg cramps, fevers, awful stomach aches, chronic gastroenteritis. And pain. Like hand grenades exploding in my gut. Once Mom even called a cab and rushed me to the hospital. The doctor smiled.

—It's just nerves, was his diagnosis.

He gave me a double shot of tranquilizers.

—This would put even a bull to sleep, he told Mom, winking.

A week later the headaches started. I rubbed my eyes until I saw spots. I would've gouged my eyes out if I thought it would make the hammering in my head stop. I tied my bandana so tightly it left a mark on my forehead. I couldn't stand up straight, I had to lean against walls to walk. Mom brought me paracetamol, Lonarid, whatever over-the-counter painkiller she could find. I swallowed them and closed the door.

I basically lived in my room. Everyone seemed like morons. I guess I had a screw loose somewhere.

You can get pretty much any pill you want online. Antidepressants and anti-anxiety meds, Buspirone, hydroxyzine, sertraline, paroxetine, venlafaxine. It's crazy. Indications, contraindications, proper dosage for facilitating synaptic transmission via serotonin reuptake. Great, as if that made any sense to anyone. No adverse effect on alertness, best results within a month. That's what the website promised. You have to get off it gradually, though, or you'll go into withdrawal. They never tell you how bad that part is.

Game over, Mom flipped out. *The door to your room is to remain open at all times*, she said. Actually, she started leaving all the doors and windows in the house open, to let in fresh air. And she made sure I got my recommended daily allowance of vitamin C, squeezed orange juice for me three times a day. She filled the house with whatever natural dope she could find: sallowthorn, ginseng, spirulina. Royal jelly, saffron tea, pollen. It all went straight down my throat.

And guess what? It turns out sunlight and exercise are all it takes to flood the brain with serotonin. All the magazines say so. Mom read that and made up her mind. For the time being she stopped bugging me about my homework, she figured my psychological well-being took priority.

Maybe it was a fear of competition, like that shrink said. To me he seemed like a nutcase himself. Mom got a zillion recommendations and references before settling on him. He asked a bunch of questions, I counted the pockmarks on the wall. He sang his little song, we handed over a hundred euros, he asked to see me again. Are you kidding me?

I mean, why don't they all get lost.

All I know is, if I ever have to take another exam in my life, I'll die.

•

Souk *entrusted* me with a list of topics to choose from. He has his own way of speaking. He never just gives you a notebook, he *entrusts* you with it. When I first had him as a teacher, back in my first year of middle school, I thought he was really tall. It took months for me to realize that he's actually what you would call average height. But in class he seemed to grow taller, until he filled the whole room. Once he suddenly spread his arms out to his sides. He was wearing black, of course, *his uniform*, we call it, since he always wears exactly the same outfit, winter or summer. And with his arms spread wide, he looked like an eagle about to swoop down on us. All the kids in the front row ducked. Souk gave an explanation of Attic reduplication in verb forms, then abruptly clapped his wings shut again. An entire class will remember *akouo, akikoa* for the rest of their lives.

Souk is the one who taught our class what a reference book is. He bought shelves, paid for them out of his own pocket, the gym teacher told us later, shaking his head at Souk's idiocy. Souk screwed them into the wall next to the blackboard one afternoon after school let out.

—This is where you'll keep your dictionaries, grammar books, and literary histories, he announced the next day.

At first we didn't give it much thought. But Souk had a plan. Instead of going home with us, the reference books stayed at school, and they got used on a daily basis. Tons of exercises. Our parents were ecstatic. Souk had earned their trust. Grandma Evthalia even came to school to congratulate him. Finally, she said, someone was correcting our essays with professional rigor, underlining our mistakes in red pen, suggesting alternate wording, teaching us new words, explaining the difference between *katarhas*, "firstly," and *katarhin*, "in principle," and quoting phrases in ancient Greek. She decided it was time to buy me Vostantzoglou's 1949 *Antilexicon*, which has antonyms, word roots, and etymologies. She put it on my bookshelf at home, beside the Triantafyllidis dictionary.

—This book will be a valuable friend. I'll show you how to use it, she promised. It will enable you to use words properly and with elegance.

She'd written a dedication on the first page:

> *To my beloved grandson,*
> *for your success,*
>
> *Grandma*

Over the next few years we had other history and language arts teachers. Good ones, bad ones, so-so ones. None like Souk, though. They all smiled more. And assigned less homework. But Souk had taught us to think—even the kids who'd never admit it knew it was true. He was the only one who'd earned enough respect to be addressed as *sir* whenever we ran into him outside of school. With everyone else, we just crossed to the other side of the street, or mumbled some incomprehensible greeting.

It didn't matter that he was a tough grader—justifiably tough, he claimed. It didn't matter that he even failed kids, lots of them.

—It takes effort to fail, but I know that won't stop some of you from trying, he warned.

And now here we are together again. It's my senior year, I'm twenty centimeters taller than him and I still feel like he's the giant.

—Georgiou, I'm entrusting you with a list of possible research topics. When you're ready, inform me of your decision.

—I'm just a kid, sir. I'd prefer if you chose for me, I dared to suggest.

—You're not a kid, you're a mule. I'll expect your decision by Wednesday.

Souk didn't mince words. He didn't give us encouraging slaps on the back, didn't try to reassure us. But with him at least you knew where you stood.

•

Souk's sheet of paper sat on my desk all afternoon. Untouched. At the top of the list was the Gris affair. Messy from the start, an unsolved case even now. I'd heard about it, but that was all.

—Don't you have Latin homework? Mom asked.

I was in the middle of a mission and didn't even lift my eyes from the screen.

—Mom, I'm going to die. Who knows when, maybe even today. Do you really want me to have spent the last half-hour of my life studying Latin?

Mom's given up. This time last year she'd have started shouting. Now she just shuts the door and walks away. She used to do that thing with her eyes, too. You know what I mean. All moms play that game. They stare at you and you're supposed to freeze. To repent, to apologize.

As soon as she left the room, I called Dad at work.

—When are you coming home?

—That's so sweet, I miss you too.

—Come on, I'm serious, when are you coming home? I want to ask you something.

—Ask me now, I'll be late.

He's always late. Something always comes up at the last minute. Something only he can take care of.

—What do you know about the Gris affair?

—Why? Is it on the exam?

In the battle over the Panhellenic Exams he's on Mom's side.

—I have to do this project for school and I thought maybe you'd know something. You're the one who told me about it in the first place.

At home Dad doesn't talk much. He sits there and pretends to be listening, but really he's just filtering out whatever he doesn't think is important. If you ask him about current affairs, though, he really gets going. *He gives way to no man*, says Grandma, who's seen him hijack plenty of family gatherings and Christmas dinners over a piece of front-page news. But when his reporter's jaw gets going, when he launches into his I-know-how-it-really-went-down routine, I just press mute. That's why I can't remember a word of what he told us about the Gris affair. All I remember is the name. And Dad on the sofa, shouting.

—A project about Gris? Who gave you that assignment? he asked, incredulous.

—Souk.

—Who?

—Soukiouroglou, Dad. My history teacher?

—Is that the guy you had in middle school? Sort of a loose cannon?

—Yup, that's him.

—I didn't think he had it in him. Turns out he's got balls.

—Dad, do you know anything or should I just hang up?

—Minas, I've got the whole file at home. Gris worked at the paper, you know.

—Great, I'll be waiting, I said and hung up.

I can picture Dad looking at the receiver. Time for his evening drink. A half glass of bourbon with a splash of water. Two cigarettes, one after the other. I don't have a hidden camera or anything, but I'm sure. That's one good thing about parents: they're predictable. Everyone knows that.

Dad got home at 12:37. Mom had already gone to bed. We'd fought and she wanted me out of her sight. Dad slipped off his shoes. Every morning Mom picks his sweater off the coat rack, sniffs the armpits and tosses it into the hamper, even though Dad complains that too much washing ruins them.

—I was waiting for you.

Dad smiled. He lifted the paper napkin off the plate on the kitchen table to see what Mom had left for his dinner. Whole wheat pasta, pesto with basil from the pot on the balcony. A chocolate turtle for dessert. A calorie bomb from start to finish, but Dad only eats once a day. Always after midnight, when he gets home from work. When Mom's in one of her moods she makes pasta, which she calls an "edible antidepressant." It's what we swallow instead of a pill. It works okay.

—So tell me about this project of yours, he said, putting his plate in the microwave.

—"The Manolis Gris case: presentation of facts, assessment of evidence, disputation of sources and views, historical context, and critical evaluation."

I held up the sheet Souk had given me so he could see it.

—Isn't that sort of a lot?

—That's how Souk is. It's no fun for him if he doesn't bring you to your knees.

—Yeah, but don't you have to study for the Panhellenics this year?

I gave him a look. He nodded. Same page.

—If I comport myself with academic rigor and intellectual gravity in the research and writing of this paper, I said, mimicking Souk's voice, I'll be excused from daily evaluation in our class.

Dad listened absentmindedly as he fixed himself a nightcap: he put some tsipouro on the stove and stirred in three spoonfuls of honey. Tsipouro with honey gives you sweet dreams, he always says. He recommends it to Grandma, too, whenever she complains of insomnia. *Lysimelis*, he adds playfully, quoting Archilochus on *limb-loosening* desire, since *meli* for "honey" sounds just like *meli* for "limbs," and Grandma adores anything having to do with ancient Greek.

—I'll need a few days to look over my files, he said.

I was so happy I kissed him on the cheek. He hid a smile. Then I sat down and kept him company for another five minutes. That's my limit.

—Minas, Dad couldn't keep from adding, you know you could get into university if you wanted to. It wouldn't even be that hard.

I didn't reply. He took a sip of his drink and turned on the TV.

If there's one thing I respect about him, it's that he knows when to keep quiet.

THROUGH OTHER EYES

The faculty meeting was scheduled for six p.m. The teachers were sitting in groups, some chatting or whispering in one another's ears, others ostentatiously bored. The principal was still in his office, rustling papers, looking over his agenda. The vice principal—a little meatball of a woman with spindly legs and a girlish ponytail, who sang songs from the resistance when she was in a good mood and always had a smile for everyone, as one of her tricks for getting things done—was already in her seat. She looked out at the warring factions before her: the dad types; the union organizers; the loners who kept their heads down and avoided taking sides; the silent, patient types; the ones who were critical of everyone but themselves; the pissed-off-for-no-reason; the arrogant and annoyingly talkative; the neutrality seekers; the politically engaged. It was each man for himself or everyone thick as thieves, depending on who had what to gain.

In the far left corner of the room, with the back of his chair tilted against the wall, sat Soukiouroglou. He had a book in his lap, a prop to occupy his eyes and hands. He held it open and turned a page every so often, though it was anyone's guess whether he was actually reading.

—Contrary to our usual practice, the principal announced on entering the room, the student council representatives will be present at this meeting.

The students filed in, the middle schoolers unsure of themselves, waiting for the older kids to take their seats first. Chairs had been set up for them in the center of the circle, exposed to view on all sides—*a spot chosen on purpose by the administration*, some would later suggest. The middle school student council president wiped his sweaty palms on his pants. The high school representatives, on the other hand, sat there with a combative air and notebooks at the ready. The girls crossed their legs almost brazenly. Some of the veteran teachers in the room took offense at that stance, though none of them said anything. Their disapproving looks were enough.

The next day some of the teachers defended them—*they're just kids, they haven't learned how to sit properly, where to put their legs*—but most of them knew that body language speaks volumes, reveals all kinds of secret thoughts. Like when Minas Georgiou, who was nearly two meters tall, stretched his gangly legs in their clunky combat boots straight out under the seat in front of him, bottoms up, as if he were mocking them with the red smiley faces painted on the rubber soles. Some were startled, others just figured it was yet another instance of ridiculous teenage fashion, one of those fads that last half a season, tops. Minas watched the meeting unfold with that passive smile kids wear when they want grown-ups to just get off their backs.

The principal scanned the agenda. Rising to his feet, proud of his democratic impulses, which some dissenters called a shocking lack of responsibility, he opened the floor to the students first.

—I'd like to share with you the statement prepared by our fifteen-member council, began Evelina, the high school student council president. We'd like your permission to organize a one-day event at our school concerning the global financial crisis. . . .

Before she'd even finished her sentence, a current of whispers had spread over the teachers' part of the room. A few snickered loudly.

—They should forget this nonsense and start studying, exam time is right around the corner, one teacher hissed to his neighbor.

But some teachers supported the idea, and a few were giving the kids encouraging looks; it was obvious that one or two had offered pointers ahead of time. Among them was the skin-and-bones physics teacher, whom her colleagues called a freak behind her back, because of her messy hair and cherry-red combat boots.

She was always getting the kids worked up over something. Once last year she even took them to a protest when they were supposed to be in class. Plenty of teachers in the room were already annoyed at how this group of snot-nosed brats had come that evening to express their political will.

The students stammered that a one-day event with presentations by economists, lawyers, and sociologists would have educational value.

—Sir, we're the ones who are going to bear the brunt of the crisis, one of the middle schoolers pleaded to the principal.

—I think we've spent enough time on this issue, the chemistry teacher broke in. He had a private lesson scheduled for eight that evening and was in a hurry to get going.

—Perhaps you'd like to propose some names of possible speakers, one teacher said, the irony thick in her voice.

The students looked at her, speechless.

—What did you think, that events just plan themselves? she exclaimed, pleased with herself.

Most of them agreed that the kids were looking for excuses to miss class.

The teachers knew that the students had been negotiating in the principal's office over the past few days. The students promised not to allow a sit-in. They'd learned a thing or two since last year's occupation, when kids who didn't go to their school had come and gone freely, and computers stolen from the computer lab ended up being sold out in the open on pedestrian streets in the city center. The punks would lay them out on torn cardboard boxes and sell them at cut prices, or break them down for parts: a motherboard on Melenikou Street, a brand-new keyboard on Athonos Square. Three months after the sit-in they were still having computer science class on the blackboard. If one kid's father, a high-level banker, hadn't donated old desktops from one of his branches, they would still be taking notes about websites with paper and pencil.

—All the other schools are having sit-ins, Evelina had told the principal in her usual blasé tone a few days prior to the faculty meeting. They're all making fun of us, she said.

—Calling you wusses, huh? the principal asked, trying to show off his knowledge of student slang.

—Something like that, Evelina muttered. How could she possibly repeat the long list of obscenities that students from nearby schools were showering on them? New compound words, neologisms, unspeakably imaginative inventions accompanied by gestures, bumping and grinding, moaning and the sounds of sudden ejaculation. The principal was totally out of touch if he thought *wuss* was the worst the inner-city crowd could think up.

—At any rate, Evelina said, we thought we could organize a one-day event.

—Or maybe two days, said Minas, who was also there, shoving her in the ribs.

—Or two days, Evelina said, without much enthusiasm.

—That way, we'll miss two days of classes, but with your permission, Minas added with utter sincerity, having decided to show his cards in hopes of getting this tedious conversation over with as soon as possible. The students will be happy to have achieved their main goal, the parents will be happy because a two-day event about the crisis sounds more educational than a sit-in. And we'll all be glad the school won't suffer any damage, he said, wrapping up his speech in complete satisfaction with how it had gone.

What Minas didn't realize (perhaps because he was a boy at the height of a raging adolescence), though Evelina did (perhaps because she was a girl with experience as the class attendance-taker), was that complete sincerity isn't always a rhetorical advantage, but on the contrary can be a political disadvantage—political in the wider sense of the word, Evelina would hasten to clarify. And while Evelina, as student council president, had been certain the principal's assent would be enough, they were now told they'd need to present their proposal before the entire faculty and put it to a vote.

Outside the office Evelina swore up and down, furious that she'd have to miss her cram school classes that Wednesday. Minas joked that they'd been issued a rare invitation from the administration to see the teachers in their natural habitat, fighting at a faculty meeting. He leaned over and whispered in her ear, laughed, then pursed his lips and blew a playful puff of air at her bangs. Evelina smoothed her hair with her fingers, annoyed. It had taken her half an hour to straighten it that morning. She started to say something, but decided against it. No matter what she said, she would still miss the explanation of the supine at her cram school. Nothing could make up for those lost hours of study.

Minas was watching an inchworm dance. As small as his fingernail, a sort of dirty color, with an agile tail that turned this way and that like a periscope. It was doing an acrobatics routine on a leaf, dangling from the green edge and bouncing as if on a trampoline. It looked like it was having fun.

—Well? What did the principal say? a first-year named Spiros came over and asked Minas. He was one of those kids who wander around during recess, desperate for someone to talk to.

—We'll see, Minas said, letting the ambiguity hang in the air and turning back to his inchworm.

Spiros, a bony runt in glasses who never knew where to put his hands, didn't budge. Better to be seen with Minas than alone.

That year Spiros had dared to sign up for the student council elections, he'd even drafted a list of proposals and passed out copies during assembly. Minas vaguely recalled something about a robotics workshop and a film club. He'd heard how the girls had giggled. But Spiros, unfazed, climbed up onto the stage where everyone could see him.

—I know I'm not much to look at, he began. I even have a limp, he added, pointing at one of his feet. Then, without any warning, he pulled up that leg of his sweat pants. It was all metal up to the knee.

—He's a fool, Evelina remarked. But Minas clapped.

From that day on, whenever Spiros caught sight of Minas in the schoolyard, he came over and stuck to him like a burr. Evelina wouldn't let it rest. *I saw you with your best friend again*, she'd tease, but Minas paid no attention.

—Well? the kid said, trying to play it cool. What do you think of our teachers?

—They're a life form, too, Minas answered, then turned back to his inchworm.

CHRIST TAUGHT AND DIED
WHAT ARE OUR TEACHERS WAITING FOR?

The slogan appeared sometime on Tuesday night, on the eve of the faculty meeting, according to information the administration gleaned from the inhabitants of neighboring buildings. The man who lived directly across the street called at eight the next morning. For years he'd kindly painted over the graffiti on the outer walls of the school. He didn't want to be paid, the principal could barely make him take money to cover the cost of the paint. But recently he'd seemed less eager to help, and at some point he let it slip that he'd been receiving threatening phone calls. The poor man was terrified. He'd just wanted to help out, he wasn't looking to get mixed up in anything. It proved impossible for them to soothe his fears, and soon enough the outer walls were once again thick with scrawls.

The school board briefly considered the proposal of a parent who was a psychiatrist at an asylum in Stavroupoli and offered to bring a few of the inmates, *non-violent ones, of course*, to return the façade to some semblance of propriety. It sounded feasible, and would have been a cost-effective solution. But what principal wants to tell parents that their children's school is going to be painted by a bunch of certified lunatics?

And so the slogans blossomed all over the building. The gutters were never cleaned, rainwater ran down the walls, the plaster flaked. And the crazies stayed locked up in their asylum. The only one who'd seen them was Minas, whose father was a journalist and often got him into places that were off-limits for other kids his age. Tasos Georgiou, usually incorruptible almost to a fault, thought it perfectly reasonable to pull whatever strings were necessary to gain his curious son access to such places—so long as Teta never found out. Minas's father firmly believed that these experiences gave his son an important, if atypical, social education. And when Minas brought up the idea of visiting the Stavroupoli psychiatric hospital, Tasos approved.

So Minas went, and sat in the amphitheater and watched as a group of psychiatrists examined the patients. It seemed to him that each of the patients before them was living inside his own fully formed personal reality, which no one could shake. And not just the patients: the young doctor over to the right had studied in Paris and was wearing the white coat of an expert, but he didn't seem much better off than the guy they were examining.

Logic, Minas decided as he watched the proceedings, was a poor tool in the hands of these obstinate people called doctors. Most of them made up their minds first, then looked for evidence. And yet they called that common sense.

As he was leaving he noticed a female inmate in the yard. A nurse was sitting on the next bench over, and never once let the woman out of his sight. *Who knows*, Minas thought, *that woman there might have killed someone.* They hadn't told him that the violent ones were kept in the basement. They locked them up, drugged them, and never let them out.

•

Minas's father was well-respected in his field. *An old-school reporter,* said everyone who worked with him. He was a deeply educated man who impressed them not with the superficial knowledge so many others had but with his steady, purposeful way of thinking, which showed he had devoted years to study. He knew how to guide the younger reporters, he gave clear instructions and sifted through their pitches carefully, choosing only the best. *A good guy, and honest,* is the first thing people said about Tasos Georgiou. At the meetings of the journalists' union people shut up and listened when he spoke. His opinion counted with friends and enemies alike. He had climbed the ladder to an important administrative position, but he never moved up the hill to Panorama, the suburb where the rich Thessalonians lived. When the publisher who promoted him suggested upgrading his car, since there was no need for the editor in chief of a major daily paper to be driving around in an old Citroën, Georgiou spat fire. The publisher didn't even get to finish her sentence. She'd been planning on offering him a very respectable Saab—this had been just a few years ago, yet in a different era, when money flowed freely—but she didn't dare continue. The Citroën remained his trademark.

Georgiou was scrupulously fair. And his friends paid the price for it, since he tried to avoid anything that could be interpreted as favoritism. He made sure everyone knew that the paper wasn't his personal fiefdom. A man of the street, he knew exactly who to call for the real story. *Just play the fool,* was his advice to the ambitious young staffers who worked under him, and who worshipped the ground he walked on. Playing the fool meant listening to everyone and keeping your mouth shut. *A reporter doesn't talk,* he counseled them, *that's for the TV anchors who look nice on the screen but don't know a thing about actual journalism.*

News was his drug. He could sniff it out like a dog, from a distance. Even in recent years when he'd held senior staff positions, he never stopped reporting. The phone calls started first thing in the morning. His cell phone was always ringing, and he always picked up, because *you just never know.* A newspaper man to the core, he loved the smell of fresh ink, the feel of the paper. He never read the newspapers his wife would flip through at home, because she messed up sections and got the pages out of order. He teased her about it, but he was half serious, too.

But while he seemed affable and approachable when you first met him—*a good kid,* as his mother-in-law would say, and she knew him inside and out—he also didn't hesitate to show his strength when circumstances called for it. And circumstances mainly called for it during staff meetings at the paper. *The staffers need to know that a steady hand is in charge,* was his motto. He barked at the editors. One well-respected staff writer was even seen crying in the bathroom after an important meeting. Everyone in the business agreed that Georgiou did his job, and did it well.

He had a say in every aspect of the paper, from the front page to the captions. Nothing escaped him, he picked the paper apart, right down to the horoscopes, which he held to the same standard as everything else. If you made some disparaging remark about their insignificance, he would cut you off in mid-phrase. Taken together, these things garnered his subordinates' respect. He was always there in difficult times, his hand on the rudder; he never left anyone unprotected. He knew who actually worked and who just sat around scratching his balls. When he gave praise, he did so out loud and in public. If necessary, he made the careless feel like garbage, but always in the privacy of his office.

For years Tasos Georgiou had worked himself to the bone. He got home late, left early. He thought he'd found a way of balancing everything. Then came Minas's first year of preschool, when Tasos came home one night to find Teta waiting up for him on the sofa. They opened a bottle of wine and Teta announced:

—This morning when I was walking Minas to preschool, he asked me, *Mom, did Dad die?* He wanted to know if you were still alive. He hasn't seen you in five days.

She set her glass on the table, still untouched.

—You've got some choices to make, she warned.

From that day on, Georgiou made a point of spending each Saturday with Minas. He took him to the zoo, to museums, to parks. The three of them would eat together off the good china in the dining room, with a tablecloth. Pork roast, rice molded into little mounds, sautéed carrots, roasted potatoes. The world could start turning backwards, but he still wouldn't work on a Saturday. He'd promised not to and he kept his word.

He watched as his child grew. A photograph of a gap-toothed Minas on the fridge, dressed as a snowman for the Christmas pageant when he was in first grade. The valentine his mother found in his book bag, written by a classmate, with the question, *Minas, will you marry me?* and a heart with an arrow through it. His report cards, all columns of perfect twenties. DVDs from family vacations. His first concert. All these things he'd accomplished.

Tasos didn't make a big deal of it, but he believed his son was special. Tall, healthy, handsome. A fresh mind, with secret fixations and unexpected flights of fancy. Minas didn't have many friends, and often spent whole days and nights in his room. But that had ceased to worry his father, who now had more important things on his mind. Teta had broken the news: Minas wouldn't be going to university. He wasn't interested in continuing his studies. Who would believe it if they heard? Cutting off his nose to spite his parents, is what he'd say if Minas were someone else's child. But Tasos knew how rough the whole thing was on Teta. Pretty soon she was going to have to admit her son's failure—and thus her failure, too—to all the other kids' mothers, whom she hated running into anyway.

The worst part was that they had run out of arguments. You won't find a job, these days a university degree is what a high school diploma used to be. You'll be uncultivated, like a raw, unfinished slab of wood. We'll sell the apartment and you can go to university abroad, wherever you want. Crisis or no crisis, we'll manage. *How on earth will we manage*, Teta secretly fretted. She watched the news and couldn't sleep for worry, twenty years of hard work and all they had to show for it was 80,000 euros in the bank. Even if Minas were to agree, that kind of money just wasn't enough to send their son to school abroad.

At some point the stress got to be too much. She withdrew all the money from the Bank of Greece, flew to Cyprus and deposited it there. The low interest rate stung. *You didn't bring it here for the interest*, the bank manager shot back. Teta grabbed the bank book and turned on her heel, cutting short all pretense and niceties. When she got back to Athens, she told Minas the money for his studies was safe.

Not that he cared. Minas had gotten his stubbornness from Teta's side of the family: Evthalia's Pontic mind never budged once it was made up. As the months passed, Georgiou realized that it wasn't an act or pose. He even went with Teta to their son's school, though he hadn't set foot in the place in years. He listened as Minas's teachers explained what the problem was, though none suggested a solution. They cared, but caring wasn't enough.

Teta went back alone the next day to talk to Soukiouroglou, who assured her he'd do what he could to intervene. She knew Soukiouroglou wasn't one to spout empty words. If he said something, he meant it—but the promises Teta wanted weren't ones the teacher was able to make.

1948 AND EARLIER

"MOTHER, THERE'S A WAR ON
OUT THERE. I'LL BE LATE."

KYRIA MARIA GRIS, MOTHER OF MANOLIS

My lips may smile, but inside there's sorrow.

We're refugees. What did we know of Greece? We used to hear the name in church, *for the good of Greece*, Father Evgenios would chant. We would cross ourselves three times. I was born in Trape-zounta. Trabzon. In a house by the sea. My hair would curl from the salt in the air. I'd wash it and iron it on the table to make it straight. I was a girl then, didn't fear God, only my father. I was in love with the psalter in our district. A polite boy. His voice trembled when he sang the Good Friday lament, *my sweet springtide*, he sang with tears in his eyes and the mothers would cry, and we cried too, the girls who'd covered the bier of Christ with flowers that morning.

One day my father brought me a man to marry. From a good family, established in the town. They shook hands. I was fourteen years old, I thought I would die. My mother-in-law grabbed the silk from my dowry as fast as she could, as if it were hers. On the day I entered her house as a bride she made me wash her feet. So I would learn which of us ruled the roost. She made me kneel in the dirt. My husband watched and didn't speak. Nor did the neighbor women who had gathered from nearby houses. I scrubbed her feet with my bare hands, tossed out the washwater, poured fresh into the tin basin and scrubbed some more. When I got tired, I lay her feet on my skirts to dry. I was wearing my best dress, my wedding dress. She dirtied it with her filthy feet. Then she pulled me up off the ground, kissed both cheeks and pushed me into the house. *Come inside, girl*, she said, yanking my braid.

We had four children. Manolis, Savvas, Evgnosia, and Violeta. Another two died on me, twins. I light candles for them on the Day of Lights, I learned that from my mother. I fill a basin with sand, stick the candles for the dead in there, so there's a light to show my little birds the way. I lost them before they even tasted milk. You people here don't know that tradition. You don't bring your dead into the house.

My husband, Stathis, worked in the fields. A farmer. Nineteen years old, what could he know, you'll say, of running a household, a beardless child himself. Quick to anger, and to punish the children. He never lifted a hand against them the way other fathers did, who hit their boys with belts. You could hear the screams from the street. Stathis just furrowed his brow and stared at us with that look of his, like a bull. It made our knees quake. He used to shut the littlest, Violeta, up in the barn with the animals, and left Manolis there to make sure she didn't sneak out. My little girl never ate much, even as a baby. All she wanted was eggs, she couldn't stand the sight of bean soup. He would let her go hungry and that imp still wouldn't open her mouth to let a bite go down.

My boys were more obedient, especially Manolis. They had respect. Stathis wanted to send them to school. He wanted to make them into men, that's what he used to say. *We may go hungry, wife, but our children will go to school*, he would shout, mostly for his mother to hear, who had other ideas. He would raise his hand and point toward the Greek school of Trabzon. *We have fine schools here, and my sons are going to learn their letters, they're going to make something of themselves.*

We made plans. We had no idea that the Turks were sharpening their knives.

My Pontus is gone, is gone, is gone.
They took my Pontus away.

Mothers fleeing with babes, stunned and dazed.
They burned my village, smoke and fire.
Where is my husband, my brother, dead with no grave.
We mourn, we mourn, with souls in our mouths we cry.

•

Don't ask me how we made it to Greece. The children hear the stories adults tell and think they remember. But only Manolis remembers. I had no husband by my side, so he became the man in the family, a boy of eight. He helped with the little ones, he took charge. I was a widow with four children. Try to imagine that.

Later on they'd come and say, *You folks were rich, you had money. You came with gold coins sewn into the hems of your dresses, whole fortunes.* Whoever hasn't lived the life of a refugee has easy words to speak.

When they brought us to Salonica, I didn't care about the hunger or about how filthy we were, after days on boats. I looked at the city and said to Manolis, *This is where we'll live.* The sea was a comfort to me.

I grabbed the girls in my arms, the boys clung to my skirts. *Hold tight*, I told them, and walked as fast as my legs would carry me. I didn't want to lose courage. I couldn't get sick, either. I had children to care for.

I bought our first eggs from a local woman at the port. She looked at my hands, hoping for rings or bracelets, but I gave her coins. The dirty thing spat on the ground. *You've come to eat our bread*, she muttered, tucking the money into her dress. She wanted more, for a pot with a hole in the bottom, but I pushed her away.

At the church of Agia Sophia I pulled the key to our house in Trabzon out of my apron. A big wrought iron key. I set an egg in the hole, it fit perfectly. I crossed myself and cooked it over the candles burning as offerings. I fed my children in the churchyard. Violeta laughed. *Mama, it's nice here*, she said, clapping her hands.

Manolis spent two years at the Papafeio orphanage learning to be a carpenter. One day a teacher came to the house and told me about the American School, said my child should study there, he'd do well. I remembered Stathis. He would've cursed me from the grave if he knew his child was an apprentice carpenter. I was ashamed before Manolis, too. His heart leapt at the teacher's words, but he just sat in the corner and didn't speak. That child never asked for a thing.

—A boy's studies, Kyra-Maria, the teacher said, are the golden bracelet on his wrist. You're from the Pontus, you understand, he added to butter me up.

That night when the other children were asleep, Manolis came and stood at the head of my bed.

—Mother, he said, touching my arm.

—You're barefoot, son, you'll freeze, I scolded him.

There was a cold like poison that night.

—Mother, Manolis said again. If I study, I'll be able to take care of the little ones.

Ai, let me take pride in my dear boy.

That's what he called them, *little ones*, though he was just two years older than Savvas. But Manolis was old from birth. *What a serious child*, others said, impressed. Sometimes even I forgot he was a child and spoke to him as if he really were the man of the house. Because Manolis took charge of things. He placed orders with the butcher, helped his siblings with their meals, with their studies. He scolded them, yelled at them if he felt the need. And they looked up to him, Violeta most of all. She'd run to him with her drawings, or in tears if something went wrong. He was the only one who could get her to eat, she would clean her plate for him.

May lightning strike me, there's not a bad word I can say about my son. He finished the American School, found work. As a reporter. He knew English, that helped. We all took a deep breath. I thought we'd been saved. I thought our worries were over. Our sadness had brought joy.

My mind couldn't even imagine.

I sent two children off to war, but only one came home. Years passed, the tears dried in my eyes. I still think about Savvas every day. I light a candle, I pray for his soul to be as light as a feather. And I don't fear death as I used to. When the time comes, my boy will come to lead me away. I'll hold him in my arms. I'll get my fill of him, my second son, the son who felt neglected.

—Mother, he used to say, you've only got the one child, Manolis.

I'd get mad, lash out at him.

Not a year had passed since he died when he came and found me in my sleep.

I opened my arms and waited. He was wearing his good white shirt, the one I'd sewn for him. The dead don't speak in dreams, that's what my mother used to say. But Savvas had a bone to pick.

—Mother, he asked. If you had to choose, who would you choose?

Oi, oi. . . . I woke in a sweat, sobbing. The ceiling struck my chest like iron. My soul ached. My heart stung, deep in pain.

Woe to me, such a great evil I never saw.

—Which son would you give to Hades, mother?

I knew the answer.

And my Savvas knew it, too.

I'd told them I loved them all the same. We would lie together in bed, and the little ones would ask:

—Who do you love best, Mama? Tell us, Mama!

It was their game. Only Manolis never asked. I would raise my hand, show them my fingers.

—Look here, at my fingers. Each one is different, none like the next. But whichever one I cut off, I'd hurt just the same.

Lies. I told them lies.

They would fall asleep amid laughter, kisses and caresses. Lullabies, songs about the sea at Trabzon.

I climbed up the hill of Poz Tepe
And saw Trapezounta below

The tears in my poor eyes
May never dry.

My Savvas was killed in the service of the country.
　—I could shit on your country, I howled, and Evgnosia ran to
shut the windows.
　I shouted at her to take down the icons.
　I wanted nothing of God in my house.
　I never had a chance to kiss the blood of my son.
　They buried him in a foreign land and sent me a piece of paper.
　I thought I would die.
　My guts turned to rock.
　If you slit me open, you'd find soil and stone.
　Any mother would understand.
　And anyone else should keep quiet.
　May their mouths be filled with cement.

An angel came, with wings.
With the cross in his hand.
He came and announced the terrible news.
What I could give I gave.
I even gave my soul,
I gave my child as a gift to God.

Light a candle, suffer no more.
Let this soul rest, wear black no more.

Manolis suffered, but he didn't show it. He had to seem strong, to
support me. That's how firstborns are, they shoulder all the weight
and never say a thing. I didn't realize it then, I thought the pain was
mine, belonged to me alone.
　I didn't forget my Savvas, but I stopped crying in front of the

children. I didn't want to poison their days. But when the children were out, when the house was empty, I brought the whole world down with my sobbing.

One night Manolis came home, sat down beside me, stroked my back. He started to say something, but the words stuck in his throat. He was a wise child, he never spoke without thinking, the way others do.

—It would have been better if I had died, mother.

I turned and looked at him, for the first time in a long while. He was hunched over as if he were carrying stones on his back.

I remembered the dream.

If you had to choose, who would you choose?

The next day I ran to church and confessed. I told the priest.

—God forgive me, Father. I'm torn to pieces over the child I lost. But if I lost Manolis I would die.

ZOE TSOKA, WIDOW OF THE AMERICAN REPORTER

He stared at my arms. A widow doesn't wear sleeveless dresses, I'm sure that's what he was thinking. They all look at me strangely, and they've called me in for interrogation eight times. I don't cry, don't beat my chest, don't wear a kerchief. I'm young, beautiful, slender. Too much the stewardess for their taste.

If they could, they would have buried me with him.

And he, the head of the Security Police, is the worst kind of village boor. A lout. I caught him picking his nose. I'd rushed into the room, I couldn't understand why he'd called me down again, just to tell him the same things over and over. He pulled his finger out of his nose and stuck the precious discovery on the bottom of his chair with an air of indifference.

Revolting.

Where I'm from men like him were my servants, they shined my shoes, opened doors so I wouldn't dirty my gloves. I grew up in Alexandria, with a silver spoon in my mouth. I had a French governess and a real porcelain tea set for my dolls. The lace from my dowry dates back three generations. My dresses were all tailored in Paris.

On evenings when she was going out to the theater, Mother would take me into her room and lay her dresses on the bed so I could help her choose. We picked out earrings and necklaces. She sang and clapped and tickled me, pulled on satin gloves, spritzed herself with perfume. She always left in a rush. She would kiss the air around me, so as not to muss me with her lipstick. She left the other dresses on the bed and the jewelry boxes open. When she was gone I would try on her clothes, her jewelry, her pumps, posing in front of the three-paneled mirror. I was pretty.

Father worried that I would marry too young. But Mother would reply that *a woman's marriage is her career—which is to say, the sooner the better*, she added, pinching my behind. When I told them I was going to become a stewardess, they didn't show the enthusiasm I had expected, but didn't object, either. Father, who had lost piles of money during the war, not to mention Mother's entire dowry, said that it was a fine job, well remunerated. *And you'll meet plenty of respectable gentlemen*, Mother said, smiling.

She was right, I did. I even came close to marrying one of them. His name was Jan, he was Swedish. He worked for his father's company, and he was in line to be president. He was polite and obliging. He entertained me for three days in Stockholm, in December, just before Christmas. We ate reindeer with elderberry sauce. It smelled so awful I thought I would vomit. But the worst part was the darkness—a thick darkness that enveloped people and houses and everything else. It was only light for three hours each day. And it was a weak, consumptive light that came out looking frightened and hid again soon after.

I made some excuse and left early. I wouldn't have stayed another day for all the world. My soul shrank in that darkness, I thought I would die.

Later on I met Jack. He was twice as old as me, and twice as tall, too. I had met very few Americans in my life, but he certainly stood out. His eyes shone as if he had a fever. He laughed out loud, and he hugged me so tight he left a mark. He danced like a movie star. He loved life and let it show. He had friends everywhere. With him the day was a thousand hours long. There was time for everything.

He asked me to marry him. He kneeled in the middle of the street one day and kissed the toe of my shoe. Passersby were watching, but he didn't care. He took the ring out of his pocket and said, *Will you marry me?* without any warning, without any wasted words. I said yes right away, and he kissed me so hard my lip split. *It'll be like sugar, the two of us together*, he promised. He wasn't one for words, he preferred actions.

After we were married he asked me if I knew any *good communists* he could talk to, if we had anyone in the family *who's in the Party, any reds, a man I can trust*, someone who could arrange an interview with the rebel General. I laughed. *So that's why you married me*, I teased.

I did in fact have a third cousin who was a rebel fighter. Jack insisted that we go visit him in jail. I still remembered Nikitas in shorts, stealing candies from me and shoving them all in his mouth at once. Stuffed, saliva running down his chin, and him laughing so hard he almost choked. The young man who came and stood before me now was as thin as a branch. His eyes had seen war, his hands had killed. I didn't recognize him. *Nikitas*, I whispered. He was only a year older than me. A vein pulsed on his cheekbone. He saw me notice. If he could, he would have ripped it out then and there.

Jack asked me to tell Nikitas he was a reporter. *An American*, he added, since that usually opened doors. He would go wherever they told him to, would follow their instructions to the letter, as long as he could interview the General.

—Your husband is crazy, was Nikitas's response. Or he's pretending to be, he added, not even looking in Jack's direction.

We left empty-handed. Jack had plenty of enemies at that point. He'd been making a stink to people in high places in the government, because the American aid packages weren't being distributed to the families of communists in the villages.

—From a political perspective it's not unjust, I heard him saying to someone over the phone. I understand your position, we don't feed the hand that bites, or kills. But, my dear friend, they're letting women and children go hungry.

Antrikos, our friend in Athens, warned me.

—You need to reel him in, he said. Two days ago, Jack met with the Minister of the Interior. They say Jack was shouting about the riots breaking out all over the country. He accused Rimaris of letting his men pick and choose where the American aid ended up. Sincerity isn't a solution or a cure, Antrikos cautioned. There are certain things we just don't say.

Jack should have known.

We could all see it: my husband was ambitious. He wanted to be the first and the only. If anyone ever said no, he simply didn't listen. His stubbornness brooked no denial.

—A reporter's job is to do the things others find impossible, he told his friends with a smile.

Antrikos disagreed.

The General was the trophy they were all chasing after. No one had ever met with him, no one had any idea where he was. An interview with the leader of the rebels in his hiding place would make an international splash. If Jack could pull it off, he would return crowned with laurels. Then maybe he would calm down. We'd go to America, have a family. He would work a desk job at the radio station, he wouldn't feel the need to prove anything to anyone anymore.

—Don't listen to him, Antrikos advised. When this is over, something else will come to take its place. The man can't sit still, don't you see?

That's when I started to notice. At restaurants he always kept his back to the wall. He slept with a revolver under his pillow. He said it was part of the job. The truth was, he lived dangerously. That's why he took pleasure in every moment. And I admired him for that.

I was a fool. I thought life owed us something. Disasters were for other people, that's what I thought. I'd never been denied anything.

I got out all the crystal from my dowry. I wrapped each piece carefully in rags, then packed them in barrels, in layers of hay. I would take it all to America, even the porcelain tea set for my dolls. I would have a baby girl and we'd sip tea and pretend to be ladies together. Our departure date had been set.

Auf Wiedersehen.

Jack had been up in Salonica for days. We'd fought, that's what the papers wrote. But I had only stayed behind to pack for our journey. Our clothes, the radio from my dowry, the embroidered sheets. The furniture he'd brought back from the Middle East. The desk, the armchairs, the bed. I had a suit made for the flight, pear green, with a cream-colored hat and gloves and a bow at the back. New clothes for a new place. A new life.

It wasn't a serious argument. We'd have settled things with a kiss. In bed, where all our fights got resolved. Jack just didn't want to bring me with him. He was trying to protect me. I arrived, as we had agreed, a few days later, and was told that he'd gone missing.

I was the only one who didn't worry. I was sure he'd return. It was a foolish but unsinkable optimism. A childish stubbornness. People commented on it, I know. Everyone else was worried, you see.

—His mule of a wife comes and goes without a care in the world, people at the hotel whispered behind my back.

I asked them to heat water, so the bath would be ready when he came back. I left him a note and went out for a walk in the town, to buy ribbon for a hem. *Make sure to shave, honey, so your whiskers don't tickle me. I miss you. Zouzou.*

That was his pet name for me, Zouzou. He would purse his lips and say it playfully. *Zouzou, will you pour me some whiskey? Zouzou, what did you do with my newspaper? Zouzou, want me to teach you to dance jazz?* He thought it was funny that I knew how to waltz but couldn't dance jazz. He was a wonderful dancer. He could dance for hours on end. He would pull me onto the dance floor, hold me in his arms, and I'd let myself go.

—Listen to the rhythm, he would whisper in my ear. With this kind of music, all the dancing happens below the waist. You're from the East, you know how it goes.

He would slip his hand under my skirt so casually that no one even noticed.

—He's handsome, your husband, Antrikos's wife said to me one afternoon when we were getting snacks ready in the kitchen.

I liked it when other people admired him. I didn't even mind all the crazy things he did, the fire in his belly. I preferred him that way, it was better than him clinging to my skirts. *A husband should be the master of his house*, my mother said. *And a wife should know how to manage him*, she would continue, embroidering dishtowels for my dowry. *Marriage takes work, little miss*, she lectured me when I was a girl. She taught me the rules, her rules. *First, always be attentive. Second, learn how to pamper. Third, provide beauty in the home and in your dress. Fourth, housekeepers and maids should be good, obedient, and fat.* If I asked why they should be fat, she would shake her head. *Because a fat woman knows how to cook, my dear. And she'll never set a house on fire*, she would continue, though she never explained what she meant by that. *Five, tell the truth to the priest, not to your husband. Six, separate bedrooms save a woman's sleep and her marriage, too. Seven, a husband should love and care for his children. Eight, your nightgowns should be even finer than your dresses. Nine, always be a lady, except in bed. Ten, marriage is a career. It takes persistence, endurance and dedication.*

Those are the things my mother taught me. If she could, she would have opened my little girl's brain and shoved it all in. The first time she met Jack, she gave him her hand and smiled. That night she pumped me for information. Where he lived in America, who was paying him now that he was working in Greece, if he'd ever behaved improperly with me, since she'd heard that Americans have no manners. She wasn't too keen on the fact that he didn't speak French. How would she tell him everything she needed him to know?

Because my beanpole, as she called him, would be taking me far from the war. We would go to live in New York. The houses there didn't have bullet holes, as they did in Athens. The shelves in the markets were full of canned vegetables and colorful candies. We would buy a car. I would meet important people. I would wear nylon slips. I would live well.

What mattered was that I leave as soon as I could. My passport had been issued. There was nothing standing in the way. Life had been kind to us.

ARIS TSIRIGOS, ENGLISH TEACHER TO MANOLIS GRIS

He was a good student. Diligent, conscientious. He took care with his homework. At recess he didn't run around in the courtyard with the other kids, he just sat and watched. He liked difficult words, the ones he thought would impress people. But he didn't know how to use them properly. When I corrected his papers I always encouraged him to write more simply, but he kept going for the big words.

He tried hard to imitate an American accent. Language requires a good ear, it's a kind of music. I tried to explain that to those hulking teenagers, but they paid no attention. Except for Gris. He tried, he studied. He worked hard. But he never excelled. He didn't have a good ear. He couldn't hear the words. A clean pronunciation, basic syntax—that's as far as he got.

To be fair, he did improve. He was one of few students who actually improved over the years. *He works like the devil*, I once said at a faculty meeting, and my fellow teachers laughed. It had gotten to where I was no longer covering his papers with red ink. His English no longer had any mistakes. But his writing was still obviously that of a foreigner, someone who would never grasp the subtle resonances, the cadence of a phrase, the way an idiom can explain everything in just a few words.

He knew that speaking English would open doors for him. That's why he improved. He didn't make any embarrassing mistakes, but he also never expressed exactly what was in his mind with the precision of a native speaker. He simply didn't have the vocabulary.

He always picked up his report card himself. I only saw his mother once: standing respectfully in the door of the teachers' office, not wanting to disturb us, since we all seemed to be busy. She was waiting for someone to look her way, to muster the courage she needed to open her mouth. The headmaster had sent for her. She left her younger ones at the entrance to the school, she must have given them strict instructions, because they stood there stock still for a long time—the guard even commented on it, said he'd never seen such obedient children. Manolis Gris's mother was wearing black, *a widow*, we all thought. Her clothes were ragged from use and from washing. The literature teacher whispered her enthusiastic praise of the velvet braid on the hem and cuffs of the woman's dress, *how lovely*, she whispered to the man next to her, *with one tiny detail, she's made that dress fashionable*. But what most of us were really admiring was her hair. Glossy and as black as a winter night. She had gathered it into a bun, but little wisps escaped from the hairpins and fell unnoticed at the nape of her neck and at her temples. She must have come at a run. Some of us raised our hands almost imperceptibly. We would happily have reached out to touch that hair. We had frozen in our seats; bent over our papers, we stole glimpses at her. After all, we were the child's teachers, responsible for his education.

Then I suddenly remembered that Gris had misbehaved, and realized that was why his widowed mother had come running, and why the headmaster had sent for her in the first place. When I entered the classroom for third period that morning, the upper jamb of the door was missing, as we later noted in the disciplinary proceedings. Holes gaped where the nails had been, and the piece of wood that had been pulled out was laid carefully to one side.

—Who did this?

I had two troublemakers in mind. Worse than troublemakers, pigs.

Gris raised his hand.

—I did, sir.

He had hung from it for a game, don't ask me why or how he got himself up there. He, a kid you'd never even notice, had pulled down the entire top of the doorframe with one motion. And he had the courage to admit it in front of the entire class.

I took him to the headmaster's office. He was quaking. I was careful to present the situation in a neutral manner. It was a tricky situation, since it wouldn't do to sully the child's record because of a single mistake.

—Punish them, don't crush them, the headmaster had told us during our last faculty meeting. We want to graduate men from this school, not hens.

Until that moment, Gris had been more or less invisible. A good kid, a good student. Diligent but unremarkable. The kind of student who continues to greet you politely in the street for years, but whose name you can never remember. The headmaster had already been informed of the incident. He listened patiently to my account of the events, then turned to Gris.

—Is he telling the truth? he asked the student.

—I did it, sir, I hung from the doorframe, I was only playing, I didn't think it would come loose so easily, the child answered in a single breath.

That same day, Gris's mother was called to the school. The headmaster punished the child—it was impossible not to—but he didn't touch his scholarship. He accompanied the widow to the gate, and gave the other children candies, *a poor reward for their excellent behavior.*

One thing I realized that day was that Gris's mother, a woman who seemed as fragile as porcelain, could withstand fire and rain. She wouldn't allow a headmaster, who'd spent his life ordering others around from behind a desk, to decide the fate of her son.

When Gris asked me for a reference letter, I wrote him one, something I rarely agreed to do. I testified to his perfect knowledge of English, though I knew he was hopeless when it came to idiomatic language. His writing was unrepentantly functional; he was going to be a journalist, he informed me proudly. So I put my hand to my heart and signed the letter. As far as a news service was concerned, he would manage. He knew how to put a sentence together, and he would work like a dog to do the job well.

And he did. Every so often I would come across one of his articles. He would write for anyone, from communists to Germans, so long as he got paid. I couldn't blame him: as his mother used to say, *words come easily to people whose bellies are full.* Gris was careful to provide actual information, rather than pepper his texts with the pretty but empty phrases so many journalists seem fond of. He nurtured his sentences as if they were plants, trimmed them, fertilized them. The poor things still came out colorless, miserable, weak, and his attempts to improve them only made them worse.

But a reporter isn't judged by the pulse of his phrases. That's for dilly-dallying poets, or so most people think. Philistines. I never shared their opinion. They supposedly care only about the news itself. But they also love bright, shiny words. Popular phrases are their greatest weakness. In his later writings, Gris didn't stitch phrases together merely to impress the ignorant. He crafted the joints of a paragraph, made sure his sentences followed one another logically and consistently.

When disaster befell him, the city buzzed with the news. People are naïve. They'll believe whatever they read, rather than trust their own opinion. Gris desperately needed character witnesses. Individuals who had known him since he was a child, reasonable citizens with unsullied names who would put their hands on a Bible for him. Who would, moreover, allow their names to be associated with his in the papers.

At certain times, little things assume significance. The headmaster refused to come forward in Gris's defense. He used the school as his excuse: he didn't want its name to be dragged through the mud. What would the students say, not to mention their fathers? He was truly sorry, but he simply couldn't do it. I suspect he slept easily after that. He didn't second-guess his decision, he dressed it up, supported it, and that was that.

The truth was, he was shitting himself with fear.

Gris asked for my help from behind bars. His sister came and found me at home. She didn't cry, didn't fall at my feet. She asked calmly, resignedly, already convinced I would refuse. She'd already been to see everyone else: colleagues, employers, old classmates. Neighbors, other teachers, the headmaster. By that point she knew what to expect.

I always try not to act rashly. Spontaneity is for Shakespearean plots, not for real life, and when the situation calls for it, I can usually distinguish between the two. I'm fairly certain even

Shakespeare wrote with a cold, calm hand, even as he tossed his characters into the fire. I told Gris's sister that I wanted to weigh things before making a decision.

Sleep is a good advisor in difficult moments. By the next morning I had made up my mind. Gris's sister kissed my hand as if I were a priest.

I'm no saint. But whatever the newspapers said, I did know Gris. During the trial they asked if I had children of my own.

—Of course, I answered. Two hundred each year. Does that suffice?

Some in the audience laughed; the papers quoted me in their coverage of the trial. For me the issue is simple. I teach Shakespeare. Literature is my life. For years in my classroom I'd been telling generations of young, impressionable students that words are actions. The time had come for me to prove it. I put my hand on the Bible and swore. If the opinion of a teacher who's paid to tame souls counts for anything, Gris never raised a gun.

THROUGH OTHER EYES

On May 16, 1948, a few hours after the body of the American journalist was pulled from the sea, the prime minister of Greece anxiously stated that he had *personally ordered the police force of the entire country to take action regarding this affair.*

The police realized right away that it was no time to drag their heels, no time for excuses or sloppiness. It was a matter of pride for the force.

Politicians and various people of influence asked to be kept abreast of developments. Some even called the office of the head of the General Security Police in Salonica to exert pressure. To make matters worse, the American government, whose forces were distributing food and promises throughout Greece, was demanding that an example be made of the murderer. They went so far as to give the prime minister a deadline. In other words, the Americans didn't believe the assurances of the Greek authorities, and issued an ultimatum.

Which is to say, no more dollars or napalm.

No more convincing argument was needed; the Minister of Justice assumed personal responsibility for the case. With an administration susceptible to compromise and unwilling to stand its ground, the nation's protectors hurriedly manned all posts in an attempt to push the investigation forward.

Foreign policy isn't a job for priests, commented those in high places, who knew how difficult it could be to keep your hands clean if you wanted to get results. *Anyone who thinks otherwise is just naïve*, they added cynically. *Words come easily to those whose hands have never been held to the fire.* Greece needed money, munitions, tanks. The war had ended everywhere else—but not here.

Jack wasn't just any foreign correspondent, which would have been bad enough. He also came from a historic and wealthy family, from old money—to the extent that there is such a thing in America. The eleventh president of the United States of America occupied an important position in his family tree. Jack had plenty of journalistic successes on his résumé, as well as a badge of honor from his days in the Navy. In Palestine he had almost killed an Arab who dared throw a punch at him. In 1947 his airplane had crashed while he was on duty in the Middle East. The nurse who tended to his wounds saw a tall, thin man smiling at her through the blood.

—There's no way I'm going to die, I've got a fellowship at Harvard, I have to get home, he whispered.

The nurse had seen people die of less severe wounds, but the young man wouldn't give up. He'd decided to live, so he lived.

And now his swollen corpse had turned an entire country upside-down. The head of the Security Police in Salonica, Thomas Tzitzilis, under whose jurisdiction the case fell, was widely praised for his work, and was considered able and sharp-witted. He was a pious citizen who took communion regularly. He crossed himself in public, always bought the most expensive candle to light at church, and took care of the poor and the weak, especially if someone else was watching. He was on good terms with God—*and even better terms with the devil*, his enemies claimed. A rabid anti-communist, he had served in the city of his birth for all the years he was in the police force. He knew all the side streets and back alleys, he knew which witnesses would be most willing to talk, he knew everyone's weak spots. He was on a first-name basis with men in high places but had ties to the underworld, too, and particularly its nightlife. Perhaps that was why some suggested that a case of such international significance wasn't for the likes of him, that he was too much the uncouth boor who knew, to be sure, how to make a man scream, but hadn't learned the art of subtlety or circuitousness.

Of course the American reporter had gone too far, had dug his own grave, as many hinted but no one dared say outright. Before he came up to Salonica Talas paid a visit to Rimaris, the Minister of the Interior, and threatened him to his face. It was as clear as day, in fact he had proof, that government insiders were selling arms to the rebels and stealing American aid. Those were dangerous words, especially when spoken by a reporter.

Jack was fighting with fire. He confided to a friend, also a well-known foreign correspondent, that in Greece there were *royalist right-wingers who are squeezing the country for their own benefit— and sending dollars out in diplomatic pouches as fast as possible.* Antrikos, who was present for the conversation, hurried to close the door. There were informers everywhere, and an American passport wasn't a suit of armor, even if Jack thought his indignation should be contagious.

The worst was that Zoe, or Zouzou—whatever they called his widow—had naïvely asked the American consul, when she heard that her husband had been killed:

—Was it the far right?

Her mother wasn't there to tug her sleeve, to put pepper on her tongue, to keep her in line. So she let it slip without considering the consequences. It took weeks for them to undo the damage.

Thomas Tzitzilis had never cold-cased a file. He tidily completed his investigations, had an unfailing instinct, and didn't waste time on bureaucratic formalities. His superiors were sure his smarts would be sufficient to solve the crime.

But certain critics—*fairies*, the men in the police force called them—were bothered by his disregard for due process. What did they know of prisons and interrogations? Greece was at war, it would behoove them to remember that fact every now and then. Due process was all fine and well, but the current political situation didn't allow for any dragging of feet.

The coast guard had catalogued everything on the dead man's person: checks and bills, in drachmas and dollars, an identification card, a watch, and a wedding ring. There was thus no evidence, Tzitzilis noted, that the victim had been murdered by a thief.

The next scenario he considered was a crime of passion. The deceased's wife seemed too refined for affairs, a spoiled, impulsive, almost childlike young woman. She claimed to be nineteen, but she had the chest and hips of a sixteen-year-old girl. The police chief questioned her no fewer than eight times. Such a thing was unheard of, the girl's parents objected, but Tzitzilis insisted on asking her all kinds of unspeakable questions—how many suitors she'd had before she met Jack, if her hymen had been unbroken on the night of her marriage, if she had a lover, if Jack might have had a lover, if they had intercourse regularly.

The girl was struck dumb. She didn't understand what all that could have to do with the case.

—It's all relevant, the police chief said sharply. If I'm asking you, it's relevant.

He offered her a cigarette. He filled it, brought it to his mouth, ran his tongue along the paper, and then held out his hand in a gesture of goodwill. Zouzou didn't even look at it; that was the last thing she needed, to lick the old man's spit.

The police chief smiled. But inside he was annoyed: this snotty kid thought she was calling the shots. If she thought the Americans would take her side, she was sorely mistaken. He'd heard what the American officials had to say on the subject: generals and diplomats alike were hoping to get Zouzou off their backs, particularly now that she had an American passport. That's why they were taking their sweet time with her visa. After all, she was no longer a spouse but a widow, so what business did she have going to America?

But Zouzou was no pushover, as Tzitzilis quickly realized. A wisp of a girl, sure, but she turned them all inside-out with her eyes and their expression of innocent wonder. Her clothes were more suited for a dance than for mourning. She walked around shame-lessly with arms bare to the shoulder. Her sweet perfume alerted them each time she walked into the station; the scent trailed her down the corridors. She threw all the men into an uncomfortable state, and they lowered their eyes when she passed, as if they were her lackeys. And that's just how Zouzou treated them, too.

Only Tzitzilis was unaffected by her wiles. He heard the snap of her high heels at the front door and her smell burned his nostrils. It was, he thought, the smell of a woman of the world, who knew how to open her legs, to move her hips expertly. He knew her kind inside and out, her tricks had no effect on him, he'd laid his hands on his fair share of society women. He wasn't interested in silk slips and perfumed armpits, he knew what a girl like that had under her skirts. Tzitzilis was more interested in whores, working girls who washed with clean towels. Smiling and obedient, grateful for a cus-tomer who finished quickly, particularly if he might tip.

Zouzou was full of dreams and caprices. *How tiresome*, Tzitzi-lis thought every time he had to question her. Only an American would get involved with her, or an over-educated dupe. Though he had to admit, the girl had spunk. Sure, her eyelashes fluttered like butterflies in spring—but on the inside she was sharp as a razor.

She cut right through you, never bowed her head. The police chief quickly realized that the hypothesis of a crime of passion wouldn't hold water, either. He needed to look somewhere else.

So he turned his suspicions on Antrikos. Everyone knew that journalists were jealous and competitive. They would tear one another to pieces for a scoop, and were always trying to get the upper hand. Antrikos was a Greek reporter, which meant he lived in Jack's shadow. There wasn't much to be done about it, he'd simply had the misfortune to be born in a weak country, and would thus never have his moment in the sun. Whereas everything had been handed to the American, ever since he was a child.

This theory seemed to hold up, but Antrikos was related to the prime minister—yes, the same prime minister who had taken personal responsibility for the case—an inconvenient fact that created significant obstacles for anyone wanting to pursue that line of inquiry. Tzitzilis called him down for questioning several times, and Antrikos was always unbearably specific and unremittingly precise. Almost insolent. He surely sensed where Tzitzilis was heading, and didn't leave him the slightest margin. He answered questions with questions, lit cigarettes without asking permission, showed that he knew perfectly well who had the upper hand. Tzitzilis soon realized he was wasting his time.

Antrikos had joined forces with Zouzou, and together they bombarded the Ministry of Public Order with complaints. Back in Athens, when she saw the reporters swooping down like vultures to pick apart her daughter's reputation, the widow's mother grabbed them by the collar and dragged them into the house, straight into her bedroom.

—Look, she told them. This is the girl you're ringing doorbells and loitering around on sidewalks for.

Zouzou was silently crying. She wasn't the worldly widow they'd been hearing about, she was just a child, a little girl sobbing in her mother's bed. She looked more like an orphan than anything else, a tiny, bird-like body, all bones.

Meanwhile, Thomas Tzitzilis was starting to worry. Every theory he'd come up with had crumbled before his eyes. The witnesses were unwilling to cooperate, no one wanted to get involved, most of them refused to open their mouths. But he had promised God and his superiors that he would solve the case. And so he would close the file. The Americans would get their perpetrator, his head served to them on a silver platter.

And if we don't have a perpetrator, well, some Greek will have to sacrifice himself for the cause. It wouldn't be a terrible blow, if it meant saving the rest of the country. Those were the kinds of thoughts that ran through his mind, though he didn't admit them to anyone else, even if he knew he was right in his thinking. The case had taken on greater dimensions. The Americans kept forming committees, poking their noses into everything, sending generals and judges to the embattled country. Congress was up in arms, newspapers and radios buzzed in New York and Washington. U.S. taxpayers weren't going to keep sending money to these barbarians if they were going to respond by murdering American citizens.

And so they threw the blame on the Greek government. Even the kindly disposed, who openly supported the Greeks for having declared a holy war against the communists within their own borders, expressed reservations.

Amid the chaos, with everyone beating his own drum yet cursing the government in unison—and the Greek police even more—for stalling and possibly covering up its own sins, Tzitzilis steadily sought the guilty party. The inhabitants of the city saw him in the churches of Agia Sophia and Agios Dimitrios, patron saint of Salonica, and in the Church of the Virgin Acheiro-poiitos, praying with damp eyes to the All-Powerful, seeking the enlightenment he needed in order to overcome American insults and Greek idiocy alike. To find a solution that would prove acceptable to all.

An American general was dispatched by Congress. He barged into Tzitzilis's office without knocking and let forth a stream of sailor's curses, as he might have cursed a lackey or an underling, not a Major of the Gendarmerie and head of the Security Police. The American had no sense of protocol, that's precisely why they'd sent him to bare his teeth, to tell Tzitzilis how things stood, without fancy prologues or arguments. Officer to officer, brass to brass. The American knew that when it came down to it, the Greek was his subordinate. So he treated him as such. And Tzitzilis swallowed the insult.

The General insisted that the crime had been committed by that hussy, Jack's widow, who had been seen dancing in jazz clubs in Athens a month after the unfortunate event. He'd heard that Tzitzilis had abandoned that obvious solution and begun to investigate the case as a political murder. Tzitzilis had in fact called a meeting behind closed doors with his most trusted men, though the possibility that it had been a political crime had been raised even before that. It suited the government, would shut up opponents, offered a ready explanation. To Tzitzilis it was clear as day that the commies wanted to discredit Greece, to bring the country's leaders down and drag them through the mud, to pressure the Americans to pack up and go home. But the investigation was still in its infancy, the evidence still a confused mess. All the different pieces would have to be brought into line if they were to convince anyone.

The General huffed.

—Your department is not doing its job, he said, pounding his fist on Tzitzilis's desk. The American people demand you find the guilty party. And in a matter of days, he ordered, and left without saying goodbye.

Whoever seeks will find.

A reporter who spoke English, former member of the communist insurgency. The last person to see Talas alive, according to witnesses. Of course the meeting only lasted five minutes, but no one cared about such details. A communist plot was an acceptable solution.

Gris had no police record. He was a calm, quiet man, almost suspiciously so. He took care of his mother and supported his sisters. He didn't spend money on things he didn't need, apart from his four packs of cigarettes a day. Sometimes he forgot and lit a new one with the old one still burning. He would hold both between two fingers and inhale them together. As tough as they come, though he didn't look it.

Tzitzilis had no intention of wasting time on preliminary questioning, corroboration, modification. This version would stick, and it was high time they were through with the case, *for the good of the country*.

All those who expressed doubt and distrust of the hurried proceedings—suspicious characters, the lot of them, and anti-Greek, in Tzitzilis's estimation—quickly learned to hold their tongues. Military tribunals took place even on weekends. Blood flowed freely. Everyone on both sides of the political spectrum had seen enough death.

The country's citizens might have learned to keep quiet, but the numbers spoke volumes. On May 3, 1948, a total of 152 communists who'd been condemned to death were executed, a fact that seemed entirely logical to the side doing the killing. Some whispered that the executions were in retaliation for the assassination of Ladas, the Minister of Justice, by the Organization for the Protection of the People's Struggle. Ladas had been the one who decided to revoke the citizenship of communists en masse. He was also the one who signed orders of execution. But the communists, too, killed indiscriminately. The two sides competed in harshness and barbarism: they burned people alive, decapitated corpses, stoned and bludgeoned and raped.

There was no end to the evil. Some executed, and others executed the executioners. Heroes became traitors and traitors heroes, depending on who was speaking. No one escaped, the traps had been set. People were condemned according to what they believed, not what they had done. Of course everyone said it was a sad state of affairs. Yet the killing continued apace. In the end political neutrality became a dangerous position. The country was ruled by paroxysms of fanaticism and intolerance. Whoever had a dissenting opinion learned to keep his mouth shut.

Those on the outside, even those who were bankrolling the slaughter, were revolted by the photographs that circulated abroad. Greece had become front-page news. One image in particular had been seen all over the world: a man on horseback with the heads of three female guerilla fighters hanging from his saddle, tied by their braids. The prime minister made some neutral comment about it being an old Greek custom, and promised the incident wouldn't be repeated—at least not with the heads of women.

The foreign journalists turned out to be some of the most easily shocked, and expressed their horror from a safe distance. Their mothers hadn't been slain, their sisters hadn't been hacked to pieces, their houses hadn't been torched. They urged people to remain calm, rattled off declarations of human rights, promoted humanistic ideals. They wrote articles, took photographs. And then they boarded their airplanes and left, and flew home to sleep easily in London or distant Oklahoma.

Perhaps it was just bad timing: the wrong person in the wrong place at the wrong time. But now things were settled summarily and speciously. The case couldn't be dragged out any longer. They were walking on hot coals, so they might as well dance.

SCHOOL YEAR 2010–2011

"WE'RE THE KIDS OUR PARENTS DIDN'T
WANT US TO HANG OUT WITH"

MINAS

They won't give me money for the class trip. *629 euros for six days is way too much*, Mom says. What she means is that it's way too much for someone who isn't going to university. *He who has ears, let him hear*, says Grandma, who doesn't let a fly shit without comment. Fine, fair enough. It's your money. Next year, when I'm an adult, we can talk again.

I don't even bother bringing up the Air Jordans, since I already know the answer: *In Africa kids run around barefoot, and you have three pairs of shoes. We don't have money to waste on nonsense.*

In our house Mom gets to decide what's nonsense and what's not. It's pretty much a dictatorship. They used to try and trick me into thinking we made decisions democratically. There were three of us, so we voted. I don't need to tell you the score. At some point I figured it out. *You guys always agree, I'll never get my way*, I complained. It was my first lesson in majority rule.

—The glory and the weakness of the democratic system, Evelina once commented in class, pointing at me, is that his vote counts as much as mine.

I can just picture her studying law. She'll rise to the top, no doubt about it. I mean, she's killer.

Last year she showed up at the debate tournament with a stack of notes and her father's Mont Blanc. She was bossing everyone around, giving orders. But when they asked her a question about the stock market crash of 1929, she froze. It wasn't in our history book. She doesn't care about anything that won't be on the Panhellenic Exams.

In the twenty minutes our group was given to prep, I went over the whole history from the crash to Lehman Brothers. It was one of the few times in her life when Evelina shut up and took notes. She was epic, though, I have to admit. She went up to the podium and pretty much smoked all the private school kids. She had her usual expression on, the one that suits her best: a German shepherd with a job to do. She didn't let anyone else finish a sentence.

—I'm sorry if I'm getting a bit competitive, she apologized, smiling at the judges.

They smiled right back. Dumb as bricks. She had them in the palm of her hand right from the start.

Evelina isn't going on the class trip, either. It's too close to Easter, she can't afford to lose even a day of studying. I'm sure she talked her dad into putting the money aside for her, so she'll be able to take a trip this summer instead, to celebrate.

No Prague for me, I might as well accept it. I won't see the old clock tower with the statue of Death, won't retrace Kafka's steps, won't go to that club I found on the Internet. I won't get to see what airplane food is like: goulash, boiled vegetables, chocolate cake. I'll just rot here in Thessaloniki. Kamara to Diagonios to Aristotle Square—the entire city center by foot in fifteen minutes. My whole life spent in a tiny speck on the map. Nine hundred steps along the sidewalk of Tsimiski Avenue. I counted.

Dad hates this city, but Grandma adores it. She's an old-time Thessalonian, she grew up on Plato Street, her balcony looked onto the Church of the Virgin Acheiropoiitos. On Good Friday she would go down and buy her votive candle as soon as the bells started ringing. For Grandma all that really counts as Thessaloniki is the part of the city inside the Byzantine walls. Everything outside the walls was just muddy fields in her day: *Don't be fooled, dear, by all the apartment buildings they've built out there, back then when it rained the whole place was one big mud pit.* Anything east of the White Tower is a foreign country as far as she's concerned, Toumba's a suburb, and Panorama up on the hill is countryside. Western

68

Thessaloniki is a parallel universe she reads about in the paper, in the articles Dad edits.

Grandma always does her hair in that poofy old-lady style. She paints her nails and smokes thin cigarettes. She has more memories than you would believe. The other people in her apartment building call her *the principal*, even though she was only ever a teacher. Whenever anyone goes out shopping they stop by her place first to see if she needs anything: a loaf of bread, some tsipouro, marinated anchovies. Grandma is a foodie. She drinks her glass of tsipouro every afternoon with the TV on. She goes out for coffee with her endless girlfriends, whom Mom describes as *tough old broads*. They talk about politics, about the city's lost splendor, about the latest movies. Grandma's a movie junkie, says Dad, who has a soft spot for her. You couldn't exactly call her a cinephile, since she loves detective films and thrillers. She and Dad always place bets on the Oscars. Nine times out of ten Grandma wins, and Dad buys her pirated versions of the winning films from the African street vendors.

—You're a godless man, she scolds him. How many times have I told you not to buy from them? Their knock-offs are going to ruin my DVD player.

Grandma considers Dad an unrepentant socialist. Too welcoming of foreigners, an armchair activist with a philanthropic theory handy whenever it's time to discuss the downtrodden. She has no patience for his kind of tolerance. In her view all black people stink, no matter what Dad says about non-Western diets and spices.

—They've turned the Rotonda into a gypsy camp, you can't walk anywhere without stepping on their handbags. I can't understand why nothing's been done. Is the mayor blind?

Dad smiles but doesn't reply. Grandma considers herself his ears in the city, *because if he tried to get any real news from his lefty friends, he'd be waiting a long time*, she says, shaking her head.

It's true, though, Grandma actually is his political barometer. She'll vote for PASOK to get New Democracy to clean up its act, or for New Democracy to punish PASOK.

—It's not that Evthalia can't make up her mind, Dad established early on. It's that she's an actual undecided voter. It's her kind who determine the final outcome. If we all had her balls, we wouldn't just vote for the same party year in and year out.

He made sure to take it back right away, though, so Grandma wouldn't use it against him.

Dad is a displaced lefty who used to believe that PASOK would save the country. Even now, no matter how enraged he gets with the socialists, he always comes through at the ballot box. He can't bear to vote for anyone else. If you think about it, it's pretty stupid to vote for a single party your whole life long, but Dad considers it political consistency.

No one at school reads the newspaper, and whatever news they watch is just STAR or sports results. The other day Souk blew up in class. Someone at the back of the room was talking, and he got us all out of our chairs. Souk never yells. His method is to turn the volume down, not up. It's incredibly effective, I wonder why it never occurred to anyone else.

—I consider it an insult, he said, staring at each of us in turn, that I have to interrupt our lesson to chastise individuals who are practically adults, and will soon be able to exercise their right to vote. An insult to you, he clarified, so there was no misunderstanding.

That day we'd been talking about the Occupation. Security battalions, collaborators, the city's own historical drama. He showed us photographs and film footage. Concentration camps, human experiments, mass exterminations. Greek Jews being humiliated in the middle of the city, in Eleftheria Square. German soldiers posing for the camera in a swimming pool built of Jewish gravestones over where the university is now.

—Sir, one girl asked, is what we're seeing a movie, or a documentary? I mean, she added, wide-eyed, did all this really happen?

—History doesn't happen in outer space, Souk replied without blinking an eye.

He pushed play. Jewish prisoners smiling at the American troops who had come to free them in a documentary about Auschwitz. Skin and bones, lying on mattresses, too weak even to stand up and walk out.

—What I mean, Souk continued, is that history doesn't happen to other people, in a distant place and time. It's happening to us, here and now. What we're living is history. Some people find that idea asphyxiating, but others find it comforting, he added as he started passing around a handout.

On Saturday night I saw Evelina at Oh La La with a group of law students. There were enough crocodiles on their shirts to stock a safari park. Evelina looked happy. I left before I would have to say hello.

Mom says I roam around like an unfulfilled curse. Well, she doesn't say it to my face, but she whispers it over the phone to Grandma. She's worried about me. She'd be proud to have a daughter like Evelina.

Whatever. I could care less.

Mom wants me to get better. Better means like her. To care about nothing but studying and grades. To go to university. To get a proper education, find a job. To smile and make her happy. So she can say, *It was worth all that effort, he turned out fine in the end.*

Mom has opinions about my opinions and beliefs about my beliefs. She knows what's right. I apparently don't.

She's a mother, which means she's clueless. She wants to help. But that's impossible: she can't help, because she's my mom.

It drives her up the wall not to know what I'm thinking.

Take the other day. I saw a dead guy, and when I told her, she freaked out. He was on the sidewalk in front of school. He had jumped off the fifth-floor balcony. The body wasn't even cold when

I got there. The neighbors came outside, got some rope from the shop across the way and cordoned off the street. The religion teacher stood on the corner telling kids to go around to the side entrance, without explaining why. The ambulance took forever to come. The first-years managed to see it all, even the guy's red socks. He wasn't wearing shoes, just wool socks, fire-engine red, you could see them from far off. The ambulance came and took the corpse away, and then during second break they came to clean up the blood. They kept scrubbing the pavement, but it still left a stain. At night the dead guy's mother came down and lit a candle. She left a bouquet of chrysanthemums, which we found there the next day. The first-years dragged their rolling backpacks around the spot so as not to disturb the little altar.

—Did that man really have to commit suicide here of all places, right in front of the school? one mother commented. It reminded me of something Souk once said: *Parents are the most despicable category of people. Childrearing does something to them, it must be hormonal.* That was last year, when a parent came into the office to bawl out the German teacher. I bet the German teacher wanted to agree, but she held her tongue.

No one knows why the guy jumped. The neighbors have various theories. Some say he'd been unemployed for a while; others say he was gay, because of the red socks; most of the teachers at school think there must have been some deeper psychological issue.

—Those aren't mutually exclusive, the woman at the kiosk said, shaking her head as if she knew.

The girls all averted their eyes and went in through the side door. Except for Evelina, who refused to change her route. She walked right by without even looking his way. I went over to see.

Right now you're seeing your first dead man, open your eyes, concentrate for once in your life.

I tried to feel something, but nothing came.

I'm a monster.

•

Yesterday Dad gave me his file with materials about Gris. Newspaper clippings, interviews, old photographs. A whole box of books, all hypothesizing about what really happened.

—These are the illustrious sources which, I take it, you've been discussing in history class, he teased.

I spread it all out on the bed and started with the photographs. Gris in profile at the trial. Ashen, though that might just have been the paper.

—When elephants dance the ants always pay the price, Dad called from the living room.

It's his favorite saying. It represents his whole idea of human justice in a nutshell. As for divine justice, which Grandma invokes, when you get right down to it Dad doesn't really care. Dad believes *justice has to be served in life, because everything else is just stories the priests make up. Religious nonsense to help them rule over the sleeping hordes.*

Mom says Dad has a *keen sense of justice*, by which she means rigid, not keen. For Dad justice is black and white. There's good and bad, right and wrong in any situation. Anyone who flip-flops must be sitting in a dirty nest. Grandma is a conciliatory type, and always says that *there are gray areas, blind spots, forces at work that we can't see from the outside*, but Dad's theory doesn't allow for that point of view.

According to Dad, philosophers and lawyers *spill ink like cuttlefish, they muddy the waters, play the venal game of Mammon. They obscure the obvious.* For him, the word justice is a holy word, *even if politicians and judges try to cut it down to their size.*

—Justice isn't a matter of procedural pirouettes, it's a basic human instinct. As powerful an instinct as hunger or thirst. Justice isn't about laws. Any child can distinguish between right and wrong without having to read the penal code.

When he talks about stuff like that his face gets all red and the veins in his neck bulge like cords. It used to embarrass me, I was ashamed of how passionate he got. Later I realized that lots of people were sympathetic to his eruptions, in fact some admired him for them. At the newspaper, barking all the time is a plus.

Truth conquers all, and if you have the truth on your side, you need to make yourself heard. That's what Dad thinks. He belongs to the generation that believed in demonstrations. Maybe that's why, when a conversation gets heated, he leaves logic behind and takes refuge in slogans and quotes.

—Sir, I don't know where to start.

—Real research takes guts, Georgiou. It's not just copying and pasting from the Internet.

—Sir, I found the books you recommended, but there are so many, and the writing isn't very clear.

Souk wasn't in a mood to rebuke me, but he did it anyhow.

—That's what historical sources are like, Georgiou. If you'd prefer, you can study for class like everyone else, but then you'd get bored of parroting back information. Did you think the critical analysis of primary sources would be easy?

He raised his eyes to the heavens. It's something he does in class when we bring him to the point of despair. It's a look I call stop-bothering-me-you-fool. I wasn't going to lay my weapons down so easily.

—Sir, I said again.

—Listen, Georgiou. How long have we known one another?

—Six years.

He nodded in agreement.

—Six years, yes. Now tell me, in those six years, have I ever given you the mistaken impression that I follow democratic processes in my classroom? Did I ever submit any issue pertaining to our class to a vote?

—No, sir.

—I'm glad I haven't created any misunderstanding, Souk said, putting an end to the conversation.

I stood up to leave.

—Georgiou, he called as I was walking out the door, and waved me back in. Listen, I know you're at sea. But you're going to have to work on your own. Study the sources, decide which you trust and which you don't, form your own opinion. Here's a book that might help you figure out how to conduct historical research. Just read the introduction and the opening chapter. That should be plenty.

That's how Souk is. He'd probably been carrying that book around in his bag for a week. He believes in the theory that you shouldn't protect kids from difficult things. That they learn from falling down and getting hurt. Learning through suffering. I don't know if it's a great pedagogical method, but it works.

Freedom is a sneaky thing. You think it's actually free, but sometimes it turns out to be pretty pricey.

I'm an idiot.

I've been reading for ages and I don't understand anything. After the first few hours I started to take notes, the way Grandma taught me. With arrows and diagrams and page numbers in parentheses. I don't know how I'm ever going to get anywhere, and that methodology book Souk gave me just confused me even more.

I've got all the events down, with dates. But I can't figure out how they're connected. Reasons, causes, effects, it's all one huge knot. Brits, Americans, Greeks, I can't keep the names straight or remember who did what. Dad insists that I need to read the newspapers from back then. He says that's the only way I'll get my finger on the pulse of the time. I have to view events through a reporter's lens, for him that's a given.

Yesterday he brought me a CD with scans of the front pages and reporting from 1949, when Gris was on trial. The newspaper was digitized ages ago, someone at the office did it. So now I've got new material, when I can't even manage what I already had.

I feel like an idiot.

Like that time Souk taught us a surrealist poem called "The Forest Boat," by Nikos Engonopoulos, in our first year of middle school. He handed out photocopies and most kids thought it made no sense, but no one dared comment out loud. I didn't understand a word, and was terrified he might call on me and realize once and for all how stupid I was.

It's something I've always worried about. *What a clever child, and so special, he's sure to go far*, my teachers all used to tell my mom. I liked hearing their praise, but it terrified me, too. I was sure someone would eventually figure out that I'm not special at all. I've got a mediocre mind, it only tricks you if you don't look too close.

The day Souk brought that Engonopoulos poem into class, he read it out loud in his usual cold voice. I had no idea what it was about. But I felt like there was something happening on the page, something important.

I was having fun.

So much fun that I forgot everyone around me. I forgot the classes, the fight I'd had with Mom that morning, the spinach rice waiting for me when I got home. And when Evelina raised her hand and started in on the poem, trying to unpack the "hidden meaning" of every single line, I felt like shoving her. What she was actually doing was changing the words of the poem one by one, so as to make it comprehensible. To explain it to us imbeciles.

—A poem has handles, Souk said, trying to guide us. Try to identify them and pick it up that way. Poetry doesn't speak only to the heart, true emotion also passes through the brain; that's what makes it so strong.

Evelina raised her hand again. She tried a second time to dissect the poem and explain it in her own words. Souk looked at her for a moment, perhaps trying to make up his mind whether or not to say what he was thinking.

—That's your poem. If Engonopoulos had wanted to say all that, he would've used other words. Poetry is a precise art.

Evelina didn't let out a peep. The others were all grateful that she had explained the incomprehensible, so they could answer the questions Souk would give us for homework. I, meanwhile, was furious at her for ruining the poem with her interpretation.

What I'm trying to do with these sources reminds me of Evelina reading that poem. I'm not studying the events, I'm looking for easy connections between them, to get it over with. I'm not letting them speak, I'm trying to speak for them. If Dad had ears to hear, I'd tell him that journalism does exactly the same thing, even if it doesn't like to think so. It takes events and wraps them up in its own voice. I already know what his objections would be. In our conversations he steamrolls me every time. He knows how to argue. I always think of what I want to say too late, when he's already left the room.

I don't know what Souk got me mixed up in, or if I'll ever figure it out. I've stuck Post-its with the names of the major players all over the walls of my room, and a photograph of Gris over my bed. Tall and pale on the first day of the trial.

—Who's that scarecrow you've got on your wall? Mom asked when she came in to clean. When I told her who it was and what happened to him, her response was:

—They burned his youth in a single night.

THROUGH OTHER EYES

THEN THERE WERE TANKS,
NOW THERE ARE BANKS

Tasos Georgiou glanced at the slogan on the wall and smiled. For days he'd been walking into the newspaper building without noticing anything, he, a man who always claimed that nothing escaped him, not even a blink of his colleagues' eyes. It had been a month since he'd joked around with the others, he just went straight to his office, shut the door, and started making calls.

—It's a tough time for the boss, said the staff reporters, his "guys," who'd learned most of what they knew from him, on the job.

They'd heard the rumors, they knew how bad the numbers were, and they were all riddled with worry. Whispered conversations in the halls centered around furloughs and salary reductions, and no one had a comforting word to say to anyone. The atmosphere at work was poisonous. No more goofing around, or workplace flirtations, or smiles for no reason. Every now and then someone would groan, it just slipped out before they could choke it back.

No one felt like doing anything. The uncertainty dragged on for days, until the days became weeks. The rumors infected everything, and none of them were ever confirmed. The girls in accounting stopped buying new lipstick. They used sample moisturizers from department stores and waited for the bomb to drop.

Georgiou wasn't sleeping well and suffered relentless headaches. Conversations with his superiors were excruciating. He was constantly weighing and calculating, trying to figure out which would be the smallest sacrifice.

—Ask your staff, suggested a veteran editor he knew in Athens who was an expert at spreading strife and breaking up alliances. They might prefer if you fired some of them. That way the rest would get to keep their jobs.

He wouldn't hear of it. He knew them all by their first names, knew their wives and children. Sure, there were some lazy guys who got away with murder, who spent all day on the phone or taking cigarette breaks, but he couldn't just send them packing. He wouldn't take responsibility for that crime.

—Only the dead don't go to work, that's how I was raised, he cut off one guy, a specialist at sick leave, who tried to call in with a cold. He dragged the lazy bum into the office to work on a piece he'd emailed in, hoping the others would fix it up.

Georgiou barked, sure, but he had no intention of biting. When the publisher called a meeting with the staff, he sat on the latter's side of the room, so it would be perfectly clear whose side he was on. The balance sheets were presented and the numbers shut people up, there was no arguing with the facts. The business side of things hadn't been going well for a while. The publisher didn't have much to add. He proposed a forty-percent reduction in wages. The staff accepted twenty percent. The union was pleased with the compromise, the staff relieved that the worst had been avoided.

The publisher wasn't one to waste words. He was a good guy, all things considered. Haggling with him wasn't an unpleasant affair: the necessary dirty work happened in a fairly above-board manner, he wasn't overly greedy for profits, he knew how to be flexible while still getting his way in the end. He pulled strings behind closed doors. He knew how to compromise and how to form coalitions. He was corrupt, of course—how could he not be?—but he would admit it readily enough, with a knowing smile, if you asked, at least to the extent that he could talk about such things. *Don't interfere, you'll mess up all my work*, his father's accountant had told him when he first assumed responsibilities at the paper. He quickly figured out how private understandings got made, how fat envelopes traveled to and from ministers' offices, how a person could ask for the most outrageous things and see them actually become a reality.

The publisher had already settled on a twenty-percent wage reduction, as per the advice of his unsmiling and extremely well-remunerated advisors, but proposed cuts twice as harsh so the union leaders would be able to boast that their multi-day negotiations had circumvented the worst.

It wasn't fun for the journalists, of course—who likes to have money snatched from his pockets?—but they felt as if the sword that had been hanging over their heads had gone to threaten someone else instead. So they all breathed a collective sigh of relief and got back to work. They were perfectly aware that their good luck was temporary, but no one was making long-term plans these days anyway.

Georgiou went out to walk the city streets. He couldn't stand being cooped up in the office anymore, his closed door made him claustrophobic. But he also didn't want to leave it open, the way he used to. He planned on walking as far as Dimitris Gounaris Street, where the downward slope of the sidewalk calmed him, even if the place was filthy. He didn't mind the muddy streets, the trash everywhere, the Pakistanis selling incense whose smell drove Evthalia crazy. All he saw was the sea at the end of the street, the glistening waves, the open horizon. That walk was his painkiller, his tranquilizer, the moments of soothing beauty he allowed himself when the going got tough. He had edited dozens of special issues about the city's waterfront, he had talked with experts about its potential uses. He'd heard some crazy ideas and some interesting ones, ridiculous modernization schemes as well as more tasteful and sensible approaches. None of the architects brought in from elsewhere had any idea what the sea meant for the city. On a design level, of course, they knew how to present their plans with the appropriate terminology. But on an everyday level, how many of those jacks-of-all-trades with their Ph.D.s from American universities knew what it meant to walk along Proxenos Koromilas Street, one block in from the waterfront, and see the sunset peeking in at every cross street? How many of them had spent their childhoods watching the sunlight dance over the waters of the Thermaic Gulf, at midday, through the windows of their schools? And how many had talent enough to make their architectural plans account for the particular gray of the city, on a rainy day, at the old port? A milky gray, with just a touch of watery blue at the end, a color all Thessalonians know—and though they might curse the dreariness of their city, if you dropped them down in the Maldives, sooner or later they would launch into endless comparisons and complaints about how exhausting all that sunshine was.

On his way he walked by Agia Sophia, where he and Teta had gotten married. Back then, Evthalia couldn't comprehend how a born-and-bred Thessalonian could want to get married anywhere else, *and not because it's in fashion these days*, she'd tried to admonish the couple, *but because it's the heart of the city, the place where so much of its history has taken place*, she said, gathering steam. The young couple didn't want to argue with her—Teta and Tasos, *the inseparable Ts*, she used to tease them. Tasos had floated the idea of a civil ceremony, which was roundly rejected on the basis of very few actual arguments. *It wouldn't bother you to have a right-wing mayor officiate at your wedding?* Evthalia asked innocently. She herself had voted for the man, but she knew perfectly well what would cut her future son-in-law to the quick. And Tasos, who considered all decisions about the wedding minor details and didn't have time to waste on skirmishes, showed up in the historic churchyard in a salmon-colored jacket and a green satin tie that he'd picked out himself, very proud of his taste. Teta smiled. She liked his wild side, how easily he got fired up, how he squeezed her hand when they were out walking and now at the church as well, the fact that he didn't give a damn about etiquette and always let his own flag fly.

—You're marrying a firebrand, Evthalia warned her with a smile.

—That's part of his charm, replied Teta, who may have seemed like an obedient daughter but always managed to get her way in the end. It was a quality Evthalia admired, though she would never admit it. She had always respected people with strong personalities. People who knew the rules and were willing to accept the consequences of their actions. Anastasios Georgiou unquestionably belonged to that category. If Evthalia had ever had him as a student, he would have been her favorite. True to his word yet mildly intractable. Diligent yet full of questions. Captain Commotion, but without a trace of cockiness.

On their wedding day they had both been radiant with joy, and Evthalia worried that so much happiness might fall and crush them somehow. She decided to light an expensive candle at the entryway to the church, just in case, to ward off the evil eye.

•

Now, at that same entryway twenty years later, Tasos Georgiou slowed to a stop. Actually, at first he passed by hurriedly, but stopped a few steps farther on, wondering what that ball of something had been, rolled up on the floor of the alcove where the candles were, by the gate to the churchyard.

Then he heard the cry.

For a moment the bustle on the square stopped. Everyone froze: the koulouri man, mothers with kids, passersby laden with bags, Chinese street vendors with their heavy loads.

It was like the cry of a large animal—a wild beast, perhaps—slowly dying. But there was no forest here, no stand of trees, no savannah. The place stank of car exhaust; vast swathes of cement swallowed up everything in sight. *Impossible*, he thought, *I must have imagined it.* A minute later the cry was repeated, deeper, as if someone were disemboweling the beast using an iron winch and tossing its guts onto the sidewalk. Georgiou turned around to look.

It was Fendi, a foreigner, a de facto errand-boy whom the regulars at the cafés on the square treated to a coffee every so often; passersby would sometimes buy him a koulouri. Always on their own initiative, since he was ashamed to ask. And now he was flailing on the ground in front of the brass tray of lighted votive candles in the alcove at the churchyard gate. He pounded his head on the cement, howling in despair.

He had no words left, or hopes, or friends.

Georgiou felt ashamed. Ashamed of himself, of the luxury of his worries, which only moments earlier had seemed to be piled mountain-high, and of his cowardice. He watched but didn't move any closer. People were passing by, others were watching the scene, smoking, chewing tiropitas. One little kid started to run toward Fendi, but his mother grabbed him by the coat—that was not a sight for a child, so she pulled him back and they continued on their way.

Georgiou took a step forward, then stopped. It seemed wrong, offensive somehow, for him to touch Fendi on the shoulder—after all, he had nothing to say, all the words in his head rang false. Better for him to just keep walking. But that didn't seem right, either, that's not the kind of person he was, he'd fought for so many things in his life, written articles full of fire, taken part in fierce protests. He stood for a moment, unable to decide. Then he walked over, left a twenty-euro bill on the sidewalk at Fendi's knees, and quickly walked away.

But he was dogged by that deep sense of shame. Shame for having too few words and too much money, shame that he couldn't reach out to touch the man, shame, shame, shame.

He turned into Pavlos Melas Street to seek shelter. He remembered going out for a walk years ago with Minas, who couldn't have been more than three at the time. They were headed down Agia Sophia Street. Minas was walking ahead, refusing to let his father hold his hand, and gazing in amazement at everything around him. Everything seemed entirely new: the bitter orange trees, the cars, bottle caps on the ground. A gypsy woman lying on a piece of cardboard mumbled prayers mixed with curses. She'd pulled up her skirts and her dark thighs were there for all to see, rotten flesh, crooked legs, turned-in ankles, a hard, yellow crust over her toenails. A little farther on a blind man was sitting on a plastic bag, playing a pipe. Minas froze, staring.

—What do they want, Dad? he asked.

—Money, Georgiou answered, but that didn't satisfy his son.

—You have money, why don't you give them some?

The question was logical enough. He tried to explain his reasoning patiently and calmly, as he'd seen Teta do any number of times when Minas barraged her with questions. He quickly realized that his explanations were confusing the child even more—how could they not, since he was only stringing phrases together? In the end he gave up. *They might be lying*, he heard himself say, *they might have even more money than we do*, and Minas finally stopped asking.

•

When Minas was little, he used to observe the adults around him with an unblinking eye. He listened in on everything they said behind closed doors. He played alone in his room, with Playmobil and Legos, knights, dragons, and pirates. He would leave notes on the fridge for his mother to read and answer in writing—it had to be in writing, in a box he would draw in the bottom right corner of the page, with the heading *Mom's Answer* in careful letters.

Teta was endlessly proud of her only child, whom she raised according to the rules she herself had learned as a child. She was constantly worrying, she always found something to agonize over: how Minas would drift off into a world of his own, lost in thought, and she couldn't tell if those thoughts were happy or sad. Or how he avoided kids his own age and sought out the company of adults, in whose presence he was particularly eloquent and outgoing.

—Don't make mountains out of molehills, was Evthalia's steady advice. The child is fine, it's your own head that needs examining.

But now that Minas had raised his banner of revolution, the ground had fallen away from beneath Teta's feet. Apparently her obedient son wasn't quite so obedient after all.

—Don't fight him, Evthalia advised.

That's when Teta exploded.

—Sure, she shot back, that's easy for you to say. We both know I was raised on prohibitions, by a mother who always had to get her way.

Evthalia refused to discuss old wounds; she had no intention of revisiting decisions she had made decades earlier. But she didn't protest: at her age she had learned to give way, to not waste energy on useless conflict but rather try and find a solution. This situation, though, seemed to have reached an impasse. Minas had dug in his heels and all Teta could do was tug at the leash.

Recently Teta had begun to resign herself. *You can't live your son's life for him, and you can't make his decisions*, her therapist admonished.

Of course Teta thought Minas was the one who should be seeing a therapist, but he refused even to discuss anything "stupid,"
a category that included therapists and their theories. Tasos and
Evthalia both agreed with the boy's evaluation, but since they didn't
have anything better to suggest, they kept their mouths shut.

Minas lived barricaded in his room. He rarely went out at night,
rarely talked on the phone. He was plugged in at all times. Teta
searched the Internet history on his computer a few times, but
never discovered anything worth worrying about. An interview
with Jacques Derrida about the instability of meaning and the
tyranny of the easy answer (good lord), poems and paintings by
Nikos Engonopoulos (lovely, but useless for a graduating senior
who should be preparing for his exams), a virtual tour of Prague
(poor thing, he'd been planning for that trip), and a statue of Justice
dressed like a rock star, with hair extensions, a sword, and a dog
collar (perish the thought).

Teta didn't feel great about spying on her son, but she also
believed she was doing the right thing. Her therapist disagreed.
What you did was wrong, he admonished, *human relationships are
built on trust, and trust is hard to regain once it's lost.* Teta didn't take
his chiding too seriously. The therapist based his judgments on
books, while Teta based hers on experience. He had no children
of his own, so who was he to tell her how to manage her son? She
still went to see him regularly, and sought his advice about all kinds
of things, but in the end she acted as she saw fit. Theories about
mutual respect were all well and good, but she needed to know
what she was up against.

When she finally went to Minas's school she was past seeking
advice; what she needed was an oracle. But most of his teachers felt
that there was nothing they could do, no matter how sympathetic
they were to her son. No one who teaches the senior class has time
to babysit parents. Teta knew that, of course—or rather, she imagined it: she may not have been a teacher herself, but after so many
years as a mother she knew a thing or two about schools.

It had been hard for Evthalia to accept her daughter's decision not to become a teacher, a decision suddenly communicated to Evthalia together with the news of Teta's pregnancy. Tasos and Teta knew that Evthalia wouldn't lose her temper in front of a pregnant daughter. And indeed, Evthalia, as fierce as knives when it came to issues of professional dignity and financial independence, accepted the blow without a single comment and held out her arms to the couple. Later, of course, when the dust had settled, she took her daughter aside.

Yes, she understood that Tasos's job was a demanding one, with no set schedule or real days off, and yes, he made enough for them to raise a child on, particularly since they weren't the type to indulge in useless luxuries—but, *Teta, honey*, Evthalia said sweetly, though she was fuming on the inside, *is that why I sent you to university, so you could shut yourself up in the house and raise a child?* She wanted to say *his* child, but at the last minute she held back, a fact for which she silently congratulated herself. Evthalia might not have been the sort of feminist who went around with hairy legs and sensible shoes, and she certainly hadn't burned any bras, but she made no bones about raising her voice and giving people a piece of her mind when the situation called for it. She hadn't quit her job to raise Teta, though her husband had tried to insist on it. Back in those days women were homemakers, each confined to her own tiny realm. Evthalia, however, wanted a salary of her own, so she wouldn't have to ask for money to have a dress made. And when her husband died young and she received his first miserable pension check in the mail, she went to his grave, and instead of crying like all the other widows dressed head to toe in black, she told him, *See, if I'd listened to you, I'd be begging in the streets*, and washed his gravestone with a deep sense of vindication.

As the years passed Evthalia started to wear the pants that her husband had forbidden. She felt beholden to no one, and particularly not to the school inspectors who visited the school regularly and always gave the widow disapproving looks. She stood her ground, though, since at the end of the day she worked as hard as ten men.

—A pair of pants is the most modest thing a woman can wear, she told the principal assigned to the school during the junta, a conservative theologian who dared to comment on her choice of attire. You can bend over as far as you want without worrying that someone might see your underwear, or even a thigh.

The theologian let the conversation die there.

Evthalia was the last of her cohort to retire. She left the school only when she had no other choice. That might have explained why it was so difficult for her to comprehend her daughter's decision to become a housewife, no matter how hard Teta tried to dress it up with various theories.

—A woman with a literature degree shut up within the four walls of a kitchen, she hadn't been able to restrain herself from saying, just once, years ago.

Teta refused to let it slide.

—At least I'll be home for my child, I'll be there to watch him grow up.

Evthalia silently accepted the jibe. Teta later apologized, but what had been said couldn't be unsaid. Even if it was unfair, entirely unfair, in Evthalia's estimation, Teta's words had rung like a bell in her mother's head ever since, marking with absolute precision how far Evthalia could go, how much she could say, and where she should take care to stop.

Thus it was that Teta devoted all her time and energy to Minas. The willful solitude of her only child had become something of a family joke. Teta liked to recount with feigned worry and thinly disguised pride a scene that had taken place at the playground. Minas, still a toddler, found a kid his age playing in the sandbox and sat down beside him, but instead of grabbing a bucket and shovel, tried to strike up a conversation:

—Do you like Miró? He's my favorite painter.

The other kid promptly picked up his toys and left, not bothering to respond.

Teta had panicked. Minas had no social skills, she fretted to Evthalia.

—Is that something people are talking about these days? the grandmother asked, and her daughter launched into a recitation from the parenting manuals she'd been reading.

While her child might have known to use the second person plural for polite speech, there were all sorts of things most people considered self-evident about which he had no idea. The guy at the kiosk, the woman at the bakery, and the man at the corner store all adored him, and showered her with compliments about how fast he was growing and how bright he was. But they belonged to the protected realm of the adult world; they wouldn't dream of tormenting a child with mean-spirited teasing. Teta was terrified of the day when Minas would enter kindergarten. She went to meet the kindergarten teacher and told her that she was particularly concerned about her child's socialization.

—He's been raised among adults, she confided.

The teacher smiled. Yet another spoiled only child.

In the end, though, Minas was fairly easy-going, or at least that's how it seemed from the outside and from a distance. But Teta's antennas were always raised. She sensed that Minas was only mimicking behaviors, imitating a child's whining or funny faces or clumsy gestures, repeating silly phrases. He was pretending to be what he was supposed to be.

The adults in his life fell for his routine, but what did they know? There was no fooling the other kids, who could tell right away that something wasn't quite right with Minas, that he wasn't *normal*. He seemed friendly and outgoing, made jokes, pulled pranks. And yet he didn't fit in, didn't conform—that's what they would have said if they had known the word. But they didn't, so the issue remained undefined, more of a feeling, a slight breeze that followed Minas around and made the other kids uncomfortable. Time passed and they got used to his strangeness. An unofficial truce developed, though only after plenty of conflict and tears on both sides. Minas wasn't one to hang back. He met confrontation head-on: he knew that was the only way to resolve things, otherwise the fools just made things worse for you. So when the class bully threw his penmanship book in the trash, a green notebook with twenty-five straight pages bearing the teacher's *Bravo!* at the top, Minas lost his cool. He glared at the perpetrator like a bull staring down a bull-fighter, grinding his teeth the way Tasos did when things weren't going well at work, and suddenly made a beeline for the other kid.

—You're a moron.

Words didn't frighten the bully, but then words are superfluous when the adrenaline is pumping through a room full of twenty-seven preteens. And so words were followed by deeds. They threw a few awkward jabs. Minas didn't know how to fight, but he was a big kid. His opponent, a nervous little runt, started landing kicks wherever he could. Minas let loose with a backhanded blow that half missed its mark, but the other half got the job done.

No one ever picked on him again. It was as if an atypical agreement had been signed that day, a secret contract that gave Minas the right to his refuge. He said hi to the other kids and they said hi back. They knew nothing about his life and he wasn't interested in learning about theirs. Of course the appropriate invitations to parties were exchanged. None of them had any desire for their parents to figure out exactly what was going on. When it comes to things like that, children display complete solidarity, cautious and resilient as steel.

Thus it was that Minas's "social skills," as Teta called them, never developed through regular interactions with his peers.

—Let the child be, was Evthalia's advice. He doesn't have any real peers at school, he'll find them at the university.

It was a convenient solution, since it pushed the problem off to a future date, which at the time had seemed fairly distant. At the time. Now, though, when the much-discussed year of exam preparation had arrived and his parents' high expectations had suddenly flown out the window, Minas's social isolation presented yet another burden—though at this precise moment such issues paled in comparison to Minas's provocative declarations concerning the Panhellenic Exams.

Teta watched as the other kids ran their long-distance race. The other mothers never missed an opportunity to update her on their children's progress. With glee, it seemed to her, though they probably thought they were just being friendly. Teta felt like a turtle missing its shell. Her brief chats with other mothers on the phone and their chance encounters around the neighborhood filled her with a dreadful guilt. No matter how hard she fought it, no matter how many times Evthalia tried to comfort her with the observation that *these things happen, just try to adjust*, she still felt that she must have done something wrong to make Minas fall apart at the very moment when the other kids were rising to the challenge, even those who were clearly not destined to succeed.

And then there was Evelina Dinopoulou, who always came in second, right behind Minas—until last year. *So diligent, so mature*, crowed her mother, who was hoping her daughter would score high enough on her exams to enter the faculty of law. Evelina's mother was discreet enough never to ask after Minas. But even that didn't seem like a kindness to Teta; it came across as a slight.

—You're imagining things, Evthalia tried to mollify her.

Teta didn't listen. She was convinced that everyone was talking behind her back. As Evthalia saw it, even if they were, that was no reason for Teta to dance to the beat of their drum.

—What did you think, you poor thing? Evthalia asked. That the hard part was the diapers and the baby food? You're only just starting to realize what it means to have a child. Now is when the real worrying begins.

Teta had already come to that realization on her own, and couldn't bear for someone else to rub her face in it—least of all Evthalia. What she wanted from her mother was comfort and consolation, a ready hug and a pat on the back. Not admonitions. But Evthalia was a general, as Tasos always said. She gave orders, not comforting words. She was a problem-solver who didn't waste time on hysterics or sentimentality.

Teta had pinned her hopes on Soukiouroglou. He was the only teacher at the school whom Evthalia really trusted. *He knows his letters*, she'd told Teta, and that was saying a lot. For Evthalia, it was everything—which is why she said it very rarely, particularly when speaking of the younger generation of teachers.

Soukiouroglou kept everyone at a distance. No one ever dared address him informally; he had no use for false familiarity. He always corrected students' papers within a day. He didn't let things drag on. If he said he would do something, you could be sure the job would get done on time.

When Teta went to talk to Soukiouroglou, she got straight to the point. She laid out the problem as objectively as she could, held back her tears, tried not to sound judgmental. Her son's teacher listened without interrupting. He expressed no sympathy. It wasn't in his nature to comfort, he believed that was a role for family members, and he was at the school to get a different job done.

—Why are you so determined that Minas go to university? he asked.

Teta had thousands of arguments at her fingertips, but the question took her by surprise. She launched into her spiel, but it sounded too much like a school essay, she realized as she spoke. She despised rhetoric and emotional blackmail, but when it came to her child, all logic flew out the window. Her weapons were the weapons of all mothers since the beginning of time.

Soukiouroglou sat there silently and let her go on. At some point alarm bells started ringing in her head: *He's testing you, stupid.* She wanted to say something clever, something to show she wasn't like other mothers, she didn't care about the diploma, what concerned her was the heart of the matter. The only problem was, the diploma *was* the heart of the matter.

In the end she said something to the effect of, *A university education will open his eyes to what's out there.* She might even have said, *Knowledge requires guidance,* or tossed in some nonsense about the joys of the intellect, a necessary awareness of the world, who knows.

Teta shook the teacher's hand and left, feeling burned. She'd been counting on him. After all, she didn't have many other options; asking Minas's teacher for help was the only solution she could think of. When Soukiouroglou spoke, Minas bowed his head and listened.

What she'd had in mind, of course, was a direct intervention, a strict talking-to that would fix things immediately, not a research paper on a topic utterly outside the program of study. When she first heard about Minas's assignment, she was dismayed, and her absolute confidence in Soukiouroglou shaken.

—Look at it this way, Evthalia pointed out, your child started opening books again. Isn't that what you wanted?

No, it wasn't what she wanted. What she wanted was for him to take his exams.

—Besides, now we'll get to see him butt heads with Evelina and her mother, your favorite person, Evthalia teased.

And since Teta didn't seem to follow, Evthalia pointed out the obvious:

—You can't research the Gris affair without talking to his lawyer from the trial. In case you don't remember, his name was Dinopoulos. He's the girl's grandfather. As far as I know, he's the only one who never spoke to the newspapers. Why are you looking at me like that? You didn't know?

1948 AND AFTER

"WHAT FOOL UTTERED THE
WORD FREEDOM?"

THOMAS TZITZILIS, HEAD OF THE SECURITY POLICE IN SALONICA

I'm the one who cleaned the Red rats out of this city. *The great benefactor of the Capital of the North*, they wrote in the history of the gendarmerie. The Americans turned out not to have a brain among them, they bought into the anti-Greek propaganda. Even Greek citizens who cared about the health of our nation, who could see the danger posed by those communist thugs, called it a *Greek outrage against an American reporter.* Their radio stations cursed our country.

A nation's leaders have to make decisions. It's their job. To make calls. To give interviews. To see the smoldering coals and call in Tzitzilis to get the job done. All of America was up in arms and the puffed-up jackasses here in Greece took up the tune. *You're accomplices, the government isn't doing anything to arrest those responsible for the murder.* Generals and journalists kept getting in my way. Suddenly they had opinions about everything. Plenty of theories but no proof.

I know how to handle those types. Those kowtowing nobodies who supposedly run this country ought to have their wits about them. Brown-nosers and slaves to foreign interests, each and every one, all scared shitless that I might offend the outsiders.

To hell with the lot of them.

Earlier that day, before the American General barged into my office, strutting his chevrons and his attitude like a cock in someone else's henhouse—a third-generation American, of European refugee stock, if you want to call a spade a spade, whose grandfather was a convict and whose mother was a whore— the Minister had called me, scared out of his wits. He warned me that the General was quick to anger, owing to his rank. He told me to watch my tongue and not say anything that might put the country at risk. I could have reminded him that he was the bootlicking fool who'd made us an international laughingstock in the first place, but ministers are all talk, they're not great at listening. They say their piece and hang up as soon as they're done.

And when the General came, he just barged in without knocking. He was wearing his dress uniform, covered in medals. A spoiled man used to giving orders at a safe distance from enemy lines. He planned the attacks on a map, wrote memos, and told other people what to do.

—Entirely unacceptable! he howled. To ask American taxpayers to support Greece, and then have Greeks kill American citizens in return!

The foreign journalists tore us to shreds. They attacked the gendarmerie, claimed we were stalling on purpose, covering up for the perpetrators.

Damn them all. Tzitzilis isn't a man of words. He's a man of action. Everyone in the force knows it, and they respect me for it.

I went into the church of Agios Dimitrios. I wanted to consult the city's marshal, our patron saint. Agios Dimitrios knows plenty about war. Friend and savior of the city, as the priests say. The commies in the mountains have no God, they don't believe in saints. Which means they've got no one looking out for them.

Tough souls shatter the easiest. Just mess with them a little and they break. Take it from me, I've seen hulking men plead, strong young men crying like babies. I see them come in for questioning and can tell right away how long they'll last.

—How do you do it, boss? the new guys ask.

They're amazed at how I'm never wrong. Because when I say a thing, it's guaranteed. And if it's taking too long I get in there myself, I don't waste time giving orders.

Screams and pleading don't faze me at all, tears won't make me relent. I know how to break the toes on a man's foot one by one. I teach the others, it's not as easy as you might think. The prisoners who have been here a while would rather be beaten, their bodies are nothing but sacks anyway. But when I start on the toes they confess right away, they piss blood. Some people protest. Fresh-faced young lawyers, judges who think they're God's gift, who think you can solve things with a few words. Smart-asses with university degrees who never had to interrogate a prisoner. They parade around town in their starched collars and spit-shined shoes. They swear by the scales of justice. As if laws were written for obedient schoolgirls. The bastards are delusional, every last one.

When I bring them the accused men who've spent time in my prison and signed confessions scripted by others, they're not pleased by my *successful resolution of sinister plots*. They just complain about broken legs and bruises. They don't believe the prisoners fell down stairs and hit their heads on the wall. They don't realize these are routine techniques used by scoundrels and crooks who want to make the police force look bad.

Gentlemen, the government is treading water when it should be punishing men, and making examples of them. We're at war. If you've got balls, you do what it takes.

Saints speak to the pious. They give you a sign so you know how to proceed. I lit my candle and waited. I sat down in the pew and studied the icon. The saint spoke with his eyes, I saw it clear as day.

I crossed myself and stood. I had my orders.

When they brought him in, I told myself this one would break in two days. Not a real man at all, push him with a finger and he'd stumble. A dandy. A bureaucrat. A sissy. Fragile bones, not much meat on him, boiling him in a pot wouldn't get you much broth.

He didn't seem to understand what was happening, he looked at me foggily and kept whining like a schoolboy. He pretended to be naïve, but it turned out he knew perfectly well what was what.

Watch out for the silent types. You think you've got them under your thumb, as soft as dough. But they're cunning. Like water. You wouldn't think it, but there's nothing more devious and cruel than water. It wears down even stone.

That's how he was, silent. Nobody you'd ever pay much attention to. With his clean suit and ironed shirt, the note pad in his pocket, his fancy words and his press pass. Quiet as a mouse in its hole.

There's no sense betting on a little lizard like him, but my guys didn't have much else to do for entertainment. After interrogating brutes all day long, they deserved a little fun behind closed doors. One guy bet three days' wages that he would break.

And lost.

None of us could have imagined how long the lizard would hold his ground. I screamed at my guys until I was blue in the face. I called them incompetent, useless.

—Drop your pants, all of you, none of your cocks is worth a thing.

In the end I had to deal with the situation myself. With words and with deeds—the usual tricks. But he was a dog. He kept his mouth shut tight. We kept roughing him up, then waiting. When he came to, he still wouldn't confess. And what we needed was a confession. Without his signature I couldn't move forward.

He didn't leave me much choice in the matter.

I told them to bring in his mother. If Tzitzilis takes on a case, he puts it to bed. For a true leader, to begin is to finish.

VIOLETA GRIS, SISTER OF MANOLIS GRIS

The well-fed shouldn't complain. I always got annoyed when my mother said that. Don't stretch your legs beyond your blanket. Only go as far as your own two legs will carry you.

—Oh, Mother, you'll go through life with your head down, you don't ask for much. And that's why they'll never give you much, either.

—Don't disrespect our mother, Evgnosia protested.

I can practically see them now, sitting by the window with their mending in their laps. Needle, thread, thimble. The tin box of spools open, the pins lined up neatly in the pincushion. They would turn the fabric inside out. Evgnosia would hold the needle to the light, lick her fingers and twirl the thread. Then Mother would take over. She never tied knots, that was for second-rate seamstresses who couldn't do better, or careless housewives in a hurry to be done, who didn't understand that each action has its time and manner. Mother took hold of the thread with dexterity, smoothed the fabric under her finger and began. There was no better mender than she, you had to look hard to see where her needle had been. With a bit of ribbon and a button she could make a dress look entirely new. She would change the collar and the cuffs, always careful about the details in the finishing.

Mother was a woman of the old style. She knew never to throw out scraps of fabric, one day they might come in handy. Even a torn petticoat would find its way into something else. If it couldn't be mended, it could be turned into a little curtain or a bag for smelling salts. All it needed was a hand to show it off in its best light.

They never made me do those kinds of jobs, because I was studying at the university. *This family's hard work has paid off*, Manolis would say. His hard work, really, only he never drew attention to himself like that. What he wanted more than anything was for someone in our family to study. That had been our father's goal, too, or so our mother would say, turning her head in the direction of the Pontus.

When I announced that I had been accepted into the faculty of law, Mother left the food on the fire and the wash in the washtub and ran to kiss me. *Come here, child, let me kiss you*, is what she said. It was a formal kiss, first on my forehead, then on my cheeks, accompanied by a stream of wishes and tears, memories and aspirations. Manolis proudly told her about my scholarship, and our mother said, *Oh my, I have to sit down*, and collapsed into a chair. With the money from my scholarship she bought Evgnosia a new overcoat, and we decided to make a few repairs to the house that we'd been putting off. We did that as a matter of course: in our house everything was common property, and we certainly weren't going to make an exception for money.

I wore Evgnosia's hand-me-downs all through my university days, I never had new clothes. That was fair, if you ask me. They'd taken care of me for years, and now it was my turn to give back. They'd spoiled me since I was a girl. I was twenty, and Mother still boiled an egg for me each day so I'd have energy to study. She would chase me down in the yard and make me eat it.

My last class of the day ended at eight. By eight-thirty I had to be home. I would walk with a fellow classmate named Crete—what a ridiculous name, I can't imagine how any mother would let her child be baptized Crete. At any rate, her family had money, so Crete could have taken the tram home if she'd wanted, she didn't have to walk. The first time I ever saw real English pounds was at her house, tossed on top of the piano.

None of my classmates liked her, but Kyriakos, first in our class, was particularly hostile.

—Violeta, he would ask, why do you go around with her? She's at university just for fun, to have something to talk to her girl-friends about between dances. She and her kind will be ordering you around soon enough. We're studying so we can work for them one day. Open your eyes.

I had no interest in comparing myself to Crete. My mother had taught me never to compare myself to anyone. My mother, the poor, Pontic, refugee widow, who knew how to dress even if she didn't have money for new clothes, who thought her children were better than anyone else in the world. She passed that on to us, too, with her praise and her chiding. It was a deeply rooted belief, something that went without saying. She didn't shout it from the rooftops. She kept both feet on the ground and prevailed in difficult situations. When bad times brought other people to their knees, we dug in our heels and clenched our teeth. We went as far as we could, to the edge of the cliff.

My mother. Harsh and forgiving at the same time. She'd be the first to point out our weaknesses, but she turned into a wild dog if anyone else dared hint at some flaw in her children. There was no job she couldn't do, no burden she couldn't bear, no silence she wouldn't impose if circumstances called for it. She blew wind into our sails. She never touched our souls with dirty hands. She gloried in us from afar and prayed for the best. She believed we could take the moon down from the sky if we wanted. She didn't care if no one else agreed.

So Kyriakos could say what he liked about us ending up part of the suit-wearing proletariat. *Degree or no degree*, he would say, *we're all the same, the same millstone grinds us all down.* Kyriakos could say plenty more along those lines, particularly when he got riled up. He mocked Crete, called her a *marquise*, sneered at her coiffed hair, at the way she pronounced legal phrases, with a calm distaste, as if they felt dirty in her mouth. Kyriakos was smarter than any of us. The law professors were always talking about the country kid who had come down from his village to study in the city and was at his books night and day.

The professors were charmed by his passion, but even more by the precision of his language, by his sound judgment and fine rhetoric. The students who came in second and third, right behind him, claimed that his brilliant wordplay in the lecture hall only showed that he was a godless sophist. His teachers, who valued such rhetorical sleights-of-hand, thought it demonstrated his admirably wide base of knowledge.

Kyriakos did well in school, and after graduating, too. Soon enough he had become one of Crete's kind, full of irony and witticisms. He bought an apartment in town for his parents and brought them down from the village. His mother stopped wearing her headscarf and robe. She blessed the marriage of her only son to Crete's cousin Sofoula, a girl with a considerable dowry and ambitions for a wedding in the Metropolitan Church.

The day I went to find him, the newspapers were on the war path, and the whole city hummed with news of the murder. I made an appointment through the secretary at his office, a young woman who sat anxiously typing carbon-paper triplicates. Kyriakos welcomed me with a rehearsed smile.

He explained to me that it was impossible. Things weren't as simple as they seemed.

—Caesar's wife must be above suspicion.

—What's that supposed to mean? I lashed out.

Kyriakos made a gesture with his hand. To him the conversation was pointless.

—He already confessed. The only thing anyone can do, perhaps, is to save your mother. Violeta, this is not a time for emotion. One and one make two. Open your eyes.

—Look at you, Kyriakos Lolos, a boy from the village, valedictorian of our class in 1937, the young man who gathered up crumbs from lunch and saved them for dinner, who studied by the light of borrowed candles, who used to say that guilt is the creation of circumstance. Look what's become of you. My brother is innocent. I know it and you know it, too.

—Violeta, you're not being logical.

—Logic isn't always the best advisor. Aren't you the one who used to say that? That the hegemony of logic is responsible for some of the most fundamental misunderstandings?

—I wish I could help, Violeta. But your brother's case has already been tried.

—It's been tried outside the courts. That's what you're telling me.

Kyriakos didn't breathe another word. It was hard even for him to say to my face what anyone with eyes in his head could see.

KYRIA MARIA GRIS, MOTHER OF MANOLIS

It was dark as tar, rainy weather.

When they burst into my house to turn the place upside-down, I had just lain down with my feet propped against the wall. My feet were swollen something awful, my knees had been killing me since morning. I heard footsteps and knew. I ran to the door. I didn't care about the pain or anything.

A mother's curse never fails.

May a bereaved mother never cross your path, the old women in Trabzon used to say. *She'll burn up your joy, poison your day.*

Those men weren't men, they were mules. Pigs.

—Hey! Don't you have mothers of your own? I shouted, but they'd come there to get a job done.

Which is to say, not even a troop of janissaries could have stopped them, much less pleading and tears.

They turned the whole house upside-down. They even searched the lamp in front of my icons. They pawed the girls' nightgowns, flipped through our books, read all our papers. They found the one about Savvas.

—One son a hero, the other a traitor, they said.

Evgnosia put her hand over my mouth.

—Don't say a thing, Mother. Our silence will protect Manolis.

But there was no way of hushing Violeta. She couldn't abide injustice. Her head had swelled at the university, she'd read the laws. She knew right from wrong, not the way we learn it at home, but how it's written in books.

—You have no right, you have no proof, she shouted in their faces.

They paid her no heed at all. They asked their questions, I answered. They made me write a paper and sign it. I told them I never went to school, I might make mistakes, Violeta was the one in our house who had studied.

—Don't worry, ma'am, said a young man standing off to one side, just write the words and don't worry about that.

When they asked me to come with them, that's when my legs started hurting again. In all the commotion I'd forgotten the pain. My mother was right when she used to say, you can bear any pain if you have other worries on your mind.

I'm bearing, Mother. I'm bearing.

And troubled years came full of tears
since the barbarians came, and took my son
and killed my race, and smashed and burned.
With fire and axes they took our souls away.

We never had anything to do with the police, we aren't communists. We believe in Christ. Later on, at the trial, they said all kinds of things. They said we collaborated with the Reds. My boy joined the Party, it's true. He needed work. Do you think he had many offers to choose from? But they kicked him out, they figured out fast enough that he wasn't one of them. I tried to cheer him up, told him it was better to keep his distance. He would find another job, he was good at whatever he tried. When anyone called, he ran to help.

I'd had my dream. I never dream anything significant, I fall in bed like a log and sleep like a log until morning. But two days before my name day, all my dead came to see me in my sleep. They crowded in on all sides. My dead babies wrapped in blankets, fresh out of my belly, with the eyes of the very old. Eyes that know life is an uphill battle. My mother, young, with a braid in her hair and a kerchief, in her best dress and an embroidered apron. My father in his burial clothes. My mother-in-law with the tin basin, the one I washed her feet in, and her wedding coins sewn to the chest of her dress. My husband Stathis with those thick eyebrows of his, and the mole on his forehead. Savvas with a starched white shirt hanging out of his pants. *Tuck that in, boy*, I shouted. He was so thin, with cheeks as yellow as kaseri cheese. All around were cousins and neighbors, nephews and distant uncles. They all stood there in a crowd, none of them said a word, all you could hear was an *mmmmmmm*, something like church, or a song.

—Why aren't you talking? I asked them right to their faces. Say something! If you've gone to the trouble of rising from the earth to visit me, you can't have all come here tonight for anything good.

I woke with them still on my mind.

I counted them and remembered them one by one, twenty-seven in all, more than the house could fit, if they'd actually come. I was angry with Savvas. The rest had been buried for years, they'd forgotten and been forgotten, I rarely mentioned them in my prayers—except for my mother, of course—but Savvas was everywhere I turned. His photograph, framed in the sitting room. My blessed child, there at every turn. I was standing in front of that photograph, ready to give him a piece of my mind, when Evgnosia called to me.

—Mother, come quick! The lamp broke.

The oil had spilled all over the good tablecloth, the embroidered one, which we used to decorate the table. Evgnosia crossed herself.

—Don't worry, Mother, I'll put some warm water and soap on it.

She scrubbed it and got the stain out. But a faint shadow remained. Evgnosia put a bottle on top so we could still enjoy the embroidery. Right there, on our good tablecloth, was where they had me write that statement. My letters wouldn't lie flat, my hand trembled, and of course there was the cross-stitching underneath. Evgnosia made sure ink from the pen didn't leak onto the cloth. The poor thing was afraid another stain would ruin the piece altogether. Those were the kinds of worries we had. Back then. Before the sky fell on our heads.

•

Kyrios Tzitzilis wanted to be done with the case, he didn't like that we were causing him trouble. He smiled when I came in.

—Your Manolis is a good boy, Kyra-Maria, but too quiet. He's not saying what we want him to.

—What is it you want him to say? I asked.

—We want him to tell us about the communists, about his friends. To admit what he's done, so we can all go home.

What had he done? That was the trouble: they wouldn't tell me, no matter how many times I swore in the name of the Virgin Mary and her holy son that my Manolis had no truck with communists, that we were godly people, Greeks of the greater Greece, refugees chased down from the Pontus, but Greeks to the marrow of our bones.

—Fine, fine, Tzitzilis nodded, and kept asking what he'd already asked.

When he saw me rubbing my legs, since it was hot outside and they had swollen something awful, *Get up, kyra*, he ordered, *you're going to climb the stairs.*

A Turk might have cut my legs off right there, but he wouldn't have put me through that torture.

Forty-three stairs, up and down.

Again. And again. All day.

My lyre can sing and sing and cry
it lets out rivers of tears
and sings of the child away at war
of the unfair, unjust fight
with a heart on fire and rivers of blood.

I didn't care about the pain. Pain you can bear. You keep saying, now I'll surely die, but it keeps getting worse and you keep on living.

When your fate has been written, even God abandons you.

O Virgin Mary, who saw your son on the cross, you understand.

You understand but say nothing. You won't come down from your throne to save a body. Your eyes may fill with tears, but you offer no shelter.

They opened the door at the bottom of the stairs and I saw my child lying in blood. As if dead, tossed on the cement floor.

—You have no God, I shouted at them, no mother gave birth to you. May you live with my curse, and die unmourned and unforgiven. May you see all I've seen and worse.

I dragged my foot down the stairs, I grabbed the left one, which hurt more, between both hands and pulled. My foot caught on the railing and I tumbled down the stairs, my knees were bruised but what did I care, it was just flesh, flesh and bone, and mine, not my child's, I could tear myself to shreds and never care, as long as I got to where he was.

—Don't worry, ma'am, a tall young man said politely, stepping between us. The best doctors will take care of your Manolis. He fell down the stairs, like you.

He waved his hand and they closed the door, closed it before I could see him from up close. And they paid no heed to my pleading, all the tears in the world couldn't reach their hearts. They stood there in front of the door, men with no ears and no eyes. They knew no pity.

The young man came over, put his hands under my arms and held me up.

—Come, ma'am, and sign the paper. For Manolis's sake.

THROUGH OTHER EYES

When they brought Gris before the district attorney to sign his confession, he couldn't even hold a pen. He kept sliding down on the chair. A policeman wrapped his hand around Gris's fingers and helped with the signature, to speed things along.

In that policeman's opinion, the American marshals, the Greek military officers, the government ministers, and the guys from Security all owed a moment of silence to the young man who had withstood all he'd withstood for so many days, and had even dared to raise his voice. He'd spoken back to the Minister of Justice, who had made a special trip up from Athens in a hurry—always in a hurry—to close the case, telling Gris that if he would just confess, *he would be offering the greatest of services to the government. The country would honor and respect him, his name would go down in history as one of the great benefactors of the nation.* At first Gris just stood in his corner like a whipped dog, but in the end he couldn't hold back:

—Sir, why don't you ask your son to sacrifice himself? To have his name go down in history as a benefactor of the nation? My family has already paid a high enough price. I lost a brother in the war. My mother can't bear to lose another child.

Look at the little half-pint, thought the policeman who had been assigned to guard Gris, the same policeman who had lost the bet over how long he would last. The Minister let loose for a while and then stormed out, slamming the door behind him, and Tzitzilis vowed to punish the prisoner's audacity.

The interrogation methods of the head of the Security Police were infamous in the city. He made prisoners stand for hours on end, deprived them of sleep and water, beat them, hung them upside-down, applied electroshock to their genitals, administered his own special concoction (no one dared mention opium), injections (of calcium, they said), promises, lies, curses, and kicks.

Tzitzilis never imagined that it would require his entire arsenal to bring Gris to his knees. The little lizard seemed like a sensitive type, a man who did the right thing, a pen-pusher with family obligations that strangled any dreams or desires of his own. A widowed mother and two unmarried sisters could un-man a chieftain, much less a reporter. Tzitzilis gave him two days at most. The policeman in charge of Gris was the first to bet on the boss—and two days later had already lost.

Tzitzilis promised the prisoner a passport and a ticket to

Argentina, as the guys at the Ministry had advised him to. They wanted to close the case as soon as possible, to get their hands on the proper confessions and signatures, to shut the journalists up. To put an end to the rumors once and for all.

Gris smoked a carton of eighty-eight Matsaggou-Stoukas cigarettes a day, equivalent to four normal packs. In other words, this little lizard had balls, though you wouldn't guess it from looking at him. So Tzitzilis decided to add hashish to the prisoner's cigarettes; after all, a little relaxation wouldn't do poor Manolis any harm, and it might even loosen his tongue.

Tzitzilis served him a coffee spiked with his special cognac, banking on the fact that the man wasn't used to narcotics. He let him light a cigarette, too, one of the ones he himself had rolled. Then he sat back to watch the show.

Gris was confused at being treated so well. He smoked his cigarette, drank his coffee, and suddenly felt his brakes fail. It was as if someone had reached a hand straight into his soul, as if he'd stepped into nothingness, as if the springs that kept his thoughts and emotions in place had all unsprung at once.

—I was just wondering, Manolis, if you might be a communist, Tzitzilis said as soon as he thought the prisoner was sufficiently dazed.

Manolis couldn't control his tongue, and his mind was stuck like a cart in mud. His limbs seemed to have been poured into the chair. Words seemed impossible—where to find them, how to pronounce them. He wasn't a communist, and didn't side with the others, either. All he wanted was to be left in peace, to not be bothered, to do his job well, to provide for his family, to make his mother proud. He certainly didn't believe that an idea would save the world. He didn't even believe that God could save him, so why would he put his faith in human beings?

His body abandoned him. All he wanted was to sleep. After so much torture, a man becomes sentimental.

•

Terrifying in his despair. That was Gris.

An egoistic individualist, those in the Party would say. In Greece, where everything was a performance, the verdict was a foregone conclusion. There couldn't be smoke without a fire, most people thought. Surely the reporter had sullied his nest somehow. Besides, there was indisputable evidence, witnesses, signatures. Lawyers came and went behind steel doors, attempting various agreements and plea bargains. They knew what they had to do, but their consciences weren't convinced. That made things more difficult.

Some claimed that the district attorney assigned to the case had gone to visit Gris's lawyer, a young man by the name of Dinopoulos, at his home, an unprecedented move for someone in his position. Rumor had it that the lawyer managed to bargain the sentence down. He would keep his mouth shut, he promised, about the irregularities in the proceedings, if in return they would rule out the death penalty. The district attorney weighed Dinopoulos's intentions, trying to decide whether he could take him at his word. The two men quickly reached an agreement, with a few sentences and a slap on the back.

A few years in prison wasn't the end of the world, the district attorney apparently hinted. And it was a holy cause, the fate of the nation hung in the balance. *My job*, he said in conclusion, *is to take responsibility for my decisions*. He didn't want to give too much ground, but he took care to calm the young, untried lawyer—who, moreover, was a member of the party in power, and therefore someone to work with rather than against. Dinopoulos swallowed his doubts. He'd avoided the worst, he told his conscience. What it came down to was, he'd saved an innocent man from the firing squad.

A few days later the young lawyer went out to walk through the city. Salonica was divided into semi-autonomous regions: the city below Tsimiski, the city above Egnatia, the city beyond Venizelou.

Urban zones whose borders were nowhere demarcated and yet were sharply cut, separated by lines of fire. Residents knew where those secret dividing lines were; they moved with ease to and from their burrows, and took care on foreign turf. Dinopoulos hugged the exterior walls of Agia Sophia, great is her grace, but decided not to cross the threshold of the church itself. An agnostic from the cradle, he wouldn't let his current difficulties defeat him. Besides, his back was covered: his mother and wife regularly lit candles at the church, so the family already had representatives before the icons.

On his walk he tried to consider the situation from a practical angle. Greece, since its formation as a modern state, had been a nation of useless, dreamer politicians who gambled away the fate of the Greek people. The country had from the start been overrun with outcasts of all sorts, worthless upstarts and coattail-riders. Why should he be the one to pay the damages, to snatch the chestnuts out of the fire? He would stand as tall as he could; he would make sure the proper formalities were observed; he would protect Gris from the worst. He had drawn a line in the sand. If he quit now—a thought that had passed through his mind the previous night—they would crush the accused man entirely. The least of all evils, wasn't that the mature and judicious approach to take?

It was certainly what Evthalia would have advised, if he'd had an opportunity to discuss the case with her. He saw her every so often in the neighborhood. She reminded him of the girl in that famous painting, her beauty all corners, hidden miracles in her cheekbones—what a pity he'd never be able to tell her. She just would have given him a sardonic look and walked off, ponytail swinging in rebuke. She had been admitted to the literature department at the university, and still wore girlish ankle socks. She didn't hesitate to correct his quotations of Cicero whenever he tried in vain to impress her. She respected the proper order of words in a sentence. His mother didn't like her, though; in her opinion, Evthalia was an obstinate girl who talked too much and couldn't even boil water, much less cook a proper meal.

If the lawyer's mother and the student found themselves side by side at the grocer's, the younger woman never ceded her place as she should have. His mother complained that the girl had no manners, she was a wild creature. And since he had no desire to argue with his mother, he'd made up his mind not to bring any unpleasantness down on his head for Evthalia's sake.

And so he married Froso. It was an arranged marriage. She was a good, sensible, respectful girl. She could darn socks and cook. There was nothing missing from Froso's dowry, not even a needle. She was obedient in bed, fulfilled her wifely duties convincingly. As for flowing conversation, that's what his friends were for.

Evthalia, on the other hand, was an untamable beast, and he needed to secure his career, he didn't have time to waste on winning a girl over or strategizing about his love life. At times, though, he still thought of how it might have been. Particularly when he saw her in her green pleated dress, her white ankle socks, and her ponytail, walking home from the university hugging her Cicero to her chest. He found Homer less exciting—Homer was a poet, all empty words—but the sight of the girl clutching her Cicero could keep him dreaming for days. That was enough for him. And it was something no one could take from him.

Meanwhile, Froso learned to cook papoutsakia the way his mother did. She wrote his name on the prayer paper in the evening, for his health, and took care of his laundry. As far as his mother was concerned, that more than sufficed for a successful marriage—and in the end, he came around to her opinion. Evthalia was the moon. You don't take the moon down from the sky and marry it. You admire it from afar. That would have to be enough.

What had gotten into him, why was he thinking about all that? He needed to focus on other things right now, things that couldn't wait. Perhaps it was because he had caught a glimpse of Evthalia's ponytail from afar. And he knew she had her Cicero class today. *De oratore.*

Oh, if only.

SCHOOL YEAR 2010–2011

"THE ONLY DIPLOMA WORTH EARNING IS
YOUR DOCUMENTATION OF INSANITY"

MINAS

Souk makes no sense. He doesn't drink, he doesn't smoke, he barely eats. His pants always look like they're about to fall off, his stomach is actually concave, I've never seen another belly that doesn't stick out at least a little bit.

Evelina says his whole body is an appendage. That it's just there to hold up his head. It's more or less what everyone says who doesn't like him, including the other teachers. They can't criticize his knowledge of the material, so they start out saying how well-read he is, only to end up saying he's *not cut out for high school. He'd do great at a research institute, or the university, but here, it's not about how smart you are, you need other skills.* They've mastered the art of the backhanded compliment. Yes, of course, but.

None of the other teachers came to Fani Dokou's concert. If they had, they'd have been stunned. Souk was way up front, all in black, as usual. And next to him stood Dokou's son—I knew it was him, I'd seen him in photographs. He's about my age and plays in a band at his school in Athens. He has a pierced eyebrow and a tattoo on the back of his neck. My mother would have a heart attack.

Anyhow. Souk looked like his usual somber self, only he was standing there with his arm around Fani Dokou's kid like it was no big deal. Souk, who never touches anyone. The tenderest thing he's ever done in class is say five nice words in a row. But there he was, all tight with Fani Dokou's son. You could tell how much fun he was having by the look of them from behind. Souk's back speaks volumes—like when he's writing on the board, he doesn't have to turn around for you to know what look he's got on his face. At the concert, it was obvious he was having a good time.

—Look who's here, Evelina said, giggling, as she bodychecked me from the side. She came over and stood right next to me, waving to some big dolt who was making eyes at her from across the crowd.

—I came with a friend, she said.

—I can see.

She raised her cell phone to take a picture, but there wasn't time. Just then the lights dimmed and Dokou started singing a folk song that everyone in the audience knew, about a jealous husband who murders his wife. The drums fell silent, the keyboard hushed. Her voice rose up from deep inside, she held the high notes, then plowed on, filling the stage, filling the whole square with sound. She lifted us up and swept us away with her. The crowd was a pulsing sea creature. Cameras flashed, cheers rang out.

—My mom used to sing that as a lullaby, Evelina whispered in my ear, her hands raw from clapping.

My mom sang it on road trips. It was so sad, but it always put her in a good mood.

—That song goes out to someone I love dearly. For you, Marinos, Fani Dokou said, pointing right at Souk.

Respect.

Maybe Souk has a body after all?

Fani Dokou hadn't given a concert in Thessaloniki in over a decade. She left in her twenties and never looked back. But Thessalonians never forget their own, particularly when someone makes a name for herself in Athens. And now Dokou is an internationally recognized ethnic singer, with concerts in Portugal and Oslo, recording sessions in Paris, tours in Israel. She popularized Greek folk songs, reworked them, added electronic touches. And in the process, she achieved the impossible: she made music that both Mom and I like.

—She's good, Evelina agreed.

That didn't seem strong enough to her, so she added,

116

—A goddess.

For real. The light around her wasn't that fake, plastic light, all smoke and cameras and kilowatt hours. Her sweat shone. She was on fire up there on the stage. Mom always talked about her concerts, the flowing skirts that fell around her like veils, the bracelets all the way up to her elbows, the bells at her ankles. Any other woman who dared to wear what she wore would just look ridiculous, but Fani Dokou pulled it off.

The concert ended, the floodlights flickered off. Most people pushed as fast as they could toward the exit.

—Should I walk you home?

Evelina hesitated.

—My friend was going to walk me, but his house is in the opposite direction. Wait a minute, I'll let him know.

We walked without talking, half an arm's length apart.

—Are you really not going to take your exams? she asked.

—Can we really not use that word today? It's Saturday, and I hear it enough during the week.

—Okay, category change. Let's turn to affairs of the heart, Evelina said, doing her best impression of a talk show hostess. Do you think they're a couple?

—Who?

—Souk and Dokou. I wish I'd gotten a shot of them with my phone. I could've put it up on Facebook.

—They were at university together, ages ago.

—You know everything, don't you? she commented.

—Yes.

—Modest as always.

—Just acknowledging the facts.

She laughed. When Evelina laughs, her whole face changes. She turns into a normal person. At school she's always got a smile plastered on her face, like a good, obedient student, pretending to be social. You never see her alone during break, the others always cluster around her. In class she rarely asks questions, she's too full of certainties. She hates philosophy but still quotes philosophers left and right in her essays. That's how people are who believe in the absolute: they need a guru to show them the way.

But now, walking up Iktinou Street, Evelina had left her shield and spear behind. She reminded me of how she was in grade school, a little girl in sweat pants and braces. She used to steal candy bars from my bag, and she once ruined my shirt from pulling it too much during a game of tag. She was always trying to engineer trades. She would grab my Scooby Doo erasers and give me chewed-up straws in return.

We were almost at Agia Sophia. Her shoulder brushed my sleeve, her hair tickled my nose. She smelled like a garden.

—Want to go in? I suggested.

—Are we allowed?

—This late at night, everything's allowed.

I hopped over the low wall around the churchyard and held out my hand.

—I bet what we're doing is against the law, she said gleefully.

I didn't tell her I jump this wall every day, to look at the sky from inside the churchyard. From in there the stars are dizzying. The way they leap out at you all at once, you can almost hear it, like a wave crashing. If you close your eyes, you can even pretend that the coastline of Halkidiki has beamed itself into the city center. Of course you're brought back to reality by the honking of cars and the stink of exhaust. But even car exhaust smells different, better, around Agia Sophia. If you've grown up with that smell in your lungs, the countryside throws you for a loop. Grandma might be right when she says Agia Sophia is the heart of the city. If you drew a circle around the city with a compass, this is definitely where you'd plant the foot.

Evelina spread her bag out on the grass and sat down.

—I wouldn't recommend that, I warned. Stray dogs shit there.

—How much of a jerk are you?

—Why? Because I'm trying to keep your pants clean?

—Now the thing I'm going to remember about being here is dog shit. What are you doing?

—Bringing you to someplace better.

I put my jacket on a fragment of marble, the one with the rosettes and the piece of gum stuck to the bottom.

—Is this part of a column? An ancient one?

—Probably. Move over so I can sit, too.

Spotlights flooded the place.

—It's like moonlight, Evelina said. All that's missing is Byron and the moon-drenched maid.

She leaned her head on my shoulder and launched into the folk song Dokou had started the concert with. She doesn't have a great voice, and she knows it. Which means she usually doesn't sing. But she's got soul. She's got a fire inside, you can tell. She squeezed her eyes shut and turned up the volume. She was living it. Her forehead glistened. What I was smelling wasn't her perfume, it was her skin. It made me dizzy.

I bent down and kissed her. Don't ask why, I don't know. She turned toward me and stuck in her tongue. Hot saliva and a sweet taste of Evelina and bubble gum.

Somewhere dogs were barking.

—Turns out you're brand-name, she said.

I didn't have a ready response, so I just shut up.

I had no choice in the matter. One French kiss and she had me on standby.

Grandpa Dinopoulos, born in 1922, was twenty-six years old during Gris's trial and is eighty-nine now. He lives in a penthouse apartment on Ermou. From his veranda he can see Agia Sophia if he twists his head. The apartment was bought with his wife's inheritance. She was younger than him and everyone assumed she would outlive him, but she set off before him *along the eternal road*, as Grandma Evthalia says.

Statistics suggest that most widowers wither away, but Grandpa Dinopoulos, a widower for the past twenty years, is living proof to the contrary. He wakes up at six every morning, drinks a Greek coffee with lots of sugar, dunks his koulouri in the froth, and sets out on his walk through the apartment. His doctor has forbidden him to walk outside, since he's unsteady on his feet and sometimes has dizzy spells.

He wears a vest and pocket watch over his pajamas. He does the rounds of the entire apartment three times. Kitchen, living room, dining room, office, bedroom. When he's done, he goes out onto the balcony to get some sun and feel the breeze on his face.

Now that his wife is dead, Elena, from Georgia, takes care of him. Her legs support the old man and the apartment, too. She's his nurse, his cleaning lady, his cook. All his relatives worship the ground she walks on.

Grandpa Dinopoulos doesn't eat much. He spends his mornings reading in his office and pores over the newspaper with a magnifying glass every evening, seated in his favorite armchair. He has opinions about everything and likes to share them with others, though these days he rarely has the opportunity. He's a walking library and a living museum. He knows everything we read about in books, only he knows it first hand. He has the equanimity of a person who's lived through a world war, a civil war, and plenty of political changeovers. Nothing phases him. He believes people can withstand pretty much anything.

He hasn't practiced law in years, but continues to advise his son, who inherited his law practice, along with a Rolodex full of clients. In the beginning his son wasn't bothered by the father's interventions, he was glad for the help. But Jesus Christ, he was nearing retirement age himself. It didn't look good for him to still be accepting advice from his father.

Evelina and her grandfather aren't on the best of terms. No matter how much her mother sang her praises, it took the old man ten years to reconcile himself to the fact that his law practice would eventually fall into a woman's hands. Only last year did Grandpa Dinopoulos finally write a card to his granddaughter in a trembling hand congratulating her on coming first in her class, and expressing his wishes that she continue to thrive and prosper and accomplish good works—even if he personally doubted how much a woman could achieve.

Evelina explained all that to me, more or less, when I asked if she would take me to see her grandfather. At first she didn't want to, he talked too much and it bored her. Besides, there was the principle of the thing, since she thought it irresponsible of Soukiouroglou to assign me a research project so close to the date of the exams that would determine our future.

—What's his deal, she said, wasting your time on something so pointless?

Evelina is as stubborn as Mom. She thinks her opinion is superior, tries to push her ideas on others, doesn't listen to anyone. It took me seven text messages and half an hour of close tracking on Facebook to bring her around, and she almost drove me crazy with her LOLs and OMGs in the meantime.

Evelina is like a lion. The lion is king of the desert, and can pretty much do whatever it wants. That's Evelina. She absolutely never backs down until she gets her way. If you try to stop her she'll tear you to shreds. I can say under oath: if there's ever a nuclear disaster and only one human being survives, it'll be her. Handling her takes skill and subtlety, not brute force. We're talking hours of conversation and negotiation.

In the end, though, she did arrange a meeting, and even came with me. Elena opened the door. We'd come during the old man's afternoon walk, and we watched as he dragged his feet through the rooms, braking at every turn, then gathering speed and racing down the hall.

—Advanced Parkinson's, Evelina whispered in my ear. It takes a while for the engine to warm up. But when he gets going, there's no catching him. If he stops, he'll fall, so he always touches the walls to steady himself, even though it embarrasses him.

The old man was approaching the living room. Elena ran over, wedged her body under his, and eased him into his armchair.

—What a wreck of a human I've become, the old man commented.

He had on striped pajamas, mustard and red, like the ones people wear in movies. His big bald head had a strip of hair around the edge, and the veins on his hands bulged. But what I noticed most were his eyes. A person's eyes don't age. Mom learned that from one of her documentaries, that the eyes are the only part of the human body that doesn't age. I checked with Grandma's, too.

—Well? he said, obviously thrilled at suddenly having an audience.

—Grandpa, this is my friend from school, Minas Georgiou. He's writing a research paper about Manolis Gris. He wants to ask you some questions.

—I see, said her grandfather.

Evelina kicked my shin.

—Say something, she hissed.

—Mr. Dinopoulos, I'd be interested in interviewing you about the events of the trial. I would want to record our conversation, to make sure I get everything right. Of course you can check the final text. It's a student paper about the Gris trial. I'll be presenting it at our school at the end of the quarter. And if you'd like to attend, you would be the guest of honor.

As I spoke, the old man pulled a magnifying glass out of his vest pocket and started examining me through it.

—You remind me of someone, was his response.

Now it was my turn to kick Evelina.

—Grandpa, she coaxed.

—I'd be very interested in recording your opinion of the events, I plowed on. You're the only person involved in the case who never made a public statement.

—What's done is done. Water under the bridge, last year's sour grapes, the old man said, seeming bored.

—That's not true, as you know better than anyone, I tried to challenge him. What matters is that justice be served.

—Evthalia, Evthalia Mitsikidou.

The old man was drumming his nails on the arm of his chair. He'd brought the magnifying glass back up to his face and was scrutinizing me again.

—If you didn't have that silly ponytail, I never would have made the connection, he said, laughing with a kind of a snort. The devil take me if you're not Evthalia's grandson. Your face is like hers, and the way you move your head when you talk. How is Evthalitsa these days? he asked.

I glanced at the clock on the wall, calculating. The Gris affair could wait. For the old man, Grandma came first.

—Grandma, do you know Mr. Dinopoulos, Evelina's grandfather?

Grandma was frying eggs in margarine. She put them on a plate and poured the extra melted margarine over them, then diced an onion for the salad. She sprinkled it with water and salt to take out the worst of its sting.

—We were neighbors. We lived across the street from one another, she answered, without pausing in her task.

—I went to see him yesterday, Evelina took me. About Gris. I told you about my project, right?

She crumbled feta over the salad with her fingers.

—He guessed right away that I'm your grandson. He says I look like you. He seemed kind of strange.

Grandma smiled.

—Well, he was a very well-respected lawyer in his day. Gris accused lots of people of intrigue, but never Dinopoulos. They had some kind of a friendship, or at least that's what the newspapers claimed. Dinopoulos used to go and visit him in prison, even after the verdict.

—What's he like? As a person, I mean?

Under different circumstances, Grandma would have put down the olive oil and the oregano. She would have sat me down at the table so we could talk *vis-à-vis and face-to-face*, as she likes to say. Grandma believes that people shouldn't talk without looking one another in the eye. I watched the hunch in her back rise and fall nervously. She fished in a jar for olives, took out some spicy pickles and went on decorating the salad.

—I couldn't say. I knew him when he was young. People change.

—Come on, Grandma. You're always bragging about your infallible instincts with people.

Grandma wiped her hands on a dish towel and started setting the table. When she answered, she seemed almost out of breath.

—He's very bright. Worked like a dog. Was never accused of the slightest irregularity. A family man, with traditional values. Talked a big game, but always followed through.

She served the food. She had no intention of continuing that conversation. Whatever else she had to say on the subject, she was already saying on the inside.

—Did you know our grandparents knew one another?

Evelina shrugged.

We've been hanging out for the past week or so. Her mother apparently considers me a good influence. When we were eight years old, Evelina told her mother, *I always have the best conversations with Minas. He's the smartest kid in our class.*

—Just look at our little grown-ups, her mother said to mine, back then. Mrs. Dinopoulou also told Mom that Evelina was the one who put that valentine in my bag in first grade, the paper heart that said, *Minas, will you marry me?* on it.

At some point, though, we sort of stopped having anything to do with one another. Evelina hung out with more popular kids; I didn't meet her requirements. It bugged her that I always got the better grades, always scored just a few points higher than she did. Last year she finally got what she wanted and calmed down. The fact that she's in charge of the attendance book this year is proof that she finally beat me. After being runner-up for years, now she's getting ready to be flag-bearer at the school parade.

Evelina's one of those people who needs constant validation. No amount of praise is ever enough. She dopes herself like a race horse. She thinks she knows the truth just because she knows how to pick the right answers on exams. Which isn't all that great an accomplishment, if you ask me.

There will always be someone who's better. Someone is al-ways going to know more. Evelina is a right-answer machine, as long as she's already learned the answer from one of our textbooks. Maybe that's why it's so hard for her to deal with Soukiouroglou—because he's unpredictable. He asks unexpected questions and accepts bizarre answers, as long as you support your position with evidence. Souk doesn't test our knowledge, he takes it as a given. What he cares about is how we think. His mind doesn't work like other people's, he's full of incendiary ideas and loves to provoke. The atmosphere in his classroom can get pretty tense. Not everyone can take it, and not everyone is interested in supporting a position. If it's in the answer key, that's good enough for them. Souk doesn't even read answer keys. Which is a big problem if you're in a hurry to find out the answers.

THROUGH OTHER EYES

—Sir, I read the pages you recommended.

Minas's tone was one of mild despair.

—So, I need to quote others' opinions and cite my sources properly.

He didn't know what else to say.

—You think that's enough? Soukiouroglou asked. Just cite some sources and you're through? That sounds like an easy way out.

—But, sir, I'm going to discuss the events, too. I've been investigating the causal relationships.

Minas couldn't remember precisely where he'd heard that phrase, but it seemed to suit the occasion, so he went ahead and tacked it on.

—Investigating the causal relationships? Where on earth did that come from? Someone less well-disposed might call your language borrowed.

He gave Minas a look and decided the conversation was worth pursuing.

Years earlier he had spent a semester of unspeakable loneliness in Bristol. The historians at the university there, or at least the ones he met, were all provocatively postmodern, and avoided mentioning events. They preferred to talk about the *narrative construction of history*. Some wore moth-eaten sweaters and ragged slacks, but others wore bow ties to class, men of privilege with no need to prove anything to anyone, who considered power dynamics the sole driving force behind history.

—Historical events arrive to us already interpreted, they're trickier than we think, he remembered one graduate student saying, a young man with a bowl cut, wire-rimmed glasses, and a healthy dose of self-confidence. The historical continuum has no beginning, middle, or end, he proclaimed. The ideology of periodization is way out of date. It's time we recognized that. We can't just divide history into neat slices. History is a construction. Narrative would be the best word for it.

None of this was entirely foreign to Soukiouroglou, but in Bristol it seemed more appealing. Perhaps it was the unbearable wetness of the place, or the solitude, the fact that he never heard Greek being spoken on the street. He even dreamed in English. It wasn't something he enjoyed—on the contrary, it was a heavy price to pay.

He wrote two articles while he was there and took notes for more, but nothing could make up for the nights he spent shut up in the cell of a room they gave him, his gaze trained on the wall. As was natural, he became even more suspicious in the face of what was commonly known as truth. So many of his fundamental certainties had been shaken. And yet deep down, he knew it was all not much more than intellectual gymnastics. He didn't see the wisdom in radical skepticism.

On his return to Greece, he was a different person altogether. Fani was the first to notice. *Your voice changed*, she'd said. *It's deeper, less certain.*

That lesson from his days in Bristol was what he wanted to share with Minas, whose paper he had conceived as an exercise in recognizing that there were multiple versions of reality. A simple statement of the various viewpoints on the case wasn't what Souk had in mind.

Souk's colleagues couldn't believe how slippery he was, pretending to be some kind of monk and then suddenly showing up in the society column in a tender tête-a-tête with Fani Dokou. The photograph that got published the morning after the concert showed them leaning in toward one another. Rumors flew, his colleagues jumped to all kinds of conclusions.

But the joking and laughter stopped abruptly when Souk walked into the teachers' office, silent and obviously exhausted. He had sunglasses on and didn't bother saying hello to anyone. They observed his entrance, exchanging glances and committing his movements to memory, as fodder for later conversations. Souk opened his locker, got out his things, and made photocopies for class. He still hadn't said a word to anyone by the time he headed down to morning prayer. He never crossed himself during prayer, a stance that had attracted comments of all sorts during the years he'd been working at the school.

He was in no mood for small talk or smiles. He stood behind the rows of students, alone, entirely alone, with an armful of books shielding his stomach.

He had missed Fani. They tried to keep up on the phone, but sometimes things got in the way: concert tours, travel, resounding silences initiated by one or the other or both. But then at some point they would simply pick up the thread again, start right where they'd left off, in the middle of a sentence, telling stories to fill in the gaps. Fani told him about experiences she'd had, things she'd done and seen, while he mostly talked about what he'd been reading. They never intruded on one another's lives, perhaps out of discreteness, perhaps out of discomfort. Souk also talked on the phone with her son. Nikolas Dokos didn't know Souk all that well, but the boy clearly had a soft spot for him. He was intrigued by the unlikely combination of the teacher's austere, almost ascetic personality and the abrupt flights of his thought—his unconventional mind, his biting irony, the way he toppled the walls of established logic, overturning everything. Souk didn't pretend to be a revolutionary, like most of the musicians Nikolas had grown up around. He never launched into long diatribes against the system, he didn't try to one-up others by being the most radical person around. He said what he thought, didn't hold back with his opinions, and didn't change them to suit the circumstances. When you asked nothing of him, he gave you everything. But if you put a knife to his throat, he'd dig his heels in like a mule.

Nikolas would accept advice from Souk that he wouldn't from Fani. Mostly because there was nothing preachy about him: his relentless irony undermined everything. Nikolas told his mother he didn't find her friend boring, like all the tutors with their fancy degrees whom Fani paid through the nose to teach her child to give the right answers. And while she was happy that Marinos had developed this channel of communication—even at a distance—with her sourpuss of a son, it worried her, too: even she preferred a more conventional approach to the issue of her son's education.

So when she saw Nikolas hanging on Marinos's every word that night after the concert, agreeing with whatever the teacher said, she sent him away. Nikolas went off in a huff. For the thousandth time, his mother was spoiling his fun.

Fani leaned toward her friend, whom she hadn't seen in a long time. He was the one she called with unwashed hair, in pajamas and slippers, when Nikolas was driving her up the wall, but also when she had some important job prospect that she wanted to discuss. She was eternally grateful that she'd never shared a bed with him, as she had with most of her friends, artists with high ambitions and low self-awareness. He wasn't a very physi-cal person, or at least that's what she used to think, when she was an undergraduate and would watch him in the lecture hall, the graduate student and teaching assistant for the course. He seemed to be wrapped in barbed wire. The other students didn't like him, called him a *leper*, or *uptight*. They made fun of her for talking to him. But Fani liked how Souk kept his distance. He shunned the crowd. Though in the end he paid for it.

—Why don't you have a job at the university? she asked abruptly that night after the concert.

He showed no surprise at the question. It was one Fani often returned to. From the moment his advisor, Asteriou, had retired, Fani wouldn't let it rest.

—I'm not cut out for that kind of institution, Souk replied.

—You're wasting your life at the school, Fani insisted.

—Who says?

—I do. What on earth are you doing there? I mean, I'm sure you're doing those brats some good, I see how Nikolas is with you. But you're made for other things.

—Mmmm, he murmured ironically.

—You're a fool, Fani said, starting to get mad. A stubborn fool. The king of fools, the fool to end all fools.

—For a bard, your prose isn't half bad, either, he teased.

Fani tickled him in the ribs. She liked touching him. Sometimes she pinched, or sank her nails into his flesh, or, like now, tested him with a tickle. She liked seeing him pull back in a panic. His body was on alert, it wouldn't stand for any incursion, even in the form of a caress.

—I'm not cut out for all that, he repeated. Running around to conferences, padding my c.v., making connections. I'm a solitary researcher.

—Okay, Lucky Luke.

Fani clinked her glass against his. After a concert a few drinks helped her relax. But even with alcohol, she could never get to sleep before dawn.

—You don't understand, Souk insisted. You think things would be better there.

—Yes, I do, Fani answered without hesitation.

He weighed her with his eyes.

—I'm not going back there, even if they burn me alive.

—Well, I can't argue with that, Fani said, and let the subject rest.

Grandpa Dinopoulos was walking slowly from the olive tree at one end of the veranda to the mallows at the other and back again. Elena helped ease him into the turn. The weather was lovely, the sun caressed his bald spot and eyes, warmed his pajamas. This brief excursion onto the veranda had lifted his mood. So much so that he was considering asking Elena to read him a few pages from the penal code. It might give her some trouble, but she'd manage, she was diligent and compliant, and her Greek wasn't bad. He was already daydreaming of the moment when he would sink into his armchair and listen.

—Could you bring me my binoculars? he asked.

Elena sat him down in his chair on the veranda. *A gorgeous day*, the old man thought, closing his eyes.

How could I have imagined, he wondered. *Back when I was so anxious all the time, when I thought work was everything. When I spent my days strategizing. When I confused unimportant things for important ones.*

Grandpa Dinopoulos raised the binoculars to his eyes. On sunny days when he could sit and daydream outside on the balcony, this was his morning entertainment: watching the passersby and his neighbors, the activity on the street and in the apartments across the way, whenever a curtain parted. He turned his gaze to the tables on the sidewalk outside Terkenlis, the sweet shop on the corner. That's where Elena bought his favorite tsourekia covered in white chocolate. She brought them home still warm in the box, and he liked to touch them with his hands, stick a finger in the frosting and bring it to his mouth. Buying a whole tsoureki for a few fingerfuls of frosting struck Elena as a waste, but then there weren't many pleasures left to the old man. The manhandled sweet would end up at the Georgian housekeeper's apartment, where she gave it to her kids and neighbors.

Grandpa Dinopoulos watched the morning customers at the tables set out on the corner of Agia Sophia Street and Ermou. Middle-aged couples, a few extremely old women, some university students. Evthalia and her girlfriends had taken a spot at the corner table. He recognized her from her knitted suit; she'd always liked bright colors. This one was a roof-tile red that caught the eye, particularly as she was surrounded by her friends' gray, sky-blue, and salmon-colored jackets. Evthalia was lecturing them, he could tell by the way her head bobbed, and the rest were listening, most likely agreeing.

Grandpa Dinopoulos put down the binoculars with a sigh. How could he possibly have imagined, over half a century earlier when work was his whole life, that the sight of a suit in roof-tile red would be enough to make his day?

1948 AND BEYOND

"WITH EVERYTHING THEY'RE DOING, THEY
MIGHT MAKE ME HAVE AN OPINION"

MARGARET TALAS, MOTHER OF JACK TALAS

Each child is born with its character already in place. Teachers and missionaries like to think they tame souls. What do they know? They're all men, and most of them childless. They think character is something you can shape, that punishments or encouraging words actually make a difference.

Bullshit, darling.

As soon as you take your child in your arms you know. From how it cries and nurses and sleeps. You know how much it's going to put you through from that very first moment. Jack is a perfect example: he was as stubborn and hardheaded as they come.

—What a beautiful baby, my mother-in-law crowed. He sleeps like an angel.

But when he was less than a month old I saw what his anger looked like: face blue from screaming, legs so stiff he looked like a dry branch. He didn't know how to talk, so he shrieked until we figured out what he wanted. In all the years that followed he didn't change a bit. If he set his mind on something, we all had to get out of the way.

My other boy, Mike, wasn't like that. He went along with whatever his older brother wanted, he didn't like to fight. They slept in the same room, shared clothes and toys. Mike used to grind his teeth in his sleep, I could hear it at night, and Jack would twist and turn so that in the morning his sheets would be tangled into a ball.

Jack excelled at everything. He was the best student in his class, and had a shelf full of sports trophies. People loved him, but they were jealous, too. At school and in the neighborhood, Jack's reputation made things hard for Mike. Everyone compared them. It wasn't fair, but that's how people are, darling. Jack just laughed, and Mike learned to grit his teeth and bear it.

The day Jack told us he was going to be a radio reporter, we were sitting right here on the sofa, listening to the radio, as a matter of fact. I scolded him for not taking off his shoes, but he was in a hurry to tell us *what was going to happen*—that's how he said it, since the decision had been made and there was no changing his mind.

We had intended for him to be a lawyer, a well-paying, respectable profession. But he went his own way without consulting anyone. He'd already signed a contract to go overseas as a foreign correspondent. Instead of being upset, his father was proud. Mike became a lawyer in his place.

Jack left for the Middle East, the other end of the earth. While I was ironing his shirt collars, he came and hugged me. *Don't worry, Mommy*, he said, *I'll be fine*. And he was. His letters were always upbeat, full of jokes. Even when his plane crashed. Anyone else would have begged to come back home, but he insisted on finishing his assignment. He had a journalism fellowship waiting for him at Harvard, he would rest on his laurels later.

It's my fault. I often think that, darling.

I never taught him what danger meant. My child hadn't learned to fear. Of course at other times I say that they're born with their character already formed. You could turn the whole world upside down, but you couldn't change him.

I went to the country that killed him. Jack's widow welcomed me. A good girl, I could see why he'd chosen her. She was made for happiness.

—Take off those widow's weeds, child, I counseled. They won't do you any good.

She insisted on wearing black. I told her to at least go sleeveless. To dress nicely, not in nun's habits. She was a polite girl, and didn't want to upset me by objecting too strongly. I talked to her mother and made myself understood: I would be bringing Zouzou to America. We would figure out her visa. I saw no reason for her to stay behind in that wild place.

Stench and filth, darling. That's all I remember of Greece. Miserable people, hungry children. You had to find the proper person to take care of the least little thing. If you found him, the job got done in seconds flat. If you didn't, door after door just shut in your face.

Before Jack went there, I didn't know a thing about Greece. When he wrote to tell me about his latest assignment, I looked for it on the map. Such a tiny place, it was hard to find. Mike helped me, moved my finger over from Asia to Greece, a tiny splotch. *It's a country with a lot of history*, he told me.

—If it mattered, we'd know about it. I bet they know who we are.

Then I saw that photograph in the newspaper. A man on horseback with a rope of severed heads hanging from his saddle. Only communists do things like that.

—That's not a communist, Mother, Mike corrected me.

I didn't listen. It worried me that my son was breathing their air, drinking their water, lying down to sleep on their beds.

Greece. Such a small country, and making such a big stink. Mike said that we should know more about them, they were important. But can you give me one real reason why?

Greeks: proud as punch of themselves, for no reason.

Greece: a country full of corpses and graves.

A place where the dead rule the living.

We're not like that, darling. Our decisions are made in politician's offices, not over open coffins.

That's life.

They think they have a monopoly on pain. They wear their

black head scarves, show their wounds like badges of honor. It's all theater. Pure theater.

I asked for respect. A closed coffin, a service read in our language, far from those bearded priests in their cassocks.

As for them, the clock is ticking backwards.

That country needs to pay.

NIKITAS TSOKAS, COMMUNIST, COUSIN OF ZOE (ZOUZOU) TSOKA

Enough is enough.

Those slippery bastards saddled us with too much, they crossed the line.

Crazy, cheating sons of bitches.

Our newspaper took a stance, came out against the accusation. Our press releases called it how it was.

They'd accused Gris, an opportunist who had joined our ranks for a while, though the Party spat him back out soon enough. We could tell he had no faith. He wasn't working for the common good, he just wanted money. To buy food, that's what he cared about. We have no use for guys like that.

Along with Gris, they accused two of our own. I know all about it, and I can tell you the charge was absurd. Neither of them was even in Greece when the murder took place, we said that right from the start, it was official. One wasn't even alive. He'd been killed earlier, in a bombing. His name had been released along with the other names of the dead. The second guy had crossed over into Yugoslavia on orders from the boss. His job was to help out when any of our people headed that way. He spoke pretty good English, they had him up there to communicate with the foreigners.

Those fascist thugs said our guys pulled Gris into it, to work as an interpreter. No matter how you look at it, that story is full of holes. Why would they need him to interpret when our guy knew better English than he did? They just cooked up some charge to cover their tracks. They wanted to close the case, and it suited them just fine to call it a communist plot.

Of course the Texan was no angel himself. There were plenty of his type hanging around back then, journalists on the hunt for people in the Party. He was desperate to meet our General.

He came to see me in prison. Zoe brought him. They were newlyweds, the wedding bands glinted on their fingers. He told me who he knew, wanted me to arrange a meeting. He was quick-tempered and harebrained and wouldn't take no for an answer. I bet his mother never taught him what no meant. He wanted to get his way, that's what he cared about most. He handed out orders and threats like they were candy.

Whatever happened to him, he brought it on himself. Think about it: he put his life in the hands of extremists. Who knows what kind of people he was dealing with. The city papers called it a murder. We believe it was an execution.

Read his articles and you'll see. Go track down his radio broadcasts. He called things by their names, didn't sugarcoat anything. He called the government corrupt and inept. He made no bones about declaring the country's elite responsible for the poverty of its people, and for the political violence. He was as upper-crust as they come, but he told things like they were.

And he didn't spare his own, either. Did you see what he wrote about Truman? That he was *uninterested in truly aiding the Greek economy and improving living conditions among the people of Greece. All President Truman cares about,* Talas wrote, *is squelching the uprising.* And supporting the corrupt administration.

The Americans called him a communist. That's ridiculous. He was as blind as the rest, even with the truth screaming right in his face. He wrote that the communists were barbarians who swept down from the north to conquer Greece. A child of propaganda, he sang the same tune they all did.

What with one thing and another, pretty soon he made himself unwelcome. To our people but also to his. No one wants a barking dog nipping at his feet.

The Brits had him in their sights, too, for criticizing their policy in the Middle East. He spooked the British diplomats, who were in league with the Americans and the fascists in our government.

How one person can make such a fuss, I don't know.

He also didn't hesitate to go head to head with Rimaris, the Minister of the Interior. In a private meeting in the minister's office, he accused him of secretly—that is, illegally—sending money to a private bank account in New York. Talas was more or less insinuating that government money, from the American aid effort, had ended up in private pockets. The minister was furious. He threw Talas out of his office, but the damage had been done, word got around. Rimaris howled that his enemies were slinging mud on his name, that *dark forces were planning his political demise*, that it was all *baseless accusations*.

What can you do, word spread.

Twenty-five thousand dollars in a secret bank account, which Rimaris's son, who was studying at Columbia, milked for all it was worth. The dollars flowed. Everything those guys own is stolen. Those Greek fat cats, the Rimarises and all the other money junkies, built their fortunes while others among us spat blood. And those others weren't members of the ruling class, that's for sure.

As for what they said about Tzitzilis, what he did and didn't do, this is a small place, there are no strangers here. His guys spread a bunch of rumors, all bullshit. That he thought about retiring so as to avoid the case. That he considered suicide—as if a pig like him could have a conscience or self-respect. That he made a pilgrimage to the island of Tinos to pray for the Virgin's guidance. That inspiration struck and he solved the case then and there.

Not even a child would believe that.

That's why I'm telling you, use your brain a little.

The Americans, the Brits, and our government—one big fascist roadblock. Jack Talas was a nail in their eye. If they could shut him up, they'd all be better off.

WALLACE CHILLY, FORMERLY OF THE BRITISH FOREIGN OFFICE

I design formal gardens and labyrinths. Here, take my card. I've worked for royalty, and for plenty among the peerage. I'm not a gardener, make no mistake, I'm not a manual laborer. I take great pride in my taste, and it's something the better classes are willing to pay for. I turn their endless caprices into inspired designs.

I have a file with magazine clippings from all over the world. My gardens have been photographed many times, as examples of fine taste. In such a hideous age, it's a form of consolation. Beauty, my dear, is what makes life bearable. It's a discriminating choice, and not everyone shares my point of view.

As for the era you're asking about, it's now a distant, vicious past. I rarely think of it. It's true, I worked for the Foreign Office. In those days we rushed headlong into the fire and didn't think twice. We thought we would live forever. Youth. I have no nostalgia for it at all.

My position: I interrogated prisoners of war. I was head of the Interrogation Center attached to the British Consulate in Salonica. The Service considered me the best informed individual, among non-Greeks, concerning the Communist Party of Greece. I knew people, I knew what was happening. I handled crises. Even Americans and Europeans came to me if they wanted to track someone down, to talk to one of the rebel fighters.

Back then Salonica was a Balkan hole in the wall, filthy and disgusting. I certainly hope you don't believe the locals' ridiculous claims about how cosmopolitan the city was. They're just trying to prettify a miserable, dreadful reality. The foreigners living there suffered, that was a fact. The streets stank, the food was suitable only for locals, the only entertainment to be found was at establishments of the lowest sort. You could perhaps tolerate the place for a certain stretch of time. But there was no high emotion to be had. Anyone looking for even a drop of civilization would search in vain.

As a British citizen I have a practical, empirical mind, I like to speak with examples. This case, for instance. Let me remind you that remains of a European dish, lobster with green peas, were found in the victim's stomach. A Scottish dish, to be precise, meant to be accompanied by aged whiskey. Talas had wine—I wouldn't have expected more from that Texan orangutan.

The investigation concluded that he'd dined with his murderers at a seaside taverna. Forgive me, but that hypothesis doesn't hold water. There is simply no dining establishment in Salonica that would serve lobster with green peas. They may know a thing or two about mussel pilaf and stuffed peppers, but that's as far as it goes. There's tangible evidence to the contrary, too: the Greek police searched the bins of every restaurant and taverna as far as Mihaniona. They turned over every leaf and found no trace of that dish.

Which means that Talas must have dined in a private home. The aspersions they cast on me later, that only at the home of a British citizen would he have been treated to a meal of that sort, that one way or another I must have been involved—these were merely attempts to blacken my name. If it ever becomes an official accusation, I'll take the appropriate measures.

As for Talas, you know what there is to know. He was aggressive and headstrong in his reporting, and uncompromising in what he wrote. An American through and through. He advertised his integrity far and wide, to the point of making himself unpleasant. Wherever he went, he left a trail of ruins and wounds. He pointedly ignored the press releases of the Greek administration. He did his own research, trusted in no one.

When he asked me for information about the General, I hesitated to answer him. I preferred to keep my knowledge for someone else, someone more judicious, some colleague of his who would have a better understanding of what was at stake. Talas was an excitable amateur, not an experienced correspondent.

Don't forget, he also wrote pieces against British policy in the Middle East. People in the British foreign service took note, and rightly so. They asked their American colleagues to rein him in. But there wasn't much the Americans could do. Their admonitions fell on deaf ears. The British weren't pleased, but they had to keep things in balance.

Whoever told you that Talas was the first western reporter to fall victim to the Cold War apparently had no idea what was really going on.

Talas, my dear, went looking for a fight. He saw the glint of the knife and rushed straight at it.

THROUGH OTHER EYES

The Americans readily accepted the explanation that the murder had been committed by communists trying to put the administration and its allies in a difficult position, with the ultimate goal of turning Americans against Greeks. This theory was challenged by a lack of forensic evidence, or hard evidence of any kind. That was the biggest sticking point in the investigation.

In those days of mayhem and rage, one well-respected newspaper published an editorial that lay the facts on the table. If, God forbid, the perpetrators were found to be affiliated with the right, the Americans would hold the entire Greek government responsible. Consequently, there was only one solution. *And as the government is weak, powerless, and sickly, having only just managed to get back on its feet, the administration is terrified that this situation might add other troubles to its already long list. So it crosses itself and prays that the murderers turn out to be communists—because if they aren't, we're lost*, wrote the shrewd publisher, and many of his readers bit their lips with worry.

Around that time, Rimaris's son, the one who'd been studying in New York and had perhaps gotten mixed up with embezzled funds, went to visit Zouzou at home. He urged her to tell the newspapers that her husband had been killed by communists. Zouzou started to cry, declaring that if she'd had a gun, she would have killed herself already. Rimaris's son laughed at the widow's tears and overblown words. He pointed out that there was a perfectly fine window for her to jump out of—he even opened it ostentatiously and stood there, waiting.

Meanwhile at the offices of the Security Police they were tailoring Gris's file to suit their needs. They made him an officer of the Communist Party of Greece, with the General as his mentor. They said he'd been trained in Moscow, and circulated a rumor that he killed a police officer during the Axis Occupation. The investigation wasn't turning up any evidence, but that problem could be solved easily enough. His refusal to cooperate became unquestionable proof of his guilt. He walked toward slaughter with his head bowed.

His statement kept changing, to come increasingly in line with the events. Once the accusation against his mother for collaboration had been dropped, none of the eminent lawyers who got involved in the case seemed to notice that the only basis for a ruling against him was a confused, nearly incomprehensible confession.

Gris had given that confession on his feet, over the course of several hours. His sentences ran amok, they had no consistency; his statement was packed with borrowed language, with the vocabulary of the security police. He spoke in the name of his country, praising its mighty past, expressing his abomination of communist ideals, taking the weight of the world on his shoulders. *I was a communist, I was a member of the Communist Party of Greece, and I declare that Greece my Fatherland is innocent of the murder of Jack Talas, which has been unjustly laid at its feet. I impeach and indict the Communist Party of Greece and Cominform and Moscow as perpetrators of this crime. When a person becomes a Greek, he speaks the truth and nothing but the truth, and I have decided to become a Greek. As I sat in my cell my eyes were opened and I became a Greek. A person becomes Greek only once in his life.*

Tzitzilis couldn't have put it better himself. It was a statement of values, less confession than manifesto. Salonica was under strict martial law. The city slept and woke with a pistol to its head. The communists had bombed it, the citizens' sleep was dogged by fear. Tzitzilis was the city's protector.

Meanwhile, foreigners living in the city recorded their impressions and sent their reports to distant, carefree countries. One of them, Wallace Chilly—a Swiss-born British citizen with a degree in classical philology from Oxford and five foreign languages on his résumé, a distinguished rhetorician well-versed in ambiguous language and sophistry, an interrogator of prisoners of war, and therefore an expert torturer *without consideration or shame*, as Cavafy would have it—had the foresight to flee to Finland and lay low. His absence was covered up, though some commented on how he'd vanished off the face of the earth right after the murder took place, indeed even before the corpse was dragged from the sea.

Chilly's superiors protected him: this was no time for Britain to get mixed up in a case that was, after all, an American affair. When his name was mentioned and the poison-penned reporters started sniffing around, the British officer under whose authority the issue fell announced—unofficially but emphatically enough for all interested parties to take note—that *Chilly had the habit of undertaking dangerous spy operations. That was the reason I requested his transfer*, he clarified, *even before the Talas case broke.*

Rumors that Chilly had murdered Talas elicited sarcastic smiles and sharp comments from those in the Foreign Office. The British often relied on unconventional characters, people who jumped out of airplanes without parachutes and didn't hesitate to use extreme measures if they thought circumstances demanded it. Chilly was a perfect example. He and his men were waging a propaganda war against the communists. Fraudulent techniques were their bread and butter.

The situation was critical. Greece considered the United States its savior, and had welcomed the Americans with hosannas and wreaths of laurel. The negotiations regarding the Marshall Plan brought hope to the broken country. NATO was just beginning to take shape, and the Berlin blockade wasn't far in the future. None of the involved parties, Greek, British, or American, wanted Talas's murder to knock any of that off course.

And so they drowned any inconvenient suspicions like a baby in a bucket. At the trial the accused's lawyer, a young man by the name of Dinopoulos, spoke at length, but avoided the strongest arguments, relying solely on rhetoric. Some supporters of Gris suspected Dinopoulos of compromise, but no one ever accused him outright.

The American general who had once given Tzitzilis a piece of his mind went along with the Greek officials. Through process of elimination Gris was the only name remaining on the initial list of suspects. Antrikos was silently crossed off thanks to a telephone call from the prime minister, while Zouzou had the fervent protection of her mother-in-law. There had been another woman on the list, a reporter, Kristen Sotiropoulos, a troublemaker with an American passport and connections in both the United States and Greece; she was the one who introduced Talas to Gris during their five-minute meeting, but she had supporters in high places, too. By a kind of *reductio ad absurdum*, Gris was the obvious solution. He wasn't a well-known figure; he had very few connections; no one would rush to his support. He was, consequently, an easy target.

The American general had earlier expressed his suspicions to the State Department that the crime had been perpetrated by right-wing forces. His superiors were concerned, as he confided in personal conversations. The general cited his sources, but government officials were hesitant to implicate the right. A development of that sort would serve no one. On the contrary, it would harm their interests in the region. The American general rightly declared that, since his own compatriots were failing to verify the information they received, they couldn't expect much more from the Greeks. His superiors chose not to add fuel to the fire. And the uncouth general, though known for his obdurate outbursts, also knew how to read the silences of his superiors. In this trial, justice was not the primary goal—political expedience had the upper hand, and anyone who imagined otherwise would do well to keep his mouth shut. Now and forever.

SCHOOL YEAR 2010–2011

"LET YOUR RAGE RUN FREE"

MINAS

Turns out we're having a sit-in after all. The first-years organized it, they hung a banner and dragged all the desks to the front entrance. We took a vote, but it didn't go down quite as it should have, since their representatives ran around to all the classrooms during the breaks making secret deals.

We decided to let the teachers into the building. The coordinating groups from the other schools say our occupation is a sham. Who ever heard of joining forces with the enemy in the heat of battle? When they found out our student council decided that seniors will still have class, so we don't lose any prep time for the exams, they were furious. But it's a school tradition, it wasn't really ever in question. The world outside could fall apart, but the seniors would still go to class. *Your only tradition is in being sissies*, Dad teases. He's a fine one to speak, making revolution from the comfort of his office.

The principal called an assembly, to give us an opportunity to share our views and articulate our demands. He invited the Parents' Association, too. Everyone needs to accept responsibility for their actions, he said.

The teachers are bored by the whole thing. Except for the party-liners, most of them are opposed to a sit-in. They shake their heads at our demands. Grandma does, too, of course.

At the assembly the principal could barely keep it together. Just the other day he had assured the citywide school board that while occupations were being staged at surrounding schools, ours was *an unwavering bastion of learning, a shining example of effective communication between students and teachers.* Now he would have to let their offices know that the stronghold had fallen.

Spiros took a piece of paper from his pocket to read off the demands. Evelina would happily have strangled him. According to her, he was a lame, uncouth idiot. His sheet of paper was covered in scribbles and torn on one edge, where he'd ripped off a piece to spit his gum into. He took a deep breath and launched into the list. After complaining about a few run-ins with teachers and our lack of resources, he hurried on to his main issue: why did we need to learn ancient Greek? He just didn't understand why we should spend so many hours memorizing the verb *lyo* or third-declension nouns. *We want a school that's alive*, he said, *we want to talk about things that affect our lives, not memorize words from a dead language.*

Evelina looked like she might punch him. In the end she couldn't restrain herself. The defender of the theoretical track of study intervened.

—Sorry for interrupting this little diatribe, she said. Our fellow student here seems to have gotten carried away by his own eloquence, when he spoke about Ancient Greek class. In order for this conversation to proceed on the basis of arguments and evidence rather than assumptions, I thought I should inform this student, who's still only in his first year of high school, of some objective facts about the pedagogy and grammar of the Ancient Greek language.

When Evelina gets going, there's no stopping her. She made a complete fool of him in front of everyone. Before the assembly started, she'd gotten the other seniors to agree to be totally ruthless with the younger kids. No way were the seniors going to get loaded down with absences just because some stupid brats wanted to play revolution in the cafeteria. The occupation had already lasted three days, and that was more than enough. The first-years had had their time in the sun. Basta.

The whole episode raised suspicions that the student council had made a deal with the administration, but Evelina had a solution for everything. She got the others to agree to floating one-hour meetings to take place during different class periods, so that the student representatives could keep track of the demands of the majority. Whatever stupid shit everyone thought up, they would bring before the teachers. The negotiations seemed to drag on forever, but in the end it was decided that the seniors would continue going to class. The younger kids could cling to the illusion that their demands had been heard. Meanwhile, the whole thing would blow over, since the one-hour meetings would diffuse the situation.

Spiros learned his lesson. Next year, though, Evelina would be at university, and there was no one else with her force and connections. He would just have to sit tight and wait.

—Well? she asked.

She was expecting me to congratulate her.

—You destroyed him.

—I'd have preferred a more generous description. I guess maybe hanging out with Spiros has brought you down to his level.

I wasn't going to give her what she wanted. I've figured out by now that it drives her crazy when I don't give in.

—Are we going to your grandfather's? I asked.

—I've got homework.

—Me too.

—You've made your decision.

—So have you. What's a few hours more or less at this point?

—It's a matter of discipline, she insisted.

—Fine. Then we can go tonight, when you're done. I'm sure he doesn't go to bed at nine.

—He doesn't sleep at all. He just sits in his armchair with glassy eyes. Dad says he's afraid of death.

It's exactly what Mom says about Grandma. She once went over to Grandma's place first thing in the morning and found her on the sofa with the telemarketing channel on, still awake from the night before. Mom gave her a talking-to like you've never heard, like she was the mother and Grandma was the kid.

The older children get, the worse they treat their parents. I do it, too.

It was a pretty wild scene in the schoolyard. The cleaning lady and the biology teacher, a fat little ball of a woman, were standing there, rattling on about the shocking indifference of parents and teachers, *who haven't stepped forward to nip this in the bud.* The cleaning lady told the teacher what she'd found at the sit-in, she was hoping word would get around, most of all to those oblivious parents. She'd picked three pairs of panties off the floor of the girls' bathroom, which meant that some girls *had gone off with their parts uncovered.* She'd found condoms and torn porn magazines. She mentioned cigarette butts, too, she apparently had no idea people were smoking pot, she couldn't tell the kids were all sky high, for her the problem was nicotine. She shook her head, *God will burn us for this, he'll burn us all.*

Some angry neighbors called the principal to inform him that kids had been drinking beer in the schoolyard the previous night, they could hear cans popping from their balconies. Those who lived in top-floor apartments had found a new pastime: sitting on their verandas, watching everything we did. Skateboarding, guitar-playing, basketball, singing. They found us fascinating, even better than the Turkish soaps on TV.

—They organized a concert, Evelina told me.

—Who did?

—The younger kids. It's tonight. To go out with a bang. That was their condition for ending the occupation early. They say they've got a band. I'm sure it's some awful cover band, she added dismissively. They're bringing backup, too, seniors from some private school in Athens.

In other words, Spiros didn't accept unconditional defeat.

Evelina weaved her way down the aisle between the lined-up desks.

—Come on, she called back at me. We're going to Grandpa's.

We've already lost the whole day, I guess I can study later.

Like most girls, Evelina is totally unpredictable. She's practically manic-depressive. Some people can't stand it, but I kind of like it. With her I never get bored. The more I want her, the more I tease her. The more I tease her, the smaller the chances that we'll ever actually hook up.

Child, you're courting disaster, Grandma would say if she saw me this way.

I trailed after Evelina like a stray dog. I gave her ass a good look and decided it was more or less a perfect fit for my palms. It lifts gently and sways as she walks. As if there were a wind, 3 or 4 on the Beaufort scale.

—We're not staying for more than an hour, she declared.

—That's three thousand six hundred seconds.

—What?

The elastic band on her thong was red. Tomato red.

—I broke the time down into smaller units, so it would last longer.

—Show-off! she cried, and picked up the pace.

I caught up with her and pulled the elastic band. It snapped back against her skin.

—Are you a complete moron? What are you doing?

—Playing.

—I'll show you what to play with, she said, pressing the buzzer for her grandfather's apartment. But words apparently didn't suffice: she spun around and flicked me with her finger, right where she meant.

Elena was waiting for us at the door to the apartment.

—Sorry we didn't call ahead, Evelina apologized. There's a sit-in at school and we thought we'd come here instead.

—Your grandfather will be happy. He saw you coming with his binoculars.

Evelina told me the other day that her grandfather has a soft spot for Elena. He's pretty harsh with his family, though. He banned all bad-tempered people from his home, he says he has no use for grumpy faces.

—Grandma was always griping about something, Evelina whispered, so when she died, he told us all to leave our problems at the door. Of course he only remembers that rule when it suits him.

Grandpa Dinopoulos was sitting in his armchair. Elena had opened the curtains wide and sunlight streamed in through the windows, warming the old man's bald spot. Life wasn't too bad up there, in one of the prized penthouses on the square. *The realest of real estate*, as Grandma Evthalia sometimes says, who values nice things and nice places as much as Mom does. *Up there you need sunglasses all day, even inside*, she likes to say. *The only nicer apartments to be found are the penthouses along the waterfront, where you feel like you're living on the deck of a ship. You wake up and see the sea, but you're stepping on solid ground.*

Grandma's house is on Prasakaki Street, just north of Agia Sophia. It used to have a view of the sea, too—if you pressed up against the balcony railing and twisted your head just right. Now it looks into the bedrooms across the way. Dad calls it *seventh heaven*, because it's on the seventh floor. But to this day Mom can't stay in that apartment for longer than an hour. The walls start to close in on her. She says it all the time, but she can't understand that I feel exactly the same way about our house. Our house has no oxygen. Sometimes I can't breathe, just sitting there in the living room.

—Welcome, the old man says. Elena, do we have anything to treat the kids to?

Evelina looked at him in surprise. In all those years her grandfather hadn't treated her to so much as a glass of water. Elena brought us orangeade and slices of tsoureki.

The old man was one of the ones who'd been keeping tabs on the sit-in, which gave us something to talk about. He knew more than we did about what was happening in the schoolyard. We spent seven minutes on boring observations. Then I lost patience and got to the point.

—Mr. Dinopoulos, would you mind if I recorded our conversation? I asked as I searched the menu on my cell phone. I knew it had a function for digital recording, I'd just never needed it until now.

—I want to see Evthalia.

Evelina started to say something. I put my hand on her knee to stop her, pushing the button to start the recording.

—Really, young man, did you think I'd talk to you without some kind of exchange? At my age I enjoy the ultimate luxury of being beholden to no one. Though I don't mind making other people beholden to me, he added slyly.

—That's precisely what I'm counting on.

—Pretty big for your britches, aren't you? Just like her.

—Who?

—Evthalia. She always had to have the last word.

I smiled. That was Grandma, all right.

—Well? Will you bring her to see me? he insisted.

—I accept your terms.

The old Methuselah smiled. He leaned his head back on his armchair and squinted against the light.

—Bring that thing closer, he ordered. If we're going to do this, let's do it right. I don't want her complaining afterward that I tricked you. If she decides to give me a piece of her mind, not even God himself can save me.

On the first day of the occupation, the first-years tossed a plastic bottle over the schoolyard wall. It was a half-empty bottle of water—not a big deal, you might say. It would burst on the sidewalk outside and that would be that. But this bottle happened to fall on the head of a passerby, a tourist, a German philhellene of the old breed, one of those who think the ancient Greeks invented the universe. The bottle smacked him right in the middle of his bald spot. It took the dazed German a few minutes to figure out what had happened. And when he did, he made a beeline for the school, enraged.

The German tourist was not mentally prepared for the sight of a sit-in at a public educational institution. He was obviously suffering from culture shock. And his English, while good, got him nowhere in terms of comprehending the situation. The students were all talking at once, the desks had been dragged into messy rows by the entrance. The German had an open mind, or so he liked to think, but the disorder before him was more than he could understand. It was incomprehensible to him that adult teachers had allowed a bunch of crazed teenagers to occupy a public space. It was even more incomprehensible that the policemen he'd seen right down the street were making no move to intervene. The students' lack of fear made an impression on him. They acted without any consideration for what the consequences might be. They had no idea what punishment even meant.

These were the thoughts he tried to communicate to the principal, who himself had only a Lower Proficiency in English, and from decades earlier, meaning that he had a sum total of about two hundred words of English at his disposal. The principal immediately sent for Soukiouroglou. When everyone else was drowning in a spoonful of water, Soukiouroglou always found a way out. True, the principal thought he was antisocial, bad luck, and a snob, and generally kept him at arm's length. Yet he didn't hesitate to call on him when circumstances demanded.

Soukiouroglou and the German shook hands and started to talk. Soukiouroglou never boasted about his language skills, the way some of the jokers on the faculty did. The principal had even gotten annoyed with stubborn, mule-headed Soukiouroglou for not turning in a résumé, as he'd asked all the school's personnel to do. What he really wanted was a list of skills that would make it easier for him to distribute extracurricular responsibilities, so he could get them all running around working on projects funded by the European Union, making him look good in the eyes of his superiors—or so his adversaries said behind his back. At any rate, most teachers turned in their résumés as he had requested. These were tricky times, and no one was willing to risk his job.

Soukiouroglou, however, wanted nothing to do with it.

—I choose not to be judged by you. I've been judged enough in my life, he said, and walked off.

The principal decided not to push the issue. It was a decision he had congratulated himself on ever since. He'd heard about Soukiouroglou long before he assumed duties as the principal of this school. *A good civil servant*, that's what they told him at the Ministry. Some might have considered that an insult, or at least an ironic put-down. For most, being a civil servant meant leading a lazy life of responsible irresponsibility, sitting pretty without having to work all that hard. People offered anecdotal evidence of the worst kinds of abuses, and came to easily digested conclusions.

The civil war between the public and private sectors had been simmering for years. Now that belts were being tightened all over, the situation had erupted into open conflict. These days it was each man for himself, all against all. The first in the crosshairs were the teachers and the university professors. Furious parents and journalists who thought they had the truth in their pockets made sarcastic remarks about the easy hours and long vacations. None of those people really knew what it meant to be a teacher. They just found a scapegoat and loaded it up.

A few days earlier one mother had come to the school to try and get her child's absences excused. She had on a T-shirt printed with the words, *THREE REASONS I WANT TO BE A TEACHER: JUNE, JULY, AND AUGUST.* While this fine specimen of motherhood had her back turned, Soukiouroglou said, loud enough that she would hear:

—Some parents are as uncultured as their children. They have plenty of time to paint their nails, but never manage to make it to parent-teacher night. They think the school is there to baby-sit their children. Meanwhile, they settle in at the hair salon and boast about how they could do the job better. But if you threw them into a classroom for even five minutes, they'd put down their revolutionary banners and run the other way as fast as they could. They can't even manage their own kids, so how could they ever control an entire class of them?

The mother blushed and turned to leave. The previous year, when her child had been in Soukiouroglou's class, he asked her to come to the school eight separate times. She was always busy. Her child's situation was discussed at faculty meetings, and they even ordered an external review of the case, but no solution was ever settled upon. The mother was always absent, never had time to talk to the school psychologist, kept offering excuses and putting up obstacles. At the end of the day, she just wanted the experts to deal with her child. People with degrees who were paid for their time and effort. People whose job it was to shape children's souls.

In other words, the mother palmed her problem off on the child's teachers. She expected a solution to drop down from the sky, without her lifting a finger. Her attitude was understandable—even excusable. Most teachers were used to listening patiently to despairing parents singing sad songs about their lot. Soukiouroglou went a step further: he tackled the problem. He tried to move forward toward a solution.

A good civil servant. It wasn't ironic, and it wasn't an insult. What it meant was, a person who assumed responsibility. Who finished the job on time. Who gave for free what others sold at a high price. Who taught his class with intellectual propriety and sound pedagogical methods. Students at the school—or rather, their parents—paid out the nose to evening cram schools for services the school provided for free during the day. Soukiouroglou tried to make his students realize how nonsensical that was. Some of them were convinced. They stopped going to cram schools, quit their private lessons, and studied under his tutelage. And in the end they got into university, just like the rest. They saved time and money. Their brains didn't rot from too many worksheets and mnemonic devices.

The principal never found out what Soukiouroglou said to the German tourist on that fateful first day of the sit-in. The foreigner smiled, jotted down some notes, and headed off with a clearly marked map, courtesy of Soukiouroglou, who went back to the teachers' office, and to the task of tallying student absences.

Everyone came to the concert. Spiros greeted them at the main entrance, handing out a photocopied program along with a little slip of paper printed with slogans. They had spent all afternoon trying to decide what to write, since they wanted their school to make a good impression. At some point Spiros realized that talking wasn't going to get them anywhere, threw democratic procedure out the window, and just wrote what he wanted.

The band was tuning up in the schoolyard, testing the distortion. The neighbors were in despair, since they could tell it was gearing up to be a long night. None of the fifty-somethings sitting on the surrounding balconies had any desire to listen to the songs of enraged adolescents late into the night—after all, music had died with their youth. The real revolution had taken place decades ago—or so they believed, these adults who had dedicated years of their lives to demonstrations and occupations. The political activities of their children struck them as a washed-out repetition of an earlier era, which they themselves had lived through in its full glory: the era when they had been building a world, which they'd now cut and sown to their measurements.

Of course they recognized these students' need to raise fists and banners, to blow off some steam with a slogan or two. But they also thought these underage revolutionaries required supervision and guidance—that it was their responsibility to impart their knowledge and experience, to instruct their children in the ways of civil disobedience.

And then there were other parents whose lives revolved primarily around the workplace, where they tried to be as tractable as they could, and who shuddered at their opponents' views. Thus parents and students alike split into two camps: those who believed that an occupation could teach an important political lesson, and those who considered the loss of class hours a serious obstacle to the students' progress.

A school has a duty to remain open regardless of circumstances; its job is to weave a protective cocoon of knowledge and understanding, particularly in difficult times, proclaimed those who supported the rule of law. Whereas experienced revolutionaries and unionists of various stripes laughed in the face of such arguments and gave their all to the struggle.

The students tried their hand at the rhetoric of occupation. Some parents disparaged it as empty jabbering, but their kids didn't care. They were just glad to have broken the deadly routine of classes. They felt they had assumed an important role, and a kind of power, particularly those who were making decisions on behalf of others—Spiros, for instance. He blurted out whatever he was thinking without taking the time to find the proper words. He loved the applause, fed off of his classmates' approval. He suddenly felt that he wasn't the school pariah anymore, the awful speller, diagnosed with dyslexia by the school psychologist. Now he was Spiros from the occupation. The one who'd made the Facebook page for the concert.

Evelina couldn't stand seeing that moron prancing around as if he were running the show. Taking initiative, making plans. Bringing others over to his side with the worst kind of demagoguery, and to top it all off with arguments articulated in terrible Greek. In her mind, it was high time he learned his lesson. So she shamed him publicly, in front of everyone, even the teachers. Meanwhile, she covered her bases by sabotaging him behind his back, too, with phone calls and secret agreements. It took time, but it worked: the occupation came to a peaceful end.

She had decided that she should definitely show up at the concert. She didn't want to give way to her opponent so easily. She pulled on a pair of ripped jeans that showed some thigh and a black T-shirt. The outfit seemed simple, but it took her forty-five minutes in front of a mirror to settle on the details that would make the difference. What color bra she should wear, for instance, since it was an off-the-shoulder shirt that revealed one strap. The string on her thong needed to be discrete, a color that wouldn't show even if she bent over. Clear lip gloss and mascara applied with a special brush, to make each eyelash stand out separately. Then she straightened her hair with a hair iron and set out, ready for battle.

Things in the schoolyard were in full swing. Spiros was running around, making sure everyone saw him. He was looking for Minas. He found him lying on a low wall, all alone. He had headphones on and was nodding to the rhythm; he seemed perfectly in tune with himself. Spiros was jealous of his indifference. He didn't seem to care what other people thought, he wasn't trying to make anyone like him.

Evelina didn't understand that at all: she wanted everyone to love her. Whenever she picked up on even a whiff of dislike, it threw her off completely. She may have seemed strong, but it was just her protective shell. And it shattered easily—or so her mother thought, who worried constantly about her daughter. Minas was of a different opinion. In his view, Evelina had surrounded herself with barbed wire, and wouldn't let just anyone in. The other girls at school were always going on about lifelong friendships and nights out and summer vacations. Evelina went along with it all, yet remained encased in her coat of armor. She seemed outgoing and friendly, but she was made of steel.

She'd been class president four years in a row. Her father was proud that his daughter was such a fighter. She was that rare combination: an excellent student who also managed to be popular. She shared her essays with the lazier kids, covered up their absences, stood up for her fellow students. Minas was the only one who made fun of her. Usually it enraged her, particularly when she knew he had a point, or if others were listening. She had a great sense of humor, but not about herself, as Minas was continually discovering.

Evelina admired his brain. She'd never admit it in public, even under the most terrible torture. Minas was sloppy and chaotic. But he knew things the others didn't. His train of thought was always taking some bizarre turn, he never gave the answer you were expecting. He liked to make his mind work, he liked to solve riddles, to pose questions. He was good at whatever he tried. But he always abandoned things in the middle. His favorite word was *ennui*. Seventeen years old and he spoke like a veteran of life. He observed everything, but rarely acted.

Evelina stood over him and pulled off his headphones.

—Everything okay, fool?

She sat down beside him. Her hair tickled his shoulder. From a distance they looked like a couple. Her girlfriends gossiped that the Evelina they knew wouldn't deign to be seen with Minas.

The band started with Miles Davis. *How pretentious*, thought Minas. Nikolas Dokos was on saxophone, and he was obviously driving the music. He had a clean sound and perfect rhythm. They were good, which annoyed Minas even more. Nikolas—with a tattoo on the nape of his neck, a smile on his face, and a ratty T-shirt—was talking into the microphone. His body was loose, he was obviously enjoying himself. He wasn't dogged by second thoughts, backtracking, or inner dilemmas.

In other words, he was way too cool.

Shortly before he came out onto the stage he'd shut himself in the bathroom with his friends. They pushed the door closed, it smelled of cigarettes, not the normal kind, but the kind that made Fani lose her shit the one time she found the stuff in the house. He promised he would quit and she believed him, but he just got more careful. Fani tried to tell him that she knew all about those kinds of things, she wasn't like other mothers. She said something about the guys in the band, how they'd destroyed their brain cells. Nikolas wasn't even listening, he wasn't like them, he could stop whenever he wanted. *They've all got one foot in the grave*, he shouted at her and stormed out of the room. *And you've got both hands on a blunt*, she wanted to shout back, but fortunately she held it in.

—He's good, huh?

Evelina was moving to the rhythm. Her hips swayed gently.

—Must be hard, being his mother's son, Minas couldn't keep from saying.

—What do you mean?

—What I said. The mother's a singer, so the son gets to be a musician. Life's all laid out for him, a ready-made career. He's got nothing to worry about.

—Maybe you're just jealous?

—Why would I be jealous?

She rolled her eyes, and made a face like Souk in class, when his students pushed him to a point of absolute despair with their idiocy and ignorance.

—Besides, you're one to talk, the son of a big, fancy editor in chief.

His father had gone to great pains to make sure Minas never

felt like the son of anyone important, and her insinuation up-set him.

—Nice, real nice.

That was all he could come up with. He was angry at Spiros for organizing the concert behind their backs, and for bringing in a bunch of private school kids from Athens to take over their school.

Minas tapped his foot nervously. The habit had first appeared when he was in grade school. It kept up for years. It annoyed his mother, who would slap his knee to make him stop, sometimes gently, with tender admonition, and other times with overflowing irritation. Soukiouroglou had been the first to notice it. The kid was stressed out about school. And that was something he could use to his advantage.

Evelina watched the tremor in his knee, his thigh quivering at a hummingbird's pace. When she was in a good mood, she would imitate him. When it annoyed her, she would kick his leg to make it stop.

Tonight she'd had a beer and felt the bubbles rising to her head, so she laid her palm on his knee. It was a gesture that could be read either as a more sophisticated version of kicking his leg, or as a caress.

He covered her hand with his. All kinds of thoughts sliced through his brain, emotions seethed in his chest, his body was at full boil. It was dark, and their classmates couldn't be sure they were seeing properly.

1948 AND MUCH LATER

"A PARANOID IS SOMEONE WHO KNOWS
A LITTLE OF WHAT'S GOING ON"

FROSO DINOPOULOS, WIFE OF GRANDPA DINOPOULOS

My mother-in-law—may she rest lightly in the earth's embrace—called me Frosoula. She was the one who played matchmaker. We knew nothing of love in those days, those were things we only read about later, in romance novels. She taught me how to make a bed the way she liked: pillows under the covers, top sheet tight at the corners. Not the slightest bit of extra fabric, so the lace at the edge wouldn't crinkle. During those first months she would come and stay at our house for hours on end, teaching me how to wash clothes and iron, how to make all the dishes Nikiforos liked. We boiled water for the wash and I scrubbed the stains with a brush, careful not to tear the fabric. Soon my hands were swollen and peeling from the hot washwater. Other women painted their nails, and had servants and seamstresses to do the work. It didn't bother me. His mother was pleased with my progress.

A stingy woman, that's what everyone said. She wore a blue dress to our wedding, with pleats at the waist and a collar. *I sewed it for your husband's baptism*, she told me, proud of how long it had lasted.

It seemed harsh to me, yet I acted the same way with my child. I didn't spend on luxuries, didn't waste hard-earned money on insubstantial things. I ruled my house, never let things slide.

The night there was that knock on the door, I leapt out of bed in my nightgown. Nikiforos was still up working. I wrapped myself in a robe and went out. Those were difficult times, no one knew what dawn might bring to the doorstep. I had a red robe, the color of tomato paste, I wore it for thirty years until it finally fell apart. In those days it still hadn't faded from the wash, its buttons still shone.

Nikiforos asked me to open the door, and as I reached for the door-knob, I thought, *I'm wearing the wrong color, whoever it is didn't come to do us good, and here I am in bright red, a communist color.*

The man came in without apologizing for the lateness of the hour, without any kind of explanation. I'd seen him once before, he'd been walking on the sidewalk across the street from us and Nikiforos whispered in my ear, *That man is an excellent lawyer.*

There was no way not to overhear what they said.

The district attorney hadn't slept in days. His notes on the case recorded *irregularities, unexplained events, suspicious lapses in logic, naïve reasoning, legal contortions, and arbitrary legal constructions.* He had gotten hold of a telegraph in which the ministry asked Tzitzilis whether or not the man in custody was likely to break *in the coming days.* Tzitzilis wasn't making any promises. He left a window of fifteen days to close the case.

Unjust, inappropriate, outside the bounds of law. I still remember the words.

The evidence is fabricated, unsubstantiated, unacceptable.

Of course the men also felt a sense of professional solidarity. They were honest and thoughtful. They wanted to sleep easily. Not to be tormented by the pillow under their heads.

But it wasn't a time for grand gestures. If they stepped down, others would come to take their places. They needed at least to make sure that Gris lived.

Prison was the least of the disasters that could befall him.

If they could just let the dust settle, they'd find a solution.

—So, guilty?

—Guilty.

Panayiotis lived in the neighborhood. Everyone knew him, and knew he was up to his ears in filth. He always looked at your chest, never in your eyes. He had a dirty mouth and no fear of God. He pinched me one day right in the middle of Agia Sophia. His fingers left a bruise on my backside. I rubbed it with rubbing alcohol ten times a day until it faded.

I'd seen him coming home early in the morning, dragging two oars and a bundled-up canvas sail. I was polishing the railing on the veranda with soapy water. Cleanliness shows in the details, that's how my mother-in-law taught me. No woman kept a cleaner house than I did. I scrubbed the floors with lye, started at dawn to get it all done.

Later I heard him boasting at the market. He said he'd killed a man with his own two hands. There was a circle of lowlifes around him, laughing. You weren't alive in those days, you don't know how it was. We all just looked to our own business and prayed that when evil came, it would knock on someone else's door.

The communists had bombed us, just imagine, they'd turned their cannons on our houses. Tzitzilis had tracked them down and killed them, so we trusted his abilities, he was our protector. People said lots of things about him, that he was a skirt chaser, that he smoked hashish, went with whores, God save him. For us what mattered was that he got the job done. He held the whole city under his wing.

I told my mother-in-law about Panayiotis, what he'd said and done. Not about my backside, I was ashamed. But I told her about the other thing, how he had blood on his hands. Nikiforos was a lawyer, he needed to know.

My mother-in-law told me to confess to the priest, but not to get her son mixed up in other people's business, he had a lot on his mind as it was. I listened to her, it was good advice. I scattered that shame under the priest's robes and forgot about it.

After all, it might have been mere boasting, empty words to impress the others. I hadn't seen any dead man or any blood. God protected me from that. Because if you see the blood, you're involved, like it or not. Like Sofoula, whose husband's a lawyer, too, Kyriakos Lolos. She'd gone out for a walk, to light a candle for her husband. She was walking up the street toward Agia Sophia and slipped in blood. They'd shot the teacher three times. I can't remember his name, but he was a communist, everyone knew. They put three bullets in him and then disappeared. Sofoula's dress was covered in blood, the stain wouldn't leave no matter how hard she scrubbed. It was her best dress, too. They kept washing the sidewalk for three days, bringing more and more water. But blood is hard to wash out, wherever it lands it stays.

Sofoula got mixed up in it just like that, and they made her go down to the courthouse to say what she'd seen and heard. The murderer admitted to holding a grudge against the teacher. He'd joined the Party himself but later renounced it, and he hadn't had an easy time. He was from Serres, a butcher. The Reds led his wife down the garden path, he couldn't talk about it without crying. They sent him to Bulkes, a communist training camp up near Belgrade, to try and bring him around to their views. He said they tortured him there, because he didn't believe what they believed. I heard him shouting all this from the witness stand. We'd gone to the trial to support poor Sofoula, whose head was overwhelmed by it all.

Dirty communist infighting, old grudges, outside interests. The Reds claimed it was a setup, that the Greek military police planned the murder, that the directive came straight from Palladios, Minister of Public Order. The murderer was given his orders and a gun to carry them out with. At the trial he kept shouting that he would fight the Turks and the Reds to the death, that not even Ananiadis, the sultan of the Communist Party, would escape.

All I know is that from then on I never walked on that side of the street, where the blood had run. The stain was there for whoever had eyes to see. Sofoula was upset about her dress, it was good fabric and a fine design. She bought a piece of wide ribbon and covered up the flaw. If you looked closely, you could see where it had been mended. But it was on the side, so as long as she was sitting down it was fine.

Time passed. *People forget*, the priest told me. A harsh thing to say, but we all know it's true. *Time is the great healer, it heals all wounds*, is what the old folks say, *it turns blood into water.* You don't feel, don't hurt, don't care. Your soul burns and all that's left is ash.

My mother-in-law would always shake her head and say, *This too shall pass.* But Nikiforos didn't think that way. If he got a thing in his head, it would stick there like a rusty nail and eat away at everything else.

After that night when the district attorney came to the house Nikiforos lost his sleep. He would twist and turn in bed like a lamb on a spit. He talked in his sleep, let out little cries. I pretended I was asleep, but just lay there praying. And some point he would get up and go and doze in the armchair in his office. He would spend the whole night there, at attention, stiff as a bayonet.

The Emmanuel Gris affair, that was the man's name. Emmanuel Gris.

He was accused of murder. He went to prison.

He lost twelve years of his life. I lost my marriage.

MAGDA KARAGIANNIDOU, NURSE AT THE PSYCHIATRIC HOSPITAL OF STAVROUPOLI, COMMONLY KNOWN AS LEMBETI

After thirty years here I know each stone like the back of my hand. When they first sent me here I was a girl in braids, new to the job. Before that they had me at the Ippokrateio old folks' home. I fed them, emptied their bedpans, took them out to walk in the yard. Then one of the other nurses had a fling with a doctor and they managed to get me transferred out.

—You're going over to the crazies, they told me. It'll be tra-la-li tra-la-lo all day long. It's easy work, they've been shut up in there for years and nobody gives a damn anymore, you could tie them up and no one would be the wiser.

At the Ippokrateio I was always bothered by how dark it was in the hallways. Outside the sunlight was as loud as thunder, but its rays stopped at the door. As soon as I went inside I would flip the switch. You might say it was an insignificant detail. People were dying and what I cared about was the light. Until they sent me to Lembeti and I learned my lesson. I saw the worst and it knocked some sense into me.

—They're not really sick, is what other people said. Sickness means pain. They don't hurt.

I don't blame them, it's something I probably said myself at some point. For most people sickness means cancer. And maybe they're right.

As long as they get their pills, they're quiet. Every so often new doctors arrive with degrees from places like Paris who think you can cure with words. For them words are cheap and they'll spend as many as they need. They're against medication, that's the first thing they tell you. But by the end of their first night shift, their fancy theories have all flown out the window.

Like the guy whose belt kept coming loose, and he was always adjusting it. He'd come to put us in order, or so he thought. With his fancy degree and his conferences in Europe and all the big words he knew. By now we've learned not to stand in their way. But behind their backs, we take bets on how long they'll last.

He was on duty one Friday night. I couldn't tell you why, but Fridays are the worst. Something gets into people, they blow their fuses. If you've spent any time at a funny farm you know.

The first hours passed quietly enough, so the doctor relaxed. He settled into a chair, stretched out his legs, even closed his eyes. A ten-minute nap, the sweetest sleep there is. But just then, a gypsy woman burst into his office with a baby in her arms, raising gods and demons, demanding morphine. None of it seemed to disturb the baby's sleep. At first our doctor tried to reason with her. He wasn't going to sign off on anything illegal. The gypsy woman lost it, she didn't have time for conversations and haggling, she threw the baby at him as if it were a sack and made a beeline for the medicine cabinet. The doctor grabbed the baby in the air, its eyes snapped open like a doll's and it started to scream, terrified at finding itself in this stranger's embrace. Soon enough the poor man was covered in tears and snot, and he was totally disgusted, but didn't know where to put it down.

A few hours earlier he'd been lecturing us about minorities, but when he found himself with a gypsy bastard in his arms, he forgot all his fine words fast enough. He literally kicked the woman out of the place, with the help of the guard, who pretended to be shocked by the whole scene but was secretly enjoying it.

The supervisor had scheduled him to examine a patient in the lecture hall the next day. Our young doctor showed up with dark circles under his eyes. He was clearly in bad shape, but he kept it under control. There was a kid there, too, a high school kid whose father had called from the paper to ask if he could observe. He sat in a corner taking notes. Strange kid. He seemed more interested in the doctor than in the patient. If I were his mother, I wouldn't have been proud.

I'd have been worried.

I'm not sure how long Evgnosia lived at Lembeti. She was already here when I came. I learned about her case from the older staff members. The hospital was Evgnosia's home. She didn't wander around unkempt like the others did. She used to comb her hair with an ivory hair clip. It might seem strange that they let her keep it, but she bit three nurses who tried to take it away. She cried and hit herself and in the end they felt sorry for her and gave it back. She used to carry it around wherever she went. The teeth were broken, but she'd stand there running it through her hair two hundred times in a row. She had pretty hair, as black as a stormy sea. But it had started to fall out, and I would pick up whole handfuls of it in the corridors. The cleaning ladies complained and asked us to cut it, *what does a crazy woman want with hair like that*, they said. Downy fuzz grew back on her forehead, thinner than before. In the end all that was left was a few tufts here and there. So she would use her broken hair clip on them, and then pat down her hair with her palm. She cleaned her face with her own spit, like a cat, couldn't stand to get water on her face, cried if I asked her to go and wash. She took her pills, stood in the corner, and never let out a peep. It was easy to forget she was there.

In all those years I only heard her voice once. It was raining, a real heavy storm, torrents of water rushed through the streets, a dirty river as high as your knees. The rain snuck in through closed windows, locked doors. The walls were covered in damp. The whole city had taken shelter indoors.

Evgnosia was pressed up against the window, staring out. It was the only time I ever saw her actually looking at anything. Don't ask me what it was, though. All you could see through the window was sheets of water, the skies had opened. She started to say something, but what came out wasn't words. She hadn't spoken in years. No one else even noticed, because just then the plaster in the entrance fell—I'm telling you, there was that much water—and we had to go and check the damage. The guard shook his head. *I've been saying it for years*, he said, *if the place isn't kept up, these things are going to happen.*

When we came back, her eyes were blank again. Whatever it was, was gone. There are no miracles in this line of work.

I've been taking care of their medications for thirty years. I take them out to walk in the yard. But never Evgnosia. Her chart said it wasn't allowed, they kept her in the basement with the dangerous ones. Someone signed off on that, took the shame on himself and forgot all about it.

K. M., SECRETARY IN A POLITICAL OFFICE, MINISTER'S RIGHT HAND

I was good at my job. Everyone knew it, even my enemies. I accomplished things and left a good name behind. That was a different cra, full of moral imperatives; our decisions affected people's lives. At Christmas and Easter when I went back to the village everyone wanted to shake my hand. They would stand in a line, each with a gift and a good word. And each with a favor to ask. They were proud that their village had a man in the middle of things. I found people jobs, I attended their baptisms and weddings. I knew exactly how many votes my party could count on, how many each head of household controlled. I took care of the large families and they responded in kind.

I remember when they came to me about Stergios, they wanted me to make him a priest. But the church didn't want him, his record wasn't clean, he had some small-time theft on his rec-ord, and contempt for the law. The bishop had dug in his heels and was refusing to sign. Stergios's uncle had eighty votes in his pocket, it was a big family, with plenty of kids and cousins.

—What you're asking of me isn't easy, I said, trying to lower his expectations.

—If it was easy, we'd do it ourselves. The kid is a bad apple, you can see for yourself, he's not cut out for working. So we figured we'd make him a priest. He'll have his salary, we can find him a wife. His mother wants him to be a teacher, but the boy never took to books. So a priest it is, and we'll wash our hands of it.

The bishop acquiesced, but he wanted something in return: I had to find a place for one of his men in the gendarmerie. That's how things happened in those days, you scratch my back, I scratch yours. Our ties were built with actions, not promises.

The minister signed off on it. He had more important things on his mind, was holding evening meetings with people in high places, while we did the dirty work.

That year things at the office were a mess. Foreigners had gotten involved in our affairs and the job was all telephone calls, paperwork, and visits. The case was of the utmost importance, the Minister informed us; there were national issues at stake. His superiors were constantly reminding him that how he handled the situation would determine not only the future of American aid to our country, but also his own career.

The Americans made statements to the press: *The nation of Greece will be judged according to how its government handles this case.* They'd lit a fire under our behinds, and we needed to find a solution.

The ministers were all at war with one another. No one wanted to be left holding the bag. Each of the suspects had his protector. They drove us crazy with phone calls.

They wouldn't let Tzitzilis do his job. In the end, though, a *suitable solution* was found. Tzitzilis should be commended for keeping them all out of the mud.

The case was closed honorably and conscientiously; stamps and signatures rained down from above.

THROUGH OTHER EYES

It wasn't long before a second-rate American reporter conducted the much-desired interview with the rebel chief. The American listened to his harangue, jotting things down in his notebook. The rebel fighters hadn't eaten in days, their bodies were emaciated. Yet their eyes still gleamed, the reporter noted. They were nourished by privation and their faith in a common goal. *The only problem is, you can't eat faith*, the reporter later commented to his editor. *It's faith that swallows your conscience and good intentions.*

The General had a script ready in his head and was determined to say his piece. *We're strong, we will prevail.* Truman had tricked the Americans, he said, into aiding the fascists. He repeatedly maligned the President and his underlings in the Oval Office, but made it clear that, in his view, *good Americans* had no part in these goings-on. And if they were to rebuild their country, the Greeks were in dire need of aid.

The General saw the reporter not for what he was—the representative of a small, regional radio station, a powerless nobody who was simply doing the dirty work assigned to him—but as a chosen representative of the entire American people. *We're ready to stop the Civil War*, the General told him, *and begin negotiations with anyone. Under one condition: that the members of the Greek government be recognized as the criminals they are.*

The American was of course not the proper individual to respond, but he couldn't restrain himself. He smiled, as much as his good manners would allow, and noted laconically: *That's one way of seeing things.*

The General wasn't fated to be in power long; the Party soon decided to depose him. He was packed off to the Eastern block to be crushed by the Iron Curtain. His old comrades rushed to renounce him, so as not to worry that they might be next. The methods were tried and true, the procedures straightforward—and the General's name immediately lost its glory. His successor, who had orchestrated the General's removal, was soon paid in the same coin. They erased him from the official books, too, tossed him into the mire and sent him packing. Others came to fill his shoes. They may have been no better than the rest, but they watched their backs more carefully and kept things in balance.

In the meantime, the interrogations regarding the murder of Talas continued. The absence of forensic evidence left almost everything to conjecture. Tzitzilis and his men tailored the findings to their needs—only their needs kept changing with the circumstances, so that the case skittered this way and that like mercury on the marble floors of the government ministries. Solutions were settled upon in secret, on the basis of phone calls from on high and pressures from all sides.

The foreigners kept expressing their desire for the investigation to follow a particular path. That bothered the Greeks, particularly Tzitzilis, who was used to being left to his own devices. His instincts were never wrong, as everyone in Greece knew. But the foreigners insisted on getting regular reports.

Tzitzilis wasn't cowed. Those sons of bitches would get what they wanted; his main goal was to close the case. He handed over a file of scattered materials, in a royal mess, as its receivers commented. The case finally reached the courts with sufficient evidence—massaged behind closed doors into proof—though also with plenty of holes that were only filled in during the course of the trial.

The General of the Greek rebel fighters fairly quickly found shelter in the Soviet Union. Forty years later, in an interview about an unrelated issue, a young, ambitious reporter asked him about the Gris case.

The General had recently returned to his native land. He had agreed—without much thought, some judged—to run for office on the ballot of the ruling party. His old comrades were appalled, but the General believed he was doing the right thing in giving his support to the prime minister who would change the country.

In the context of a national reconciliation, he was photographed with his adversary from the Civil War. The old enemies shook hands, but the photographers weren't satisfied, and so they embraced. Flashbulbs popped. *It's all an issue of symbolism*, the prime minister had stressed when arranging this meeting. *The old Greece, riddled by divisions of all sorts, has to be forgotten. What this country needs is change.*

The General understood the need for old hatreds to be buried with the dead. He smiled when his old enemy pronounced into the microphones that the General *had been his most worthy opponent*. But he refused to make peace with the former head of the

Communist Party, the one who had kicked him out of Greece. *Bastard*, he called him, *opportunist*. The reporters were pleased to get a front-page story out of it.

The ambitious reporter approached the General after his colleagues had left. He was hoping for something more than the official statements they'd all jotted down. He reminded the General of the Gris case and asked for an exclusive interview. The General was tired, he was no longer the young man who had moved mountains and deployed entire armies. But something in the reporter's eye gave him pause. He told him to turn off the recorder. With a single sentence, he cleared Rimaris and the right. He muttered something about *dark forces*, but gave no further explanation. The brief interview was useless to the reporter, who made sure not to show his disappointment.

The General took his leave, certain that he would be seeing the young man again, in a higher position, very soon. And sure enough, within the year Tasos Georgiou was promoted to editor. By the time he became editor in chief, the General was only a name.

The Gris trial occupied the interest of journalists for far longer than it was front-page news. For many years, whenever a reporter wanted to try his hand at a difficult case, he would open the file on Gris. Every so often new evidence came to light. The journalists were primarily interested in intrigues and conspiracies. They went looking for abuses of political power, secret agreements, contradictory evidence. Lawyers sifted through the proceedings, pointing out gaps and contradictions.

Those who believed in the rule of law, particularly those who liked to think the police force does its job, were exasperated by these jeremiads. The case was closed. Anyone still trying to unearth evidence wasn't to be trusted.

•

Ach, said the people in the neighborhood, who fed on others' misery. *It destroyed his mother, she couldn't bear it.* The old goats who'd shunned the family all those years only remembered Evgnosia after the fact. The poor thing, shut up in the nuthouse, an unmarried girl. They sat by the fire with their needlework, pouring out expressions of compassion and warmth. Her misfortune kept their conversations going for years.

As for Violeta, *she became a lawyer, just think of it. Running back and forth to the courthouse all day long, how could she take care of a husband, she must have ended up an old maid.*

The family house was boarded up after Evgnosia was taken away. The paint on the shutters flaked from the rain, the garden ran riot, weeds sprang up everywhere. Eventually it was rented by an accomplished seamstress. She opened the curtains to let in the sunlight, held rows of pins in her mouth, kneeled on the floor to take in hems. There was a table beside her sewing machine covered with a tablecloth of starched finery, embroidered with flowers and edged with lace. Whenever a customer commented on it, she would say that she'd found it in the house when she came, along with a bunch of old things, torn clothes and unused scraps of fabric. She washed it with green soap, scrubbed it for hours, and in the end the handiwork shone through. It was tarnished by a faint shadow, an old stain that had seeped into the fabric. There, under the box with her spools of thread. She couldn't bear to let such a fine piece of work go unused. So she set the box over it, to hide the flaw.

An old woman who'd lived in the neighborhood her whole life told the seamstress that the tablecloth had been part of Kyra-Maria's dowry. The rest of the women nodded their heads, and said Kyra-Maria's laundry had always been sparkling white, all the neighbors used to remark on it, and the linens so orderly on the line, clean white nightgowns and underwear tucked away on the back lines where it wouldn't be seen. She had unmarried girls at home and took care. *Perhaps that's why the gypsies stole her laundry, it was too clean, and the embroidery too fine*, added one woman who still remembered the event.

Ever since disaster had struck the family, everyone had only good things to say about them. An old woman with white hair remembered the day of the funeral. Manolis had been in prison only a year and they brought him to give his mother a last kiss. The house was full of neighbors, still there from the vigil the night before. The coffin was on the table in the living room, and the older women crossed themselves and raised the icon to their eyes. They'd been reading prayers all night—someone had brought a Bible and they flipped to random pages, it didn't matter, they were all holy words, anything would suit the occasion. The two girls sat on either side. Their eyes were dry; they had run out of tears.

Outside it was pouring rain, a true storm. Water came in through the cracks and the walls ran with damp, droplets licking the whitewash. They had put out rags at the front door, but no matter how much people wiped their feet the mud still stuck, covering the floor.

Manolis came in.

His hands were tied with rope. That detail struck them, and they talked about it later in their homes. There was a dull look in his eye, like the bottom of the sea in the afternoon. His eyes were snuffed candles and his skin was pale, since now he lived locked up in basement cells. The widows bit their lips. They knew he'd adored his mother, and worried he might die on the spot and be left on their hands.

Manolis leaned over the coffin as if it were the hull of a boat. People later said the police had gotten him drunk before he came, Tzitzilis had made sure he wouldn't know what was happening and wouldn't feel a thing. Manolis never cried a tear.

He paid no attention to what his sisters said, just stared straight into the coffin at his mother, who smelled of soap. Evgnosia had insisted on bathing her corpse with a clean towel. Violeta was wracked with grief, incapable of helping. In the end Evgnosia got out the tin basin, the one her mother used to fill with sand where she'd plant candles for the dead on the Day of Lights. She found the grave clothes Kyra-Maria had chosen ahead of time, *This is what I want to be buried in*, she'd said, and wrapped them up in the shroud. It's what her mother had done before her, Evgnosia's grandmother from Trabzon whom neither of the girls had ever met. The women of their family never left loose threads to their children.

Evgnosia turned the house upside-down but couldn't find Kyra-Maria's wedding ring anywhere. The girls never realized it had been sold. Lawyers cost money, even the most compassionate have expenses of their own. And then there were bribes to be paid to clerks and various intermediaries for some document or a few minutes of visiting time. That's how mothers were in those days, particularly refugee mothers, Pontic women who had come to the country with nothing but their souls in their mouths. They held their families in their fists. Whatever needed to be done, they did it themselves.

Kyra-Maria was buried in a cheap box, they had no money for a better one. Nails poked out of the sides and the unfinished wood was rough to the touch. It didn't matter, it would do the job. There were fresh flowers from the garden, roses their mother had planted with her own hands, red and so sweet that the smell of them in the living room almost made you faint. There were chrysanthemums and daisies, too, that the neighbor women brought from their yards—especially those who had spoken badly of her in the past. And it was they who supported the girls in their trouble. They knocked on the door every day, brought food, whatever each of them had cooked for her family. They found excuses: wanting Evgnosia to try a new recipe, or celebrating a name day or holiday.

After her mother's death Evgnosia quickly let things run to seed. She would visit the grave each morning and evening to polish the marble with a clean cloth, and yet the house gathered dust and grime. At first in the corners and under the beds, though the whole floor had shone while their mother was alive. Then everywhere. The elder daughter simply withered away. She lived on water, prayers, and a handful of crumbs a day.

Violeta returned each afternoon to a cold house. Her last name now carried a stigma, there wasn't a person left who didn't know whose sister she was. She heard them whispering behind her back. Her pride became a suit of armor—but when she got home and took it off, she would collapse in a heap.

For a while she kept setting the table as their mother had taught them, with a tablecloth, a jug of water, forks and knives laid out on the napkins. But Evgnosia no longer sat with her to eat. And so bit by bit the tablecloth was forgotten, the napkins went unwashed, old food stuck to the fabric; Violeta didn't have the patience to scrub at the stains. Soon enough she just came home and ate bread and cheese in bed, not even bothering to shake the crumbs from the sheets.

Evgnosia was spirited off, the old women in the neighborhood said. *An evil shadow stood at her side, she was touched by the angel of death.* Eventually she stopped talking: no matter how hard Violeta tried to insist, not a word would cross her sister's lips. She wasted away from crying and lack of food. The neighborhood women still knocked on the door, but Evgnosia no longer got up to answer. She spent her days in a chair. She no longer even went to the cemetery. She just sat and stared at the flaking whitewash on the wall, and combed her hair, not with a proper comb, but with an ivory hair clip. She wore the same nightgown day and night. She stopped washing.

Violeta tried to feed her. Gently at first, and then not so gently anymore. She stirred the soup with a spoon, told stories to coax her older sister. Once, tired of sweeping up fallen hair, she tried to take the clip away and Evgnosia bit her hand, hard enough that it bled. Violeta had been raised with caresses. Her family scolded her, even punished her, but no one had ever raised a hand against her. They suckled her *on milk and honey*, as her mother used to sing as a lullaby.

At some point the younger sister recalled that the clip had been their mother's. In fact, she had been wearing it on the day they fled from the old house, in Trabzon. Its teeth had broken long ago, but their mother kept it in a drawer for years, she couldn't bear to throw it away. In those days women rarely threw things away, mattresses and pots and pans passed from generation to generation. Who knows what Kyra-Maria was thinking in holding on to that broken comb. She ran a tight ship, took care of her belongings, didn't waste. She turned old rags into cloth bags for storing hilopites and trahanas. She saved leftover bits of thread in case they came in handy somewhere. Spoiled fruit became compotes and spoon sweets. The lentils Violeta turned her nose up at got passed off on the third day as lentil rice. *We don't throw anything out*, was the law of the household.

Violeta didn't want them to take Evgnosia to the asylum. But the older sister stubbornly refused to open her mouth. It was as if someone had sealed it shut with a trowel and mud.

At night, when Evgnosia closed her eyes, Violeta's stayed open. She felt as if the walls were closing in. There was only one solution, and she knew it. She signed the paper.

Evgnosia was shut up in Lembeti a year after her mother's death. Manolis, in solitary confinement, never heard the news.

The outside world was far away. If you were to ask him what life was like before the event, he'd have forgotten.

SCHOOL YEAR 2010–2011

"GET YOUR HANDS OFF OUR BRAINS"

Evelina started crying during Latin class. We were doing grammar exercises, which is her forte. A boring subject, just like our teacher. Grandma says classical philologists *know their letters, which is more than you can say for the rest of those backward literature teachers.* So what? Sure, they know all about the optative and the supine, but if they have to talk about something besides the lesson plan, they throw up their hands in despair.

Dad says most teachers haven't read a book since they were at university. As soon as their diploma is in its frame, they abandon learning altogether. They teach everything and study nothing. *For their kind, that's not a contradiction*, he says, just to annoy Grandma. And it works.

Grandma is aware of their shortcomings, but she still supports her fellow educators. *Teachers can be ignorant know-it-alls, but they also tackle a challenge no parent dares attempt: to walk into a classroom full of raging adolescents and keep them glued to their seats for forty minutes straight.* Grandma's claws come out if she thinks someone's attacking her crew.

At any rate, Evelina was sobbing, actually sobbing. The Latin teacher just nodded. *It's that time of year*, she said. Every year after Christmas the seniors break down. They suddenly hear time ticking backwards, and the sound of the second hand can drive you crazy if you know you're not on top of your game. Tears, shouting, nerves, it's all part of the program, as anyone who teaches the senior class knows.

But Evelina isn't the type to cry. Not in front of other people, anyway. Nothing even happened, the Latin teacher just told us to write out the abstract supine of *vixit*. It didn't matter what the exercise was, she could've said "Good morning" and Evelina would have burst into tears. Before she even got a word down on the paper, it was soaked. Her back shook, and you could hear the sobs all the way in the very last row.

That's where I sit. No one bothers me there, and I can stretch out my legs. I can stare at her bra strap all I want. She wears brightly colored bras, cherry red, or purple with little butterflies. Her skin is the color of a peach, it makes you want to take a bite right out of her. Right there, on the curve of her shoulder.

The girl next to her gave her a hug, and the Latin teacher paused her lesson. She had a speech ready for the situation. Blah blah blah, *composure*. Blah blah blah, *I'm confident you'll all do well.*

Evelina sniffled, the teacher handed her a tissue and then wrote the future passive infinitive of *vidit* on the board. We had lots to get through and she wasn't going to waste any more time on nonsense.

During break the other girls crowded around her. Evelina couldn't explain what had happened. She shook her hair out, lion-style. For the first time, I noticed her foot tapping. *It's cram school*, she said, *four hours every day, not even a donkey could work that hard, much less a human being.* And those practice exams every Sunday, the alarm clock ringing in her ear, it was too much, all she dreamed of anymore was for the fucking exams to be over so she could sleep. The other girls nodded, *what the fuck*, they all knew exactly what she meant.

I know what's wrong. In two months she'll be eighteen. You can't be eighteen years old and always do everything right. It can't last. Grandma says it, too, but Mom gets mad and shuts her up with a look. She thinks it won't occur to me on my own if I don't hear it from Grandma.

Souk was on recess duty. He'd heard what happened, but he didn't run over to offer consolation, or to see Evelina's puffy eyes from up close. It might have bothered her that he didn't, but I respect it. Souk doesn't turn other people's lives into theater. He talked to her in class, but only to quiz her on something. World

War II might not be the best way of making conversation, but Souk doesn't know how to talk to you when things get personal. He never shows you he cares, doesn't waste his breath on sweet talk, never reaches out a hand.

Grandma calls it *the Socratic method*. She considers it *the highest pedagogical technique.* I call it cornering a person. Instead of just telling you what I want you to know, I ambush you with questions. You try to escape, but you can't. You can run whichever way you like, but in the end you'll fall right into my trap.

Souk tried to make the most of the opportunity, though. He talked about *conditioned mass behavior*, about *demagoguery* and *emotional manipulation*, though of course not on a personal level, always in reference to the historical subject matter we were dealing with. And there was more: the *cost of choices, on a political and national level*, and *the upholding—and betrayal—of responsibilities. He who has ears, let him hear.*

Souk knows everything about World War II. And he looks at the world through that lens. It's what Dad calls *intellectual autism* and Grandma calls *embedded knowledge.*

Evelina doesn't care about any of that. All she wants is to get the exams over with. If she could she would take all the subjects in a single day. *A soul that's ready to leave should leave.* Grandma says it, too, and she's usually right.

It's exactly how I feel about my presentation. Souk reminded me that next week is the last week of the quarter. He handed me a slip of paper with the date and time of my talk. He's going to put an announcement up on the door of the teachers' office, too. If I want to invite someone, I should do that now.

In other words, my days are numbered.

If I talk for more than twenty minutes, he'll cut me off. I have to leave time for questions. *Don't mince words*, he advised. And if I want to use PowerPoint, I have to take care of the technical side of things myself. Souk isn't good with computers. He sometimes uses one of the school laptops in class, but he's as helpless as Mom. He goes to Athens by way of Tokyo. Speed and adaptability aren't his forte.

The greatest wisdom is in simplicity, as Grandma says.

Twenty minutes. I don't know what to say and what to leave out. Souk told me to turn in a typed version, too, with a cover page and list of references, and a blank page for him to write his comments. I asked for last-minute instructions, but he mocked my request.

—That's the danger with freedom: it's an abyss. Will you fall in? It'll depend on you, Georgiou.

Mom and Dad both threatened to show up for my presentation. Grandma was the first to invite herself. She wouldn't go to visit Dinopoulos at his house, but said she would see him there. The old man listened with his eyes closed as I relayed her message, then let out a little laugh. I'm pretty sure he's not going to die before he at least talks to Grandma again.

It's hard to believe, but they've got lives, too. Our parents, and our parents' parents. A biology teacher once said that, one of those low-on-the-totem-pole teachers who get transferred to our school at the last minute, right before classes start. The older teachers treat them pretty badly, and none of them ever sticks around for a second year. Anyhow, the biology teacher was annoyed at us over something, and said:

—You know, your parents have lives. They're not just parents, they're a couple, too.

Evelina laughed. The biology teacher had no wedding ring. We used to run into her at bars sometimes. Her hair was always mussed, and she came to school on a bicycle. In the schoolyard it was easy to mistake her for a student. So who was she to talk?

But what she said got me thinking: if my parents are a couple, when precisely do they do it? There are no locked drawers full of condoms at our house. Though they do have a roll of toilet paper hidden under their bed. That might *constitute evidence*, as Grandma would say.

•

Evelina said she would take care of my handout.

—You're already wasting your time on this presentation, so you might as well do the job right, she snipped.

She spent a whole twenty minutes making copies on beige paper she picked out herself, without consulting me, of course. For an exam-obsessed senior with her ambitions, it's a lot, actually.

Evelina doesn't need to think, she decides. She knows what she wants and works like a dog to achieve it: a law degree, her name on her grandfather's office. She's got a ten-year plan.

She doesn't get it.

She's trying to plan her life. Which she'll live once everything is in order. When she'll have free time.

She just doesn't get it.

Life doesn't sign contracts. It doesn't make treaties. You'll never get back the blood you spit. And you can't store it up in some piggy-bank, either.

What you end up with is a big fat nothing.

Zero, zip, zilch.

As for me, the dribbling, the passes, the excuses, the procrastination, it's all over. It's time for me to face the music.

THROUGH OTHER EYES

The news wasn't good.

—The worst is yet to come, Evthalia prophesied when Teta told her what had been going on. Things at the newspaper had been bad for months. Tasos was having insomnia, his acid reflux had flared up, and his palpitations, and the shouting in the shower. No matter how you looked at it, the situation was fucked.

There was no way he could avoid firing people, it was now clear. As for voluntary redundancy, which once struck him as a professional indecency and an insult to his co-workers, it now seemed like a dream solution, no longer an option.

When Teta pressed him to tell her what was happening, he lashed out.

—What do you want to hear from me, Teta? Don't you get it? It's like we've got the dead man's coffin sitting there in the living room. It's like that every day at work. It's too much.

And it was. Georgiou had gotten used to winning the war, to calling the shots, to being flexible, when circumstances required. But now his hands were tied behind his back.

—You should resign, his mentor bellowed over the phone. An old-school reporter from the Pleistocene age, he had supported Georgiou more than a few times when the going got tough. Editors in chief are chosen for how they'll respond in a crisis, he continued. They should know how to run a paper, and they should know how to step down, too.

Georgiou hung up the phone in a poisonous mood.

—When you have a child, you're willing to swallow your pride, Teta murmured. We don't have the luxury of abandoning good jobs when the world around us is burning.

Tasos wanted to shout that it would be easier for him to support his staffers if Teta had some job of her own that brought in a steady wage. He knew it wasn't fair, the two of them had made that decision together, having a family means being present, a child doesn't just grow on its own, like a cactus. At the time it had seemed like a logical decision, one that supported him in his career and soothed his guilty feelings. Now it felt like a noose around his neck, at a time when the foundations of his world were being shaken.

The able and the incompetent were all in the same boat, they could all lose their jobs: the numbers simply didn't add up. Friendships that blossomed during happier times withered overnight. Even smiles suddenly became suspicious, since anyone who smiled surely had a protector somewhere. They all slept and woke in the same haze of anxiety.

For a while the adults in his life left Minas to his own devices. They had other worries on their minds, more important problems to solve. Salary cutbacks, the unpleasant task of firing friends, taxes that were bringing everyone to their knees. At first Minas was taken aback by this sudden lack of interest, particularly on the part of his mother, who stopped keeping track of his lost study time and glued herself to the TV. *She's more interested in floating-rate bonds than in gerunds*, he told his grandmother.

Evthalia was the only one who kept her cool in the chaos. She was infuriated by how the administration was handling the situation, and discussed their royal mess of a country with Teta over the phone and over morning tea with her girlfriends at Terkenlis. And then she would shake off these unpleasant thoughts with a *this too shall pass*—she wasn't going to lose sleep over it, she had seen plenty of catastrophes in her day, wars, people killed, and she certainly wasn't going to take too seriously this game of Monopoly unfolding before her eyes.

—It's money, dear, it's only money, she kept telling Teta.

—I don't think you really understand, her daughter would shriek, on the verge of hanging up the phone.

Evthalia had learned to ignore Teta's hysterics, which were only exacerbated by the news coverage, the front-page articles, and the confidential information Tasos brought home from work. She circled the date carefully on the calendar. On February 25, a Tuesday, Minas would present his research paper. Her grandchild took priority.

Evthalia put on her favorite knit suit, bordeaux colored, and painted her nails a pearly white. She'd had her hair done at the salon and was carrying a purse Minas had given her, though it wasn't her style. Her grandson was the only person who gave her gifts. Modern bags with removable pouches, colorful bead necklaces that hung down to her navel, or more rarely an asymmetrical shirt or pareo. Teta had settled years ago on simply giving her money, which she considered more practical.

Tasos was fretting about being late for a meeting at the paper, but Teta shut him up with a look. In the elevator she grabbed his cell phone, put it on silent, and tossed it in her purse. Without his phone Tasos had no idea what to do with his hands. When they got out to the street, he put his arm around her.

Grandpa Dinopoulos came in his wheelchair. Elena had trouble getting him into the building, since there was no ramp, but the guard was friendly and the old man as light as a feather. They managed to get him into the lecture hall in plenty of time. Evelina had never seen her grandfather wearing a suit—even when they went to see him on New Year's he always had on pajamas. He looked good in dark blue, with a handkerchief tucked into his breast pocket. His heavy glasses kept sliding down his nose and his right shoulder looked slightly hunched where there was too much fabric. But a good close shave had done wonders, and you could smell his cologne from a distance. Elena waved at Minas, who hurried to introduce Mr. Dinopoulos to his teacher.

Soukiouroglou had put up the announcement, but none of the other teachers had come. It was no time for experimentation, there was too much material to get through. The principal was preoccupied by the recent developments, and the guidance counselor couldn't find a way to make Soukiouroglou's initiative count in her file. The teacher's proposal that students from other sections be invited was rejected. No one had any desire to babysit a bunch of teenagers outside of class.

The auditorium, the crown jewel of this old, palatial building, was an amphitheater designed by some enlightened architect eighty years earlier, before the task of building schools was turned over to contractors. Soukiouroglou led Minas's parents into the higher of the two sections, to have a complete view of the events. Then he steered Evthalia to a seat in the front row beside Dinopoulos, who had been smiling at her from a distance. Evthalia gave a coquettish wave as she neared. A spark glinted under her eyelashes—the same spark that flashed in Minas's eyes when he was misbehaving, when he was consciously disobeying the rules.

Evelina distributed the handouts and Minas plugged his thumb drive into the school computer. Soukiouroglou sat down in the audience and signaled for his student to begin.

Nineteen minutes and thirty-five seconds, timed on his cell phone. Minas's classmates burst into applause. Some out of boredom, others out of interest, most because they considered it part of the process.

—You're now free to ask questions, Soukiouroglou opened the floor.

Utter silence. The students had been trained to listen. Their years of schooling had taught them all kinds of useful things, but how to formulate questions was not one of them.

Soukiouroglou turned to Dinopoulos.

—As one of the individuals immediately involved in the case, might you want to ask something?

Evthalia nudged the old man, who licked his chapped lips.

—If you want to discuss the case of Manolis Gris, Dinopoulos answered, keeping his voice as steady as he could, by all rights you should acknowledge that making sure justice was served wasn't the primary consideration. Or rather, while it may have been a concern for those individuals immediately involved, it certainly was not for the country as a whole. As with all vital decisions that affect large groups of people, you do the best thing for the greatest number. We did something for the sake of something else. It may be complicated to explain, but it's self-evident in the moment of action. Which is why a neutral assessment of the events is the safest and most honorable approach. I agree with the young man's method. It's wise to present events as objectively as possible. No one can verify exactly what happened on the day of the murder, if you want my opinion, he concluded.

Soukiouroglou caught fire.

—In my class students are taught to take a position. Neutrality is a myth.

Dinopoulos shook his head. He'd never had much respect for high school teachers. They were all talk and no action. They lived at a remove from the tumult of the real world, in an alternate universe built of words and ideas. Evthalia with her practical mind was, of course, an exception. Be that as it may, the lawyer was tired of arguing the self-evident, as he'd been for doing decades.

—Neutrality, my dear sir, has existed since the creation of the world, he answered.

—Neutrality is a dangerous ideology. Pontius Pilate's washing of his hands led a man to the cross, Souk said, unwilling to let it go.

—A man? You mean God incarnate, Dinopoulos corrected.

—Still.

Tasos, who had first-hand knowledge of Soukiouroglou's back story, how and why he'd been expelled from the Faculty of Philosophy, checked the watch of the student sitting in front of him. There was no way they'd be out of there anytime soon.

He had spent an entire afternoon explaining to Teta why their child's teacher had been kicked out of graduate school. Some people said his stance was *full of integrity*, but most called it *idiotic and incomprehensible*. If you roll around in the chaff, you're sure to be pecked at by hens. The young scholar took on the lions—and got devoured.

And now old Dinopoulos was praising the virtue of neutrality before this man of all people. He was willing to admit that a *conspiracy of good intentions*, as he called it, had ruined the life of an innocent man. But he refused to lay the blame at anyone's feet, and refused to try and identify the guilty party.

To Soukiouroglou it was clear as day that the old goat was in league with the government back then, and with Minas now. The boy had chosen the easy path of simple description. He refused to risk any commentary, evaluation, or interpretation. He just sang his song and waited for the applause.

The teacher weighed the circumstances. He glanced at Teta in the upper section of seats, then at Evthalia. In the seat next to hers Dinopoulos was trying to control the Parkinson's in his hands and head.

—I'd like to ask a question, too, he finally said. Mr. Georgiou, have you in the course of your research, he continued, addressing himself to Minas with the utmost formality, settled on a version of the story you might consider the most plausible, in light of your findings? If your ten-year-old brother were to ask you exactly what happened, could you answer him in just a sentence or two?

—I don't have a brother, Minas answered, and the audience laughed.

Spiros had requested special permission from the religion teacher to come and watch Minas's presentation. Evelina didn't even deign to acknowledge him when she saw him entering the auditorium. Spiros had heard a lot about Soukiouroglou, particularly from Minas, and wanted to see him in action. He didn't understand how that scrawny man could bring an entire class to its knees with a single glance. How such incredible awkwardness could elicit such love and respect. From his seat at the top of the auditorium he felt as if he could hear Minas's heart pounding. Why was everyone just sitting there, why didn't anyone intervene?

He raised his hand bravely.

—Yes, in the back, Soukiouroglou said.

—I don't get it, Spiros said, getting off to a sloppy start. I mean, why do we necessarily have to decide? It's not like this is a courtroom or anything.

Evelina rolled her eyes. Sure, the moron had a point, but the words he chose were all wrong, weak tools in the hands of an incapable rhetorician.

—What he means, she spoke up, trying to correct the situation, is that perhaps the precise description of events that Minas attempted is enough. The search for the perpetrator and the attribution of guilt are the responsibility of the justice system. Pointing out contradictions in the evidence is enough to indicate the problem. An interpretation of the events and indication of the guilty party is far more than you can expect from a student paper.

—Ms. Dinopoulou believes you capable of description but not of interpretation, Soukiouroglou commented, still sticking with his ironic formality. It remains to be seen whether or not her evaluation is correct.

Tasos clenched his fist under the desk. The process, *mutatis mutandis*, was familiar to him. Soukiouroglou was a carbon copy of Asteriou, his dissertation supervisor. That's who he'd reminded Tasos of from the very start, and the impression had only gotten stronger. Soukiouroglou's famous professor, the one who had sent him packing from Aristotle University to go and teach at a high school, had a corrosive effect on his students. Tasos had sniffed it out from his very first semester as a student, which is why he'd made sure never to enroll in Asteriou's classes.

The biting irony, the pressure, the pursuit of that one perfect word that would bring a smile to the professor's lips. The metaphorical flogging of first-year students for supposedly pedagogical purposes. The perversion of the obvious. The incredible joy of discovery, and the high price it carried.

Tasos had endured the teaching of the most famous professor in the Faculty of Philosophy for precisely one week. During the second lecture, Asteriou addressed him directly. He called Tasos *wily Odysseus* and Teta *Elpinor*, after Tasos had dared to answer some convoluted question that made simple things appear more complicated than they really were. He, unaware of the danger and with a false sense of security, had answered correctly. And that set Asteriou off.

Whatever Asteriou said was God-given truth. His witticisms burst like bombs in the lecture hall, his insightful observations left students dumbstruck. His arguments weren't watertight, of course.

Nor were his ideas original, as you found if you actually went and dusted off the bibliography. But certain turns of phrase stuck in the minds of his listeners. He used their emotions to his advantage, knew how to handle his audience, had inimitable technique as a lecturer. He was a consummate performer, a silent wave roiling under a smooth surface, and he pulled students into his undertow. He was precisely what he spoke so vehemently against: an iron-fisted ruler, an oppressor. He was quick to anger, rarely listened, mostly just spoke and led the entranced crowd to whatever point he had decided on ahead of time.

Tasos figured all that out during the first week of lectures, and never set foot in the class again. The power games the professor played with his students were obvious, try as he might to hide behind rhetoric and provocations. Tasos talked Teta into dropping the class and taking it with him the following semester, with a different professor. He managed to graduate without ever crossing paths with Asteriou again.

Asteriou consumed whatever got close to him. No grass sprouted where he stepped: his students ended up carbon copies of him, none with a strong personality, even the ones who were supposedly at the top of their field. Soukiouroglou was a perfect example. Tasos had to admit, Soukiouroglou had dared to go head to head with his professor. He raised his voice, stood tall, and paid dearly for his decision. But here in this high school auditorium—a step down on the educational ladder from the ambitious Faculty of Philosophy, with its inscription, in ancient Greek, *Sacrifice to the muses and graces*—Soukiouroglou wielded the power of his position just as Asteriou had: a Scottish shower, hot and cold, biting irony, and an abruptness that left no room for discussion.

—Well? Soukiouroglou repeated the question. Will you attempt to offer an interpretation of the events? Or will you limit yourself to safe, painless description?

Tasos counted the seconds on the inside. He was on the verge of getting up and tearing the guy to shreds. Teta pinched him.

—I don't understand.

Minas had spoken almost in a whisper. Soukiouroglou gestured for him to speak up.

—I don't understand why I have to present my paper the way you want me to, and not how I've decided. Description is a form of interpretation, too, he added, his voice gaining strength.

—An interpretation that doesn't take many risks, Soukiouroglou shot back.

Evelina couldn't contain herself anymore. Enough was enough.

—Sir, you're the one holding the grade book, she said. You make the rules, and you demand obedience. If that's a critical appraisal, I must be missing something.

Tasos smiled for the first time since he walked in the door. The girl had balls. He leaned back more comfortably in his chair. Well then. It was time for him to practice what he often preached: he would put his trust in the younger generation.

Before Soukiouroglou could respond to Evelina, Minas spoke up in a clear, steady, confident voice, running once more over the possible scenarios. An English secret agent, irregularities committed by the right-wing parastate, the collusion of dark forces who had something to gain from the tumult the country was experiencing. The murderers may have been right-wing extremists trying to prevent the reporter from meeting the General. Or British agents seeking to undermine American hegemony over the country. Or, as Tzitzilis had argued, communists trying to make the administration look ridiculous and convince the Americans to pack up and get out of Greece.

Grandpa Dinopoulos nodded from his wheelchair. Once the kid got going, there was no stopping him. It was clear as day, a career in law would suit him perfectly. Grandma Evthalia was proud. She had raised that child. And he had managed on his own, without anyone's help.

•

—Here you go, sir.

Minas handed Soukiouroglou a typed version of his paper.

—Certainly, was all the teacher deigned to reply.

The kid stood before him, waiting.

—Eighteen out of twenty, Souk said. There's some excellent work here, but I can't ignore the gaps and oversights. As for taking a position, I would suggest that you leave the kind of hesitation I saw in your presentation to older, more experienced scholars. You're still young. For the time being, you should take a stance.

Minas shrugged.

—You obviously don't care either way, Soukiouroglou muttered.

Minas lowered his head. He turned to leave, but then turned back again. He might as well say what he had to say now, rather than to himself later in his room.

—Sir, why do you insist on laying blame? If we accuse one person, we let everyone else off the hook, and there were lots of people who played a part. Sure, none of them actually lifted the gun. But the situation was created by friends and enemies both. Right or wrong, the result is the same: an innocent man went to jail. Case closed.

Soukiouroglou looked at him.

For the entire quarter, Minas had been reading Souk's favorite books, packed to the gills with words and ideas, which the teacher had recommended as a secondary, though still useful, bibliography. In studying them carefully, in marking passages with his high-lighter, Minas had come to realize that justice is an abstract concept. Perfect on paper. But in practice, riddled with qualifications, asterisks, interpretations, clashes of opinion. History books of-fered no catharsis, as tragedies did; there were no happy endings, as there were in fairytales or soap operas. What he would have liked more than anything was to talk to Souk about that. But his teacher wanted to have the upper hand. And with Minas that wasn't always an option.

1948–2010 BEFORE AND AFTER

"THINK BEFORE YOU LEARN"

NIKIFOROS DINOPOULOS, LAWYER FOR MANOLIS GRIS

I don't underestimate power. I don't judge anyone for having it. What troubles people—and rightly so, if you ask me—is how a nation's leaders shirk their responsibilities. They insist on blam-ing outside forces for the country's woes rather than their own deci-sions. They refuse to acknowledge their own failures.

Justice means each individual getting what he deserves. And virtue is the pursuit of justice. At least that's what Aristotle tells us. It sounds old-fashioned, doesn't it? Today's lawmakers are less strict about such things, more willing to water their wine. *Legislation has a responsibility to be neutral*, they all say. It has no right to convert, or to try to force good on anyone. Virtue isn't about coercion. Justice, above all, implies freedom of choice.

All sorts of things were said about the case, which most people separated into lies and truths. The reporters who got involved never considered what we might call inexactitudes. The ignorant fools couldn't tell the difference. Whereas the lawyers' evasions clearly demonstrate respect for the law. They took care to package the evi-dence well, to keep up pretenses to the very end. Sometimes they departed from the law, other times they took refuge in legal fictions, or interpreted the law in a particular manner. But they never flew in the face of the law, they always paid tribute to the obligation to remain honest. They maintained their professional dignity.

They made their decisions. And since the situation demanded it, they moved forward into action. Hindsight is always twenty-twenty, and it's easy for people to pass moral judgment. But those involved in the case never acted outside the law. They simply be-haved like people who would.

Please don't return to the issue of truth. If you think carrying a law book around ensures that justice will be served, I'm sorry, but you're being naïve. Life is so much more complicated than that.

As for the evidence you refer to, I can't help but laugh. I lived through two wars and witnessed plenty of military tribunals, and the idea that reality is single and undeniable amuses me. Reality is the ultimate construction—just ask the lawyers and journalists, whose careers rest on that construction. Other people have trouble understanding that. What they summarily call truth is rarely sufficient. Even more rarely does it offer any kind of solution.

The dictatorship of the truth. The tyranny of good intentions. There's nothing more dangerous for a family or a country. Historians show up after the fact. They rummage through locked drawers, discover forgotten papers, conduct their research, pass judgment. When precisely did the Gris case begin? With the murder of Talas, or with the decisions that were made behind closed doors? In history there is no such thing as progress, change, advancing toward the good or sinking into the abyss. I don't care what the survivors say.

Before and after. That's all there is. And between, a chasm.

Anyone who investigates the Gris affair needs to understand one thing: no one made any decisions without agonizing over them first. But everyone felt that the country's future was at stake. The greatest good for the greatest number, that's the basic rule of governance. You weigh the options and settle on the least of all evils.

Words rarely help. They can't separate right from wrong. In situations like these everything is a matter of diplomacy. Intentions often have some degree of dignity. Documents don't. That, perhaps, is the fundamental difference between the two.

It would surprise you how easily a piece of evidence can disappear, a signature can be forgotten.

The Gris case: *Res ipsa loquitur.*

Marinos Soukiouroglou hated the school. He felt an instinctive disgust for all educational systems, and for the Greek one in particular. He considered it spirit-crushing, obsessive and megalomaniacal. He despised its shallow formalism. The classes in ancient Greek language and culture—which the overwhelming majority considered the crown jewel of the humanities—primarily served, according to his more rarified understanding, to bolster national pride.

What dismayed him most was how history was taught. Students learned to think in a static manner, as if issues had a diachronic, unchanging character. For the Greek school system historicity was a theoretical concept, essentially unknowable. Meanwhile, most people Souk knew, particularly his colleagues but others as well, had received some reflected version of the European reception of ancient Greek glory and invested it with existential meaning, rather than trying to understand it as a historical construction. A sense of humor about such things was high treason. False modesty oppressed everything. He suspected that the root of all this was an unmentionable—yet systematically cultivated—puritanism that wanted knowledge to hurt. To be unmixed with pleasure or joy.

Even more annoying was the school's simplistic notion of competition, as something limited to final grades. The holy ritual of the Panhellenic Exams gave an official form to the ambitions of students and parents alike. How you scored determined everything, or so most people believed.

For Soukiouroglou the exams were just a hazing ritual, a humiliation students had to endure in order to be initiated into the next stage of life. These days the average person on the street was fully convinced that the only option for a bright kid with a desire and ability to learn was to go to university, that anything else would result in certain disaster. Reality, however, didn't correspond to that collective figment of everyone's imagination—and when that dawned on members of the entering class, they ended up spending their days at the cafés on the edge of campus.

A combination of Greek provincialism and nationalistic narcissism sustained the vicious cycle of the Greek educational system— which, rather than opening up toward the outside, systematically closed in on itself. Kids were raised in a corral where knowledge was kept separate from empirical observation, and where learning was presented as a kind of torture, rather than an exciting or pleasurable adventure. They were taught to have an uncritical respect for textbooks and for a teacher's authority. Any impulse toward independent thinking was crushed before it ever raised its head.

That was why Minas had rebelled. His other teachers called it *adolescent anti-conformism*. And they had another, easy psychological explanation, which Souk more or less agreed with, though he knew there was more to it than that: they'd all seen Teta in action and had an inkling of how much pressure she put on Minas. For most of them a single conversation with her was enough to make them shake their heads and exchange meaningful looks of despair with their colleagues. Teta had staked her life on her son, as was clear to anyone who had experience dealing with parents.

But Souk knew there were deeper roots to Minas's violent reaction to the institutional framework of education. Sure, Teta was annoying, but that wasn't a sufficient explanation. Minas had taken on the system itself, and was sure to get what was coming to him. His response was irrational, physical, and absolute.

No matter how hard Souk tried to approach Minas calmly and neutrally, there was always a note of exasperation in his voice. Even he, who seemed on the surface to have made peace with his decisions and had learned to limit his intellectual ambitions to this sheepfold of a school, continued to be enraged by the idea of failure. He wanted Minas to succeed. He'd have forced him if he could.

Souk knew argumentation would have no effect whatsoever, so he tried to get Minas emotionally involved in a case that was a lost cause from the start. Most people considered Soukiouroglou distant and detached. None of them could have imagined how he caught fire in the classroom. It wasn't just his sardonic wit, his cautious cynicism, or his emphatic precision, the combination of a strict literalism and the most unexpected metaphors. It was above all the way he drew, sometimes in an almost punishing manner, on the emotions—his audience's but also his own. He knew how to touch a chord, always at precisely the right moment. He managed to mine those emotions the students tried so hard to hide behind their silly grins and stupid comments. He ruled his class like an enlightened despot—which is to say with an oppressive hand disguised as something else. After a year in his class, students had difficulty accepting a different teacher.

Of course he hadn't lived his own life nearly enough. He'd shielded himself from the experiences that had burned so many others his age. But in the classroom he could finally be himself, become the person he believed himself to be. Most of his students were entranced by this transformation, swept up and carried off by the wave of his performance. Yet when the bell rang they were left hanging. The teacher's thinking and rhetoric may have been the creations of an austere geometry, but the tsunami of his explosions—part performance and part collective psychotherapy—elicited their admiration while also striking them dumb. They set out on the path he carved for them and didn't dare raise their heads.

Very few ever refused to dance to the beat of his drum. Minas was one of them. And it was strange, because Minas lived and breathed for Souk's sake. Yet he kept his core well protected, didn't let it be crushed by external pressures. Minas's strength had been a continual surprise to the teacher, from his first year of middle school until today. Yet Minas also annoyed Souk to no end, precisely because his defenses were impossible to break through.

Minas was destined from the crib to be every teacher's favorite. He knew how to learn from others, from real-life situations. Souk tried to explain to the others what Minas already knew well, because he'd been taught it at home: *in learning a book isn't enough, you need a mind, too.* A mind to distil information, to bring things together, to settle on a point of view. *There's no need for students to become carbon copies of their teachers*, Souk repeated at every opportunity. He used Plato and Aristotle as his example. He loved telling the kids at school—who listened carefully, though who knows how much they understood—that Plato's absolute idealism, which denied the senses all rights, had been overturned by his student, Aristotle. Sensory grounding, that was Aristotle's upending of Platonic thought.

Minas listened in silence. A flammable adolescent but worthy interlocutor, he was intellectually tolerant yet obsessive about his ideas. Soukiouroglou loved him, but also found him hard to bear.

THE THINGS THAT HAPPENED BEFORE AND AFTER, AND THE THINGS THE OTHERS NEVER LEARNED

There are good endings and bad ones. In books, that is. In real life, things aren't so simple, and the victims never get to say their piece. Yet those who judge shall also be judged. History is a boat whose hull is deep under water, and when it capsizes, everything is overturned. That's what Soukiouroglou struggled to show them, with examples and radical claims.

When a top student who was considering military academy said something about the brutality of the Turks, calling on sources and eye-witness accounts, Souk—a third-generation refugee from Asia Minor with first-hand experience of victimization and loss, who certainly could have told his own stories of Turkish brutality, yet judged it a good opportunity for a stern lecture about objectivity, the chimera of so many historians—let loose on the boy.

—Let's take the familiar case of an airspace violation, Souk said, and the students in the front row nodded. The other day, for instance. It was the third story on the news. The Greek minister made some statements, et cetera et cetera, he continued, feigning boredom.

But if you spoke Turkish and could read Turkish newspapers, you'd see that their approach to the situation was different. They spoke about the obstruction of military drills, illegal infringement, and so on.

Souk himself spoke Turkish fluently—he'd learned from his grandmother—and so he quoted a few headlines with perfect pronunciation. That small bit of showing off made it all more enjoyable for him, like a peacock fanning its tail.

—So, he continued, not breaking stride, let's say fifty or a hundred years from now a Belgian historian decides to write about the incident, and has those sources at his disposal. What objective reality can he offer?

—That the sky exists. And that maybe some airplanes flew through it.

Minas had spoken without raising his hand, a bad habit he'd had since middle school. Souk had chastised him for it countless times. Then last year Minas withdrew to the very back row and stopped speaking at all, and the class had lost its thrill for the teacher, became boring, even. But Soukiouroglou couldn't encourage that kind of behavior. He ignored Minas's comment and offered yet another example: how Greeks talk about the fall of Constantinople and the Turks about its conquest.

Ever since the fateful day of the presentation (which Minas considered a debacle and Soukiouroglou a teachable moment, while Evelina's and Minas's mothers agreed that it had been a huge waste of time), Minas had been an absent presence at school. Not that things had been much better before.

So much precious time wasted, Teta complained to Evthalia, *the child's energies spent on useless things, people shouldn't play those kinds of games with a graduating senior*. Evthalia didn't have much to say in response—Teta was right, in a way, but then again *the boy showed everyone what stuff he was made of*, as Nikiforos had said. He stood his ground at a moment that would have destroyed so many others, even adults. They all had their degrees, and Minas was just a poor little eighteen-year-old in a General Education class. Which is to say, a nonentity.

TASOS

Minas gave his father back the box of materials that Tasos had selected to share with his son. Georgiou put it away in the storage space in the basement, next to his pile of front pages and the cassette tapes of interviews he had amassed when he was still wet behind the ears and had tried to bring the case back into the public eye. He'd talked to all kinds of people back then; his persistence opened doors. Two veteran reporters with access to those close to the trial even entrusted him with rare material. They saw the progress he was making, and thought there was some chance he might solve the case—and might mention their names when the unveiling finally came.

He would have, too, since he always honored his sources. Only events didn't unfold as he expected them to. Georgiou's mentor was a man by the name of Vatidis, whose connections and influence were universally recognized, who held entire administrations in the palm of his hand. When Vatidis found out about his young protégé's new passion and, more importantly, about the material he had in his possession, he made it clear that *resolving that case wasn't among the newspaper's immediate priorities, much less those of the country*. Georgiou got the message loud and clear.

A year later, Georgiou was promoted to editor. He deserved it, of course. He worked like a dog, anyone with eyes in his head could see that. What they didn't see were the boxes of suppressed evidence in his basement. Even he forgot, eventually—after all, he'd made his choice. Though when Minas took on the project, for a moment his father felt tempted.

Just for a moment, and then it passed.

In the amphitheater that day, he listened as his son ran through

214

the possible scenarios, some crazy, some unsupported, others with evidence to back them up, and still others that were fairly obvious. Two decades earlier he had known them all, down to the smallest details. In the silence Soukiouroglou imposed during the ritual of the presentation, Tasos watched Minas anxiously. His boy had grown up.

When the applause died down, he ran down the stairs two at a time, grabbed his son by the shoulders and shook him.

—Good job, kid.

That's all he could say. Then he kissed him on both cheeks.

Teta didn't share her husband's excitement or the emotions of his response. But then she had never bowed before necessity, and had no boxes hidden in the storage space.

DINOPOULOS

Grandpa Dinopoulos's shoes were pinching him. He'd asked Elena to leave the laces undone, but she thought that unbefitting a formal appearance. And now his bunions were paying the price. At least the pain made him aware of his feet—that was something, he comforted himself. Besides, his whole getup made him uncomfortable, from head to toe: his wool suit tickled him, and the way it rubbed against his thighs was a torment.

Evthalia had complimented him on his appearance, though: *Look at you, decked out like a groom*, she said. He could detect no accusation in the phrase, just a gentle jab at ancient history. That's how Evthalia was. She'd make a mountain out of a molehill but swallow a skyscraper without complaint.

Like the time she stopped him in the street to congratulate him on his marriage. He'd started to cross over to the other sidewalk, he knew he hadn't been straight with her, even if he never made any promises.

But there she suddenly stood before him. *May you live long together*, she said, swinging her ponytail. *You suit one another*, she hastened to add, which bothered him, because he knew she believed it. *And may you have wonderful children*, she said, and Dinopoulos reddened, thinking of the activity that would inevitably precede a child—an activity he would gladly have undertaken with Evthalia.

All that seemed so close at hand, even if whole decades had passed since that day. He could feel Evthalia's breath on his shoulder. Today, in the discomfort of his tight shoes and itchy wool, that breath was a comfort to him.

EVELINA

Evelina held her breath. It was an exercise she'd learned from her mother's yoga book. She concentrated all her energy on her bellybutton, which wasn't easy, dammit. That asshole Soukiouroglou had found a fine time to assert his authority. Minas stood there, limbs dangling awkwardly, staring at the teacher. He'd gone into battle without so much as a knife, with just his bare hands.

Minas was handsome, tall and lanky, slightly hunched as if he were embarrassed by his height. She'd fallen in and out of love with him twice during grade school, once in first grade and again in fifth, both times in spring, when her mind wandered to such things. Then it passed, thank goodness. That's how she was, her crushes never lasted long, even if her mother praised her emotional constancy.

She could have kicked Soukiouroglou. The only thing she and that idiot Spiros had in common was their disgust—fine, call it skepticism—for the teacher.

Soukiouroglou played this game with his voice, like a snake charmer. He would drag out sentences, let his voice drop, and then it would suddenly explode. His voice was his toolbox, his winch and his blade, which carved out the emotions of adolescents, and ruled over parents as well. He chose his sentences with the care of an entomologist; he knew how to use pauses and silences to best effect. His rhetorical abilities were the school's invisible monument: quotes from his lectures got passed down from generation to generation.

When you spend hours every day with a teacher, you stop speaking like a normal person and end up sounding like him. It sounds like an exaggeration, but it isn't. Sooner or later Souk pulled them all into his orbit; even the ones who never did their homework were transformed into little Soukiouroglous.

Evelina watched as Minas tried to hold on to his own personality, to keep beating his own drum, to keep his out of the teacher's force field. She liked how stubborn he was. He dug his own grave with dignity. He never took a step backwards.

She'd met many ambitious law students, but none was as bright as Minas. They could memorize a legal code, sure, but there was no ingenuity in their thinking. They spoke in paragraphs; they were predictable to the point of despair.

Soukiouroglou's voice thundered in the audience. Up on stage, the student tugged at his already shapeless shirt and stood his ground.

TETA

Teta had no idea what made things snap back into place. Someone must have done something, it couldn't have just happened on its own. She lit a candle of thanks to the Virgin, great is her grace, as Evthalia taught her to. Her son handed his Xbox over to his grandmother—not to his mother, that would have been going too far—and said he was going to attempt *the experience of the exams*. And that was that. He set himself to studying, according to a schedule of his own devising. He calculated the days, pages, and hours of work that would be required, divided it all up and taped the resulting schedule over his bed, in place of Gris' photograph, which he took down but didn't throw away. Now he used it as a bookmark.

Teta didn't comment on the new state of affairs, she was afraid of destroying the delicate balance. Minas lived like a monk in his room. He subsisted on wafer cookies and grilled cheese; she would find them half-eaten under his bed, among dirty socks and chewed-on pencils.

Evthalia took charge of quizzing him. *Time is of the essence*, she told her daughter, and she was right. Sending him to cram school would just waste time on the back-and-forth, and he had his grandmother, he didn't need the faint lights of some recent university graduate to show him the way. Eventually Minas more or less moved into his grandmother's house, and the two of them celebrated with a meal of roast pork and fried potatoes, thin and crunchy, the way he liked. While he was setting the table, Minas recited his history book back to his grandmother, from page 45 to page 67, as she followed with one finger on the line of text, mixing the salad with her other hand.

At first Teta complained, *did he really have to leave home just to study for his exams, or was he just flying a flag of independence?* She was annoyed at her mother for siding again with her son. But Tasos shot her an angry look, tossed out a couple of choice phrases, reporter's language, the kind he usually saved for meetings at the newspaper. Teta let the issue drop. After all, the most important thing was her son and his exams, she didn't have the energy to bicker with her husband.

Meanwhile Minas set up shop in his grandmother's dining room. He studied there, ate all his meals there. The farthest he strayed was the bathroom, just far enough to shake out his legs, and then back to work.

He stopped complaining about the memorization, he'd made his peace with it. *He realized there are more important things at stake*, whispered his grandmother, who impressed upon him that memorization was in fact a *creative means of letting important things resonate*. His body became an amplifier. He even refrained from commenting on the content he had to memorize, all the stupid shit he would have to be able to reproduce in order to achieve the desired result.

—That child is a creature of extremes, Teta remarked over the phone, and Evthalia agreed, pleased.

At night he would go out and walk around the block. Evthalia had seen him from her balcony hopping over the wall of Agia Sophia. What he did in there, she had no idea.

One night when Minas had gone out, she raised her eyes and looked slantwise at Dinopoulos's top-floor apartment on the opposite corner. The living room lights were on, so he must still have been up. She hurriedly lowered the blinds and put some tsipouro and honey on to boil according to Tasos's recommended dosage.

Minas was gone for ages, and when she finally heard the elevator coming back up, Evthalia crossed herself. She had promised the Virgin that she would take communion three Sundays in a row, as long as the child came home safe. Before she started calling around to all the hospitals.

—There you are.

Bright red cheeks, glazed eyes, the biggest smile she'd ever seen.

—Hi, Grandma, Minas said, taking off his shoes in the entryway.

Evthalia was dying to ask him.

—Were you with someone? she said with feigned nonchalance. Minas smiled.

—With Evelina. We thought we'd take a break. It's Saturday. Besides, he added, imitating his grandmother's voice, well-considered breaks produce superlative work.

Evthalia smiled. Proper use of the passive participle of the present perfect and of the superlative "superlative." That was her Minas.

—What did you talk about for so long? she asked, her eyes trained on the TV screen. She was lying on the sofa under a checked blanket she got for free with a box of detergent. There was a mystery on, and the scene was just beginning when the detective would finally unraveled the plot.

—Nothing.
—For three hours?
—For three hours.
—So what did you do?
—We kissed.

He needed to tell someone, and he did.

SOUK

Souk's graduate education had been a trial-by-fire affair. Asteriou knew how to push his students to the limit, to test their resistance and resilience, to provoke them and bring them right to the heart of the matter. No matter how hard he tried to scrape off the residue of Asteriou's pedagogy, his own method was troublingly similar to his professor's. He didn't believe that knowledge came without a fight.

Minas would have to prove his mettle, tear his wings on the Sympligades. That was the only way he would get to where he was going—or so his teacher believed, having generalized his own personal example into a rule of thumb. Obstacles excited Souk, and so did hard work. But the boy was made of other stuff, even if Souk couldn't see that: focused on the similarities, he overlooked the differences. It wasn't only the decades that separated them—YouTube, Facebook, the low-slung jeans that looked like they might fall down at any moment—but also what each of them was made of.

In the commotion following the end of the quarter, Minas decided to take the exams—though in doing so he overturned all of his previous declarations. *That's how kids are*, Evthalia told her daughter with a smile, *they say things and unsay them the next minute, there's no point in ever taking them at their word.* She wasn't the least bit interested in the reason for the change, whether it had been his teacher's pedagogical strategy or the depth of Evelina's kisses. She wasn't blind, she saw Minas come home from his nightly walks with swollen lips and eyes staring off into space. How he ever got back to work was a mystery.

And yet he did. His mind was a sponge that soaked up rules and exceptions, figures, diagrams, every wrongheaded statement his textbooks contained. Souk thought it was because the blood price had been paid, and the young man finally realized what was at stake. And, of course, because he'd tasted the fruit of knowledge, reached out a hand and touched the tree of good and evil. Fireworks had gone off in his brain—and after you've experienced that feeling, there's no going back.

Souk thought Minas was born to go places. Souk divided all of humanity into two categories. He and Fani belonged to category of people who make things. The other was for everyone else, for people who just sat around all day. Nothing really got under their skin. What they aspired to was a carefree life.

It annoyed Souk that Minas was letting his talents go to waste. There were people with half his brain who managed to accomplish five times as much. But Minas didn't dance to the same rhythm as other people did. *If you stray from the sheepfold the wolf will eat you*, said people who were wise in the ways of the world. Souk himself knew the high cost of straying from the sheepfold. But he also knew he wouldn't get anywhere trying to give advice. Experience isn't something you can share.

EVTHALIA

Evthalia believed that romance was a sickness of the young. She'd never thought much of it, she shook herself free of that kind of love early on. She didn't like to feel her legs trembling beneath her, or that haziness in her head. She could still remember how her heart used to pound, as loud as thunder. She would see him walking toward her nonchalantly, but Evthalia was convinced he could hear her heart from a distance, because he swung his lawyer's briefcase to the rhythm as he rushed to greet her.

At the end of the day, he was the one who'd been in such a hurry to get married, and to Froso of all people, my Lord, a girl as silly as they come. Evthalia never forgave him for it. But she swallowed the insult as best she could—after all, they had never exchanged promises, only looks, which is to say nothing at all. And the more she saw Froso mopping her balcony, the very image of a perfect housewife, the more she counted her lucky stars. Love comes and goes, it fizzles out and leaves your heart barren. She wasn't cut out for that kind of adventure. She liked to know where her next footstep would land, to be wrapped in a cocoon of order. She lived for small things: a glass of tsipouro by the sea, teaching a beautiful poem in class. Big things frightened her. She knew that life isn't served on a platter, she had learned that lesson early on—it's just struggle and more struggle. She cinched her heart and moved on. She began each day in a suit of armor: a severe smile and a handbag full of textbooks. Plato and Cicero, ancient wise men who were above suspicion, who taught her a great deal, which she in turn taught to her students. Concepts, rhetorical structures, the layers of commentary—in the classroom she was unstoppable. She chewed gum, which her students liked and her colleagues didn't. Yet she kept chewing her gum and testing her students according to a rubric of her own devising, with fractions of a point earned or subtracted for reasons comprehensible only to her. And while she prepared for each class with outlines and notes, in the classroom she had a genius for putting all that aside, improvising answers and questions, talking about anything and everything, particularly prohibited subjects such as love and politics. The students at the girls' school put away their mirrors; at the boys' school they would do anything for her, they even studied the pages on syntax at the back of their Greek textbook, because she'd convinced them it was a crying shame that young men two meters tall could solve multivariable equations but couldn't diagram a sentence if their lives depended on it.

She took pleasure, then, in the small things, an hour on Antigone, or the Epitaphios, or Julius Caesar's *De bello civili*. Always on guard in the classroom, she managed to find all their cheat sheets during exams. No matter how inventive the seniors got, nothing escaped her. Once she pulled a strip of paper two and a half meters long from the cast on a student's arm. He had copied out the entire passage they were being tested on, complete with a translation and grammatical notes. She found the boy waiting for her at the main door that day after school. He knew she would keep him from graduating that year, but instead of giving her some sob story, he said, *I'm sorry, Ma'am, I'm sorry for letting you down.*

At home, however, all her comfort in her role flew out the window. She was a strict mother, as Teta often complained. Evthalia paid no attention, her daughter could say what she liked, what mattered was that she listened and obeyed. Evthalia was a young widow who was managing all on her own, and without crying over her fate, either. She ruled, she didn't coddle. As far as she was concerned, taking care of a household meant governing it.

With her grandson, though, things changed, her severity evaporated, she showed understanding about everything, particularly the things that made no sense. It drove Teta crazy: Evthalia always kept her mouth shut in front of the child, but he knew his grandmother was on his side. And that was enough.

One Sunday at dawn Minas went down with a can of spray paint in his back pocket and wrote on the wall outside of Agia Sophia:

EVERY GIRL HAS HER TRUMP CARD
DIAMONDS TO SPEND, STYLE IN SPADES
BUT IT'S EVELINA'S SMARTS
THAT CAPTURE MY HEART

Evthalia knew Minas had written it, but it just made her smile. It was a desecration, to be sure, illegal, improper, a peacock move, as Tasos would call it. But she found it sweet, her grandson's version of a moonlit serenade: Evelina's house looked down onto that wall, so she would see it even before she left the apartment in the morning. The exams were fast approaching, and spray-painting a slogan was better than the hysterics all the others were experiencing. And perhaps, she thought, it was time for the child to burn a few feathers. She just hoped he wouldn't get too hurt. Because her grandson could be a lumbering oaf sometimes. *He's a boy,* Teta said dismissively, *he has no sense of tactics, he just jumps into the fire with no armor on.*

Evthalia may have guarded her own feelings and kept herself far from the dust storms of love, but she still felt compassion for the suffering of others. Perhaps because she herself had once felt that pain. She knew very well that the body is an armory packed with gunpowder, ready to explode at the strike of a match. And so she watched as Minas fell flat on his face, hoping he'd pick himself back up again with no more than a few bruises.

Once, when he was rushing out to meet his young lady, with his shoelaces untied and his pants magically hanging below his hips, Evthalia thought she heard a thump—the thump of his heart suddenly kicking against his ribs. She knew that sound, she recognized it. It was how her own heart had pounded, coming home from class, knowing without a shadow of a doubt that she would see him with his lawyer's briefcase and his wide smile, and he would ask her something about Cicero.

De oratore. Even today, if you woke her from a deep sleep in the middle of the night, she'd still be able to recite that text from start to finish.

WHEN ELEPHANTS DANCE

The situation in Greece had reached full boil. Meanwhile, all of Europe was on fire, Spain, Italy, Brussels. New words peppered the speech of the grocer and the guy at the kiosk; the prime minister made statement after statement.

Evthalia couldn't stand to watch. *Get lost, you shit-eating dog*, she'd shout at the television screen, then go out onto the balcony for a cigarette. Her hands trembled and the lighter wouldn't stay still. It wasn't so much the cutbacks to pensions that upset her as the blatant dishonesty unfolding in full view: sacrifices of all kinds being thrown out the window, workers' rights suddenly vanishing with no hope of return. And meanwhile the scandals in the administration broke one after the next. The country was immune to shock, nothing surprised anyone anymore, not the kickbacks or the obvious lies. What left them speechless was the lack of foresight in how the situation was being dealt with: laws were written on the spot, amendments put to a vote in the midnight hours.

—This city smells of gunpowder, Tasos kept saying.

He watched as shop after shop lowered its shutters; the main artery of Vassilisis Olgas Avenue was deserted, Agia Theodora Street a wasteland. Empty shelves, signs in shop windows, advertising fliers in unused piles. Filth and abandonment. Tasos walked through the streets with his head down, since there were no window displays to look at anymore, only a long line of *FOR RENT* signs.

And then there was that entourage of talking heads on TV: men in suits with their Ph.Ds. and their academic papers, unionists who'd made a career out of demonstrations, guys who were all talk and no action, rabble-rousers with other people's money and votes in their pockets, demagogues and dynasty politicians.

—You're the one who voted for them, Evthalia accused, though she knew it was no time to bickering, to weigh all the mistakes that had been made over the years, from the ancient to the current-day, and try to determine which had tipped the scales. All together they had brought the country down.

Tasos tried not to take sides on the issue of foreigners coming in to help them clean up their act—a blessing or a scourge, depending on what side of the political spectrum you were on. There were endless statements and articles, commentary from all sides, pretty words to disguise dirty deeds. Meanwhile, off stage, behind the cameras, hard bargains were being driven: I'll give you this if you give me that.

That's how it had always been, from the creation of the world. Someone was always making the decisions, while others were left holding the bag. In the Garden of Eden, God was boss. In the European Union it was the Central Bank.

Minas heard it all, since these days the television was always on in the house. His father even managed to put his favorite on the front page of the paper: the caption *WHEN ELEPHANTS DANCE* beneath a cartoon showing all-powerful presidents, unfazed prime ministers, bankers and industrialists, all with elephant trunks—*give them elephant trunks and thick legs,* Tasos had told the cartoonist, *like the trunks of palm trees, but make sure you can still tell who's who*—and in the cartoon these huge pachyderms were prancing around with the country under their feet, raising a cloud of dust, with citizens like tiny ants, so small you couldn't make out any faces, they were all just smushed ants. The economists all had theories of their own, and most sounded logical enough—the only thing was, they all contradicted one another, so people quickly gave up trying to understand. The biggest problem wasn't their specialized vocabulary, which every hairdresser and kiosk guy now parroted all day at work—it was that their theories were only theories, empty words that shed light on things for an instant, with a flash, but fizzled just as quickly. So the wise simply kept their mouths shut, particularly the intellectuals, who watched the developments from their homes, discussed the situation with friends, but refrained from making predictions. The few who did mostly just stated the obvious. And so the TV stations and the blogs shouted, *Where are the intellectuals to come and save us?*

Tasos didn't believe in national saviors. He believed in

hard-working people. In people who knew how to divide wheat between two donkeys, who understood what was at stake, who saw solutions to problems and had the endurance and fortitude to work toward them. Intellectuals and academics were all fine and well, some were even willing to put their hands in the fire, and they certainly knew how to dress up their ideas in pretty words. But *just because you write about cancer, doesn't mean you know how to treat it*, he commented to Evthalia. *We need a doctor here. A surgeon who knows what he's doing.*

She agreed, in part. But she also believed a little theorizing never hurt. *Theories offer a frame*, she reminded him, *without a theory, you're just shooting into the air.* Sure, a hatchet would do the job, and a scalpel would be even better, but you still had to know where to cut. *Injustice has become an institution*, Tasos said, shaking his head, *perhaps the only institution that actually functions in this fucking country. Enough already with the violence. Institutionalized injustice is a form of violence, too*, he would shout, and Evthalia knew he was right. So they would launch into one of their endless conversations, about representational democracy and rhetoric and philosophy. And when the comb finally reached the knot, Tasos would run out of quotes to borrow, and she would, too. The conversation would end abruptly and they'd turn back to the television. It was somehow less painful to speak to the screen.

MINAS

Minas felt all-powerful. Indefatigable. Triumphant. That was how Evelina made him feel. He swallowed entire pages, memorized the exceptions that proved the rule, read and took notes the way his grandmother had taught him.

He listened, watched, and didn't speak. Only once, walking past the television as some panel of experts ran on about the national good and how much was at stake now that the situation had become so critical, did he let out a *pfff*. When his mother asked him to move over so he wouldn't be blocking her view, he nodded but stayed right where he was.

—Sure, we have to save the nation, he said in a voice dripping with irony, quoting the phrase they kept throwing around on the screen. I'm so sick of hearing that. It's just what they said when they threw Gris to the dogs. Fifty years of the same stupidity. From people who are perfectly willing to watch as other people sacrifice everything. We've hit bottom, great, we got it. But it's the same old shit all over again. Ideas above lives, the country above its people. As if that could solve the problem. Who do they think they're kidding?

He has his *Dictionary of Irregular Verbs* under his arm. For now, all he cared about was his exams and Evelina, studying and making his next move. And the time had come for both those things. Enough with the flirting and kisses.

—Why aren't we going to Agia Sophia tonight?

She wasn't asking, she was teasing. Her eyelashes fluttered.

—Because I said so, Minas responded.

—Oh, really? And what are you, the man?

Minas grabbed her around the waist and lifted her into the air. He carried her all the way to the statue of Venizelos. It was late spring and the grass smelled sweet, even here, a few steps from the cars on the street. There was a padlock on the fence around the ancient agora, the museum had been closed for months, there was no money at the ministry to pay a guard. They hopped the fence. Minas pulled her by the hand to the little theater, then backstage. Darkness, stones, everything deserted.

Evelina was used to cosmopolitan coffee shops, trendy bars, fancy restaurants. The law students she went out with, all top students with a family practice waiting for them, took her home at night in their cars, faithful protectors of female virtue. She sampled their kisses and then hopped out of their cars, leaving them with the sense that they'd been used, which was strange, since she was the girl—but perhaps it was her smile, or the look on her face, like a lion or tiger taking pity on a herbivore.

Minas took off his T-shirt and spread it out on a low wall. Evelina lay down on top of it, the shirt with the poem by Catullus on it protecting her back—*Odi et amo*, that's the kind of thing Minas wore, and he would recite the lines in the back alleys around Navarino Square, and she would shout, *Show-off, pretending to know Latin!* A soft spring breeze was blowing, and brought smells to their noses, lifting up soil, and the hairs stood up on the nape of her neck as he fumbled with the button on her jeans and finally managed to pull them off, together with her underwear, in a movement that seemed planned but was actually just luck. He bent down and paid homage to her belly-button, licked its hollow as if seeking water. With anyone else the girl would have pulled away, but with him she liked it. When he lifted her legs onto his shoulders as if it were the most natural thing—which in fact it was, as Evelina only at that moment understood—she didn't close her eyes. He didn't, either.

Her back counted the stones beneath it.

—Jesus, the sky smells like pussy! Minas shouted.

Evelina laughed, her nipples hard and cold, and only then did Minas realize that he hadn't even touched her, just rushed straight there like a glutton. And now there was no way he was coming out.

Evelina thought about all the stupid pickup lines she'd heard, and all the dirty talk and insistent I-love-yous designed to coax a girl right into bed, but Minas's words made her dizzy. As did his body—particularly from the waist down.

And because she was a girl who respected words but judged according to actions, and who didn't like to leave anything half done, she pulled him toward her again and squeezed her calves against his back. Minas felt her legs, reached out his hands and grabbed her ankles, wrapped them around his neck and surged forward.

—Fuck it, I like you, he said.

Evelina bit his ear.

—I bet we'll do great on our exams, she whispered.

—Those are not the words I want to hear while I'm fucking you.

—Oh! I thought you were done, she teased.

She flicked her eyelashes against his chest.

—When I'm done, you'll know, he said, and gave her a hickey, where it would show.

The night before the Panhellenic Exams, Evelina went out. Her mother started to say something but her husband gestured from the sofa, so she buttoned her lip again. Evelina took the stairs, high heels clacking—she was too impatient to wait for the elevator. She found Minas waiting for her in the churchyard. The bitter orange trees smelled wonderful, spring got under everyone's skin, made the stray dogs go wild. Minas had been dying to see her but didn't say anything, just let her decide. Finally she sent him a text: *Downstairs in 5*. She didn't need to explain and didn't need to ask twice, he just ran down the stairs to meet her.

They kissed before they even looked at one another.

—Where are we going? he asked.

Evelina shrugged. They didn't have much time, she wanted to go over her notes one last time, she knew that would calm her down. But Minas would calm her even more, with his talent for turning everything into a joke, particularly the things everyone else took so seriously.

—To the sea, he decided.

They headed toward the waterfront at a run, laughing like crazy people, two university hopefuls who should have been studying, or at least sitting with a book open on their laps, now that the seconds were ticking backwards.

Darkness. The sea, a diamond blue, stretched before them like freshly ironed fabric. The lights of the city shone like lanterns, and those in the distance like broken mirrors. Minas grabbed her from behind and wrapped his arms around her, and they walked like that together, or perhaps they were dancing. His breath was warm on her neck. And when he dropped her off at the door to her building, he said:

—Tomorrow. Tomorrow, together.

GRIS

Grandpa Dinopoulos had a habit of falling asleep in his armchair. Elena would fluff the pillows on his untouched bed, and dutifully changed the sheets, but he always greeted the dawn from his spot in the living room. During the early years of his marriage with Froso he would lie down and wrap his arms around his wife, listen to her heart beating in the silence of the night. Then he would turn onto his stomach, burrow under the covers, and bury his face in the pillows. His sleep was a lonely affair. Froso would search out his feet in the night, tangle her legs in his. He, meanwhile, would be solving cases and resolving loose ends in his dreams, and sometimes he would leap out of bed to jot down some note to himself, and Froso would complain, *You never relax.*

When the Gris case fell to him, his sleep became even more troubled. Particularly after the night when the district attorney knocked on his door. He knew that taking the case was the right thing to do, that he was saving a man from the firing squad. That was the bitter truth. He believed time would take care of things, that the storm would pass, the political situation would settle down, and a retrial might then yield a better result. It was perfectly clear that the confession was false, the evidence fabricated; everything about the case was an insult to the intelligence, particularly to that of the lawyers. Even if they had expressed the opinion that Gris (the *defendant*, as the legal documents had it) *knowingly and purposefully collaborated with those who committed the crime, both before, during, and after its execution.*

The deviations from procedure were obvious, the professional negligence of the lawyers and judges was impossible to miss, and yet the district attorney's office saw nothing, heard nothing, understood nothing.

And when Gris was sentenced to life in prison—an indication to those in power that the country had managed to avoid the worst, had punished the wrongdoer, had put its best face forward and acted properly—rather than transferring the prisoner to the jail, they kept him in the holding cells of the General Security Police, under Tzitzilis's keen eye. There, many prisoners, *momentarily escaping the notice of their guards, rush to the window and hurl themselves out. Others, shouting and shrieking, cause bruises and cuts on their own persons, with the aim of exposing the defenders of our nation to calumny.*

Whether in prison or in a holding cell, the years passed. Gris served his sentence and was released. Appeals for a retrial were constantly being filed. Lawyers introduced new evidence in attempts to prove the obvious. 1977, 1999, 2002, and 2006: four appeals, all rejected. The judges demonstrated evident solidarity with their colleagues. The new arguments were sent back and the verdict stood, as did the flawed documentation, written in *katharevousa* or in demotic Greek—but though the language changed, no one dared touch the content. Those who disagreed, who felt the case damaged the country's reputation and offended the sense of justice they held so dear, distanced themselves, sometimes silently and sometimes with a fuss, from the committees, resigned from the bodies that made the relevant decisions. It didn't matter: they were the minority, their opinion never determined the outcome.

Over the years Dinopoulos realized that good intentions are worth nothing, actions are what matter. Gris was released and Dinopoulos went to see him. The man's emotions seemed raw, tears came easily to his eyes, he spoke with his soul in his mouth from the very first phrase. After twelve years behind bars, he wouldn't rest unless his name was cleared. He could forgive the suffering, but not the injustice.

The lawyer, who knew that justice is won and lost in first impressions and that words matter only when they're written, shaped the appeal with mastery and patience, yet it didn't have the result they had hoped for.

Gris died without finding justice. And Dinopoulos was no longer sure whether he'd acted rightly back when he made his decision. What he did know was that he couldn't have acted otherwise.

What's done is done. One man was sacrificed to save a country. All that nonsense about the pursuit of justice was better left to a student essay. The machinery in place was all-powerful. Whoever believed otherwise probably hadn't lived long enough to know better.

FANI

—Fine, I understand your not being on Facebook, you think it's childish. But Skype is totally different, I'll be able to see you when we talk. I don't understand why you're so resistant, I'd even find someone to set it up for you. You wouldn't have to lift a finger. You're acting like a crotchety old man, you know that, right?

Fani had been trying to convince Marino to join the present moment for a while. The stone age had ended, he couldn't just ignore advances in technology. At least not the ones that made life easier and more enjoyable. Marinos dug his heels in like a mule. *I don't have time*, was his excuse, *I don't have time to waste on things like that.* And when she, who wasn't one to beat around the bush, asked him straight out, *You mean you don't want to see me when we talk?*, he answered, in a tight voice but sure of his response, *No.* And while he could still hear her breathing on the other end of the line, he hurried to add:

—It's not enough for me. Screens aren't real, Fani. Don't mess with things. Leave them how they are.

Fani let it go.

She sent him a plastic yellow duck, by courier in a bubble envelope. It was the duck Nikolas used to have in the bathtub when he was little. It had a big round belly, so it wasn't easy to balance on a flat surface, it would rock back and forth, you kept thinking it would tip over but eventually it found its footing and settled down. The right wing had collapsed, you could still see where the baby's thumb had squeezed out the water. She didn't know why she'd held on to it, she was a person who threw things out, or at least gave them away, she didn't fill cupboards with memories. But the duck had stayed, and if you'd asked her she couldn't have said why, just that whenever she tried to get rid of it, her hand wouldn't obey. She kept it in a desk drawer with a pile of old demos and photographs. It lay there forgotten, gathering dust. Though sometimes when she was worried about her son, an unbridled foal who ignored her prohibitions and her advice, she would open the desk drawer and pull out the plastic duck. She would let it wobble on the surface of the desk until it found a spot it liked, where it would balance for a few seconds and then fall.

As she was putting it in the envelope, she stopped for a minute and almost changed her mind. The duck was her good luck charm. If her mother had known what she was doing she would have stopped her, there are things you just don't do. But Fani did whatever she pleased; she never saw the signs that stopped others in their tracks.

And so she sent it, and Marinos opened the door to an envelope with an odd bulge: usually she sent him CDs, sometimes books, the occasional postcard when she was on tour. He saw the duck and smiled, remembered Nikolas squeezing it with all his might in the old home videos. And his mother standing over him, trying to rein him in but just getting soaked for her trouble. There was nothing else in the envelope, and he liked that, not even a word to accompany the gift. Then he noticed some tiny, glistening slivers of ivory, and remembered that when Fani was on tour in Africa, she had described the beach beside a lake called Kivu, or something like that. *Strewn with ivory*, she had told him, *you've never seen anything like it, it cries out for you to walk on it in bare feet.* Marinos spread the ivory out in his palm and watched as the duck rocked back and forth on the table. That day he didn't crack a book, not once. It was something he never did, not even on New Year's, and certainly not on his birthday.

ONE TEST IS ENOUGH

Teta had planned to camp out at the entrance to the school with the rest of the mothers, but Evthalia dissuaded her.

—All you'll do is annoy him, she warned. Can't you just wait it out? Go out on the balcony and wait.

Some students had brought pens that the bishop himself had blessed. Others were wearing their baptism crosses, while the more extreme carried icons of saints. Minas, meanwhile, had on his lucky underwear, blue with Japanese manga characters. His grandmother had secretly splashed a drop of sainted water into his glass of orange juice that morning; you never know what might help, and it was no time to be closing any doors.

Evelina was standing in front of Agia Sophia. They hadn't arranged it ahead of time, but they left the house at the same time and looked for one another in the street, to walk over together.

Minas grabbed her cheeks with both hands and gave her a quick kiss. His pants hung below his hips and the laces were loose on his Converse hi-tops.

—Just think about summer vacation, he whispered to her as they walked through the gate.

He reached out a hand and squeezed her hip.

—*Pimplimi*, she said, quoting the ancient Greek present transitive for *fill.*

—*Gemo* and *plitho*, he quoted back the two possible intransitive versions of that verb, with his usual confidence in his ancient Greek, and they laughed conspiratorially.

Evelina Dinopoulou, Minas Georgiou. They were sent to neighboring rooms.

The exams would be distributed in ten minutes.

The mothers were frantic, the students chewed their pens, trying to concentrate. The whole place buzzed with nerves.

Tasos, meanwhile, watched as the danger marched toward them. At the newspaper and out in the streets, he took the city's pulse. Anyone with eyes in his head could see. Decisions were being made and those making them were thousands of kilometers away, playing Stratego and Monopoly; they'd set out the pieces and were rolling the dice.

If you looked down Agia Sophia Street toward the water, you would see a snippet of the tranquil sea that hugged the city. It was a bright, beautiful day. Old folks with bypasses were out taking their constitutionals along the waterfront. Others lazed in the sun. Spring was in the air.

On a day like this, living here felt like a privilege, not a prison sentence or a curse.

AND ALL THAT MIGHT HAVE BEEN

If Greece were a country where silence wasn't hereditary, like genetic material.

If Gris had a protector.

If Greek politicians had more backbone and the great powers less of a tendency to impose their will.

If money and influence—that is, everything—hadn't been at stake.

If the past taught us lessons; if there were play, fast forward, and rewind buttons for historical events.

If the answer were single and final.

If passivity in the face of injustice were a crime, and punished as such.

If Georgiou hadn't given in to common sense.

If Teta had a life and not just a child.

If Dinopoulos aimed for the best case, and didn't just avoid the lesser of two evils.

If Evthalia's wishes were commands.

If Soukiouroglou lived his life with his body and not his mind.

Then, perhaps.

"I like my country," the villager told the CBS correspondent. The statement seemed entirely logical and made no particular impression on the foreigner. He looked across the way at the eternal mountains. Spring was bursting into bloom. It smelled of damp soil and blossoming petals.

A triumphant light.

The American pressed the button.

Click.

He wanted to remember that moment, that place.

A Note from the Translator

The Scapegoat takes place during two key periods of recent Greek history: the Civil War in the late 1940s and the current financial crisis.

The Greek Civil War (1946–1949) was the final stage of a bitter civil strife that broke out shortly after the Axis occupation (1941–1944). With the support of a full-fledged British military intervention in December 1944, Greek anticommunists ousted left-wing resistance forces from a provisional National Union government. As a consequence, the former resistance fighters faced political persecution and a wave of "white terror" by royalist squads. This situation turned into an open civil war in late 1946: on the one side, the Greek government army, created by royalist officers and other far-right elements, including former Nazi collaborators; and on the other, the Democratic Army of Greece, comprised of former pro-communist guerrilla fighters who had meanwhile fled to the mountains. The Greek Civil War was one of the first episodes of the Cold War. After the Truman doctrine was announced in early 1947, the Greek government received financial, military, and political support from the U.S. administration; on the other side, the left-wing guerrillas received a much more reluctant and covert support from the Soviet Union and the neighboring communist states.

In the midst of the civil war, an American journalist for CBS, George Polk (the model for Jack Talas in this book), was killed in circumstances that remain unexplained to this day. Polk was investigating atrocities on both sides, as well as calling the Americans to account for their support of the Greek government. His uncompromising attitude toward the truth has been honored post-humously in the George Polk Award, which is given annually to "intrepid, courageous reporters committed to doing whatever it takes to uncover matters of critical importance to an informed public and the very foundation of democratic society" (from the Polk Award's website).

After Polk's death, American diplomats, the military, and journalists placed considerable pressure on the Greeks to close the case. Two members of the Communist Party were accused of the crime, though it was later discovered that one was himself already dead at the time Polk was killed, while the other was not in Greece. The journalist Grigoris Staktopoulos (the model for Manolis Gris) was also accused, quickly tried, and convicted on very thin grounds. He served eleven years of a life sentence, was released in 1960, and died in 1998, having filed a petition in 1977 for the Supreme Court to overturn his conviction, claiming that his confession had been given under torture. His widow filed three more petitions after his death, in 1999, 2002, and 2006, each of which presented new evidence that challenged the prosecution's case; all three petitions were rejected.

There are other layers of history in *The Scapegoat* as well. Thessaloniki, the city where the action is set, only became part of the Greek state in 1912, when it passed from Ottoman rule. Ten years later, the failure of an expansionist attempt in Asia Minor brought about 1.5 million Christians, most of them ethnically Greek, to Greece from Anatolia, while some 350,000 Muslims were deported to Turkey. Part of that population exchange involved the survivors of the genocide of Greeks in the Pontus region—among them Staktopoulos's family. The story Manolis Gris's mother tells in the novel of her family's flight to "Salonica" (another name for Thessaloniki, used in this translation to distinguish sections set in the past from sections set in the present) reflects that experience.

The novel's second central narrative, that of high school student Minas Georgiou, takes place in 2010, in the midst of a financial crisis that has also become a deepening social crisis. Social services in Greece—including the public education system—have been gutted in response to conditions set by the European Central Bank and the International Monetary Fund to loans extended to the Greek government. Minas's reluctance to attend university can more fully be understood in the context of the bleak unemployment rates and sense of hopelessness facing his generation (in 2010, 33 percent of adults under twenty-five were unemployed; that rate has now reached nearly 60 percent). Many of the chapter titles in the book—"Schools Enlighten Only When They Burn," "Get Your Hands Off Our Brains," "Mother, There's a War On Out There. I'll Be Late"—are taken from graffiti painted on walls in cities all over Greece in recent years. The sit-in at Minas's school, meanwhile, echoes the wave of student sit-ins prompted by the murder of fifteen-year-old Alexis Grigoropoulos by a police officer in central Athens in 2008. In the riots that followed Grigoropoulos's death, Greeks, especially of Minas's generation, expressed their frustration with the Greek state and the country's uncertain future.

Perhaps most important are not the details of these historical settings, but the sense of history as a lived present that saturates the novel. In putting the story of Manolis Gris alongside the current crisis in Greece, Nikolaidou implicitly argues that the injustices of the past are still with us, and that scapegoating of all kinds—of political opponents, of immigrants, of the youth who will bear the brunt of the current financial crisis, even of Greece itself within the European Union—pervades the current moment.

Author's Acknowledgments

Thodoros Papaggelis stood by my side from the first draft of this book to the last. I thank him for the words, the thoughts, and the love he has shown me. Edmund Keeley, Yiorgos Anastasiadis, Grigoris Staktopoulos, Yiorgos Kafiris: their books provided fuel for the writing of mine. Dimitris Tompaidis and Tatiana Halidou supplied me with Pontic words. Most of the graffiti I quote as chapter headings comes from buildings along Agios Dimitrios Street, Armenopoulou Street, on the campus of the Aristotle University of Thessaloniki, on Agia Sophia Street, and on Theogenous Harisi Street. And my students—from the Korais School, the middle and high schools in Kato Poria, the middle schools in Provata, Skouratea, the Pallatidio middle school of Siderokastro, the Music School of Thessaloniki, the Experimental School of the University of Thessaloniki—taught me so much. I thank them all from the bottom of my heart. Eleni Boura is my editor, which is to say my person. I bow before her professional passion.

Sakis Seferas makes my life easier and more fun. Thus, I can write.

Translator's Acknowledgments

A novel like this one, which involves extensive research on the part of the author, involves just as much on the part of the translator. I thank Sophia Nikolaidou, then, first of all, for giving me cause to delve into moments in Greek history that had been obscure to me—and to revisit the streets and alleyways of Thessaloniki, a city dear to me. I thank her, too, for her generous reading of this translation.

I would also like to thank Evi Haggipavlu for first handing this novel to me so excitedly, for carefully reading over my finished translation, and for the many, many conversations about pedagogy and politics in between; Panayiotis Pantzarelas and Andreas Galanos for always being willing to join an impromptu book club; Dimitris Kousouris for his help with historical details; Amanda Doxtater, Lanie Millar, and Marc Schachter for their truly amazing edits on parts of the book, and for the community of thinkers they have been for me over the past few years; and, as always, David and Helen Emmerich, the most dedicated of editors, whose generosity as parents goes beyond what any child could ever hope for.

Reading Group Guide

1. At the heart of this book is the issue of scapegoating and sacrifice: how is it that individuals and nations end up taking the blame for events that have many complicated causes? Can this ever be justified? The novel explores these questions from numerous perspectives. Were there some you were more sympathetic to than others? Are there any circumstances where convicting an innocent man like Gris could be the right, or best possible, decision, in your opinion?

2. The character of Manolis Gris remains something of a cipher—we learn about him through other characters but never hear from him directly. What do you make of Nikolaidou's decision to present him in this way?

3. The different female characters of the book have made very different choices when it comes to career and family, and have had very different fates. And, surprisingly, the younger characters are not necessarily more committed to a life outside the home than older characters like Evthalia. What do you think of the choices each individual made, and the results?

4. Minas refuses to consider going to university in part because he's sick of tests and the effect of testing culture on his education (the pat answers, the hours spent cramming). The value of a college degree in an uncertain economy is a real question for Greek students like Minas, but also for Americans, especially given the cost of higher education. What are your thoughts about an education geared towards tests and a degree? Does it leave students ill-prepared for the real world?

5. One aspect of the book that may be surprising is the student sit-ins at the high school, which are a far more common occurrence in Greece than in American schools. What did you think of the student occupation? Were you skeptical about it, or did it seem like a legitimate form of political protest?

6. In the novel, the charismatic teacher Marinos Soukiouroglou initially seems like a champion of independent thinking and an unconventional approach to education. But that view is challenged when Minas presents his final report on the murder of Jack Talas. How did your understanding of Souk's character change over the course of the book?